Krunzle could not help letting his eyes go to the half-orc, who now opened his lips to reveal teeth like tombstones. The thief had an inkling of what Sheshakk would do with his body, once the others had removed anything of value. At the same time, the traveler's right hand had gone behind his back, where the short sword still hung, clear of his knees. The weapon seemed to press itself into his palm—no, Krunzle thought, there was no seeming about it: the smooth wood of the grip fitted itself exactly to his hand. He felt a tremor pass from the sword to his arm, as if he had laid his hand upon the neck of a warhorse just as it heard the horns blow the charge.

Before he could think another thought, the sword was in his hand, and his arm was out in front of him. Though he was famished and sleep-bereft—and more than a little worried about the outcome of the next few moments—the weapon's point did not quaver.

The Osirian made a tsking sound, drew back his arrow, and let fly. They were so close that Krunzle would have taken a bet that he could spit and hit the man's shoes. There was no time to duck; there was barely enough time to flinch. But even as the thief was helplessly twisting his head away from the missile's flight, the sword twitched in his hand. Krunzle saw a blur of motion, followed it to his right, and saw that the black flights of the arrow were now half-embedded in the Ulfen swordster's throat . . .

The Pathfinder Tales Library

Song of the Serpent

Hugh Matthews

paizo
PUBLISHING LLC

Cover art by Adrian Smith.
Cover design by Andrew Vallas.
Map by Robert Lazzaretti.

Paizo Publishing, LLC
7120 185th Ave NE, Ste 120
Redmond, WA 98052
paizo.com

ISBN 978-1-60125-388-0 (mass market paperback)
ISBN 978-1-60125-389-7 (ebook)

Publisher's Cataloging-In-Publication Data
(Prepared by The Donohue Group, Inc.)

Matthews, Hugh, 1949-
  Song of the serpent / Hugh Matthews.

  p. ; cm. -- (Pathfinder tales)

  Set in the world of the role-playing game, Pathfinder.
  Issued also as an ebook.
  ISBN: 978-1-60125-388-0

  1. Thieves--Fiction. 2. Treasure troves--Fiction. 3. Adventure and adventurers--Fiction. 4. Imaginary places--Fiction. 5. Fantasy fiction. I. Title. II.Title: Pathfinder adventure path. III. Series: Pathfinder tales library.

PR9199.3.H763 S66 2012
813.54

First printing February 2012.

Printed in the United States of America.

For Spencer Hughes.

Chapter One
The Uncharmed Tree

He called himself Krunzle the Quick. Others had called him Krunzle the Incorrigible, Krunzle the Corruptible, and once—the fault of poorly chosen associates and a line of retreat that included one roof too far—Krunzle the Incarcerated, though the experience was brief and never to be repeated.

He spent his second day in Kerse wandering the gently curving streets of the upper city, where the grand homes of Druma's elite stood behind their walls of stone or brick and their imposing gates whose gaudy locks were so obviously pickable.

But it would be a fool of the first magnitude who would pick such a lock, and Krunzle believed himself not to be a fool of any magnitude. Thus, whenever he came across a tempting venue—some wall whose bricks were gaudily inset with emerald and ruby, or a bellpull whose pendant handle was a fist-sized nugget of dwarf-mined gold—he would doff his broad-brimmed hat ornamented by a gaudy panache and fan himself against the heat of the day.

And, while so doing, he would inspect the color of the large cabochon set into the hat ornament's spiral of debased silver. Invariably, the uncut gem glowed red; never was it green. That meant that something magical guarded the riches so casually on display—if not the householder's own wards, then the all-seeing eye of the city's corps of scryers, crouched over their balls of crystal, plates of isinglass, or pools of quicksilver.

Touch one precious thing with larcenous intent and, somewhere, a chime would sound—or, for all Krunzle knew, an ensorcelled imp would bleat—and all too soon the next sound the toucher would hear would be the ring of iron-nailed boots on Kerse's cobbled thoroughfares as a squad of Blackjackets came pounding along at the double. Then the malefactor would be seized, routinely battered, kicked toward the nearest penitentiary, battered some more, and thrown into a dark cell that still stank of its last tenant's bowel movements, only to be hauled out and battered some more when the next shift of the Mercenary League's black-uniformed men-at-arms reported for duty.

Even an attempt at theft was so rare in Kerse that weeks, and even months, might go by between opportunities for the League to brutalize a captured burglar or cutpurse. Sometimes, a Blackjacket would interrupt his annual leave and hurry back to the barracks for a chance to lay his truncheon against the ribs and joints of a taken-up thief.

The prospect of such treatment, for the alleged crime of relieving some overstuffed merchant of the odd bauble or knicky-knack, offended Krunzle's sense of propriety. Even more, it activated his well-honed instinct for self-preservation. Thus, by the end of the second day of tramping Kerse's steep suburban avenues—the residents either came and went in horse-drawn carriages, or had themselves carried in palanquin-chairs born by four huffing, sweating Kellid slaves—Krunzle was almost beginning to doubt his wisdom in having relocated to the capital of Druma.

The descending sun still drew beads of perspiration from his narrow brow and bristle-sprouting upper lip. His feet ached and his calves had swollen with the effort of propelling himself up one vertiginous street after another. He came upon an intersection of two broad boulevards with a low-walled circle of green at its center, surrounding a decorative fountain. He sat on the fountain's tiled lip and watched the liquid pour, laughing and bubbling, from the smiling mouths of four metal dolphins rendered in the rococo style of a past generation. He removed his hat and cupped his hands beneath the flow from one pair of ever-amused lips, threw the cold water over his head and nape, then took another double handful and splashed his face.

Refreshed, he wiped the liquid from his eyes and took a closer look at the statuary. Surely, the pale metal from which the figures were formed was platinum—rarer even than gold—and their huge blue eyes must be sapphire. *Put out in the street like that, there for the taking*, said a voice in his head. Reflexively, his hand went to the heavy-bladed knife sheathed in the inner lining of his right buskin; a quick insertion, a practiced twist, and the stone would be in his hand.

But his eye fell on the gaudy ornament in his hat, where he had laid it down on the fountain's edge. The cabochon seemed to look back at him from within its baleful crimson glow. His hand came away from the hidden knife and dipped instead into the water, bringing a palmful up to his parched lips and tongue.

He drank two more mouthfuls, then slipped off his soft-sided, supple-soled buskins and peeled away the sweat-soaked socks beneath. For a while, he sat, cooling his angry feet until they merely grumbled.

A shadow fell across him. Krunzle turned his head and looked up to see a pair of Mercenary Leaguers regarding him in a manner that he recognized from the times he had spent in a city that maintained a constabulary. In his experience, such men rose up each morning already suspicious of all who were not of their own ilk, and let the distrust grow stronger as the day advanced. By this time in the late afternoon, these two were probably ready to pounce on any hapless passerby who could not account for himself in triplicate with a personal reference from the Prophet Kelldor.

Krunzle removed his extremities from the fountain, swiveled to face the Blackjackets, and rose to his feet. These being unshod, and he being of less than impressive height, he found his eyes could not meet theirs on an even plane. He bent his neck backward to smother their hostile gaze with a wide-eyed innocence and spoke before they could. Krunzle believed that most conversations needed to be steered, and he steered best who seized the rudder first.

"Gentlemen," he said, "such good fortune to have found you! I had almost despaired."

Two sets of eyes blinked in response. Blackjackets were not used to being gladly received by apparent vagrants. The senior of the two, a dark-complected Kersite, said, "Oh, really?"

He surely would have said more, but Krunzle was not prepared to relinquish the tiller. "Indeed," he said, "I have been tramping all over these streets searching for the Mercenary League's recruitment center."

More blinking met this declaration, then the junior Blackjacket examined Krunzle from his down-plastered hair to his pale and wrinkled toes and said, "You want to be a man-at-arms?"

"Such has long been my dream," said Krunzle, his rounded chin striking the air in a gesture of determination. "I have come to Kerse determined to fulfill it." The older one snorted, and the thief rounded on him. "You laugh? I warn you, I am a gentleman of resource and accomplishment. One day I might well be your superior officer."

"You are a little short," said the Blackjacket, "in the crucial area of not being too short. We prefer men of stature." When Krunzle began to bluster a reply, the man-at-arms spoke over him, "Besides, the recruitment center is on Bay Street, down near the docks. You've come a long way out of your way."

Krunzle plunged his features into a mask of disappointment. "Ah," he said with a sigh, "I believe the white-robed dignitary to whom I applied for directions led me astray."

"Not unlikely," said the junior Blackjacket. "The elite of Kerse have little regard for the impecunious outlander. If the only profit they can wring from you is a laugh at your expense, then that is what they'll take." He clapped a sympathetic hand to Krunzle's shoulder and said, "The center will close at sundown and you won't make it there from here by then. Where are you staying?"

"An inn on Front Street," Krunzle extemporized. "I disremember the name, but I'll know it when I see it."

"Well, then," said the younger man-at-arms, "go on back there and report to the recruitment center in the morning. I'll be off duty but I'll come in and put in a word for you if the underofficer in charge gives you any difficulty."

"Wait a moment, Follix," said his partner, "this fellow's—"

"Showing the right spirit, Gladrius," the younger one said. "And he strikes me as a man who has both feet on the pavement, even if his head doesn't rise all that far above it." When the older man made a derisory noise, Follix overrode him again. "There's more to man-at-arming than cracking heads and booting fundaments. Sometimes you have to outthink the bad fellow."

"Very well put," said Krunzle. He seized the younger man's hand and said, "I'll look forward to seeing you tomorrow. Now, I think I should cool my feet some more, before I ask them to carry me all the way back to the lake."

And thus, with gestures of amity—though Gladrius's carried an overtone of irony—they parted. Krunzle waited until they had turned a curve in the serpentine road, then replaced his socks, footwear, and hat. He did not, however, depart in the direction of any inn on Front Street, but wound his way farther uphill, to where he could see a park that might offer him a less comfortable, though definitely less costly, bed for the night. In any case, a space beneath a bush would have fewer vermin than any hostelry he could afford at present.

He found such a spot and disposed himself within it as comfortably as he could. He made a traveler's meal from the contents of his satchel: a cob of bread, a wedge of cheese, a handful of black Keleshite olives. He wished for a beaker of red wine to wash it down and warm his inner being, but had to content himself with cold water from another fountain near the entrance to the park. This public utility was also crusted with wealth, but again his hatpiece glowed a fiery hue when he brought it near.

By the time he had eaten and drunk, the sun was well down. Shadows crept across the open space, turning the green of the grass to black, and converting the elegantly trimmed topiary into hulking menaces. Krunzle wrapped himself in his cloak and lay down beneath his chosen bush, his folded hat for a pillow.

It was as his eyes closed that he caught the gleam of something in the darkness, beyond the high hedge that rimmed the park. He blinked and it was gone. A moment later, it was back—a tiny glint of light that came and went, like reflections from a faceted jewel hung, rotating, from a string.

Krunzle remembered what had lain in that direction when he had made his way up yet another hill to find the arched gap in the hedge that led into the park. A blank wall ran the length of the block on the opposite side of the street, with fully grown shade trees at intervals along the grass verge between the paved path and the cobbled roadway. Whatever was winking at him must stand in the grounds enclosed by the wall.

And is probably guarded by a half-starved wyvern, he thought. He shut his eyes and sought for sleep. But in a moment his lids popped open again. The sparkle came again, and now it was joined by another—this one the deep crimson of a blood-ruby.

The thief reached for sleep again, but it evaded his grasp. Again, the glimmering came. Something in its insouciant glistering drew him; he could not keep his eyes off it. A moment later, hat upon head and satchel slung from shoulder, he was marching across the lawn to the park's exit, though he could not remember forming the intent to do so.

As he got closer to the archway, the gleam beyond the wall across the street grew brighter. He saw now that one of the trees that punctuated the grass verge extended a substantial branch over the top of the barrier. An enterprising and nimble fellow could be up that tree and over the wall in the time it took to draw five breaths, he thought.

And be ensorcelled and flung to the Blackjackets in another five, he told himself. This is no town for an honest thief. Still, when he stood in the shadows beneath the tree, conveniently hidden from any casual glance, his dulled optimism revived itself enough to cause him to remove his headgear and see what the cabochon had to say.

It glowed a soft green. Perplexed, scarcely daring to hope, Krunzle shook the hat and looked again. Still green. He tapped the rounded gem with two fingers. Green again. He held it toward the wall and still the green glow lit up his wrist and forearm.

Five breaths later, Krunzle dropped silently into the space beyond the wall. He clung to the shadow beneath the limb of the overreaching tree and surveyed the grounds. He saw a formal garden with walkways and occasional benches of a pale stone that was probably marble, surrounded by low hedges and banks of flowers, the latter filling the air with heady scents.

Beyond the garden was a patio, and beyond that the rear of a fine mansion, its lowest story coated in a stucco of sparkling gemlets, the wall above patterned in a checkerboard of onyx and alabaster tiles. The ground floor was unlit, and only a faint light shone from one upper window. Krunzle studied the layout, then held out his hat. The cabochon glowed a faint pink. He took a step toward the house; the color deepened even as the gem glowed more brightly.

The house was warded. But what about the glittering thing in the garden? Krunzle extended the hat in its direction and saw the red convert to green. He made the appropriate deduction: someone, for some reason, had neglected to weave a protective charm around the thing that had called him here. Perhaps some minor mage, charged with safeguarding the garden, had mispronounced a line in the warding incantation, and had gone to bed without noticing that a gap had been left where there should have been none.

Having found the gap, Krunzle's obligation was clear. He strode across the grass to where the prize glittered. For prize he was sure it must be—now that he was over the wall he could see that the two gleams that had called him were but the topmost of a host of sparkling lights. And they sparkled because they were gems of purest ray serene, he now saw as he neared the spot— gems of all kinds, and many of surpassing size, dangling from a multibranched tree that grew out of a large and ornate pot. Indeed, overgrew was a more appropriate word, he thought, seeing as how the plant's fibrous and gnarled roots had spilled over the container's rim and, in places, burst through its sides.

Now he stood beneath the tree. A ring of small floodlights were set in the soil within the pot, their beams directed upward to catch the facets of the gems. The jewels grew from the ends of thin tubules that in turn sprouted from the tree's limbs. Some slow vegetative force caused them to spin slowly, first this way, then that, even in the absence of a breeze. Lit from below, the ten thousand facets threw a kaleidoscope of colored beams in all directions. Krunzle looked down and saw his torso and arms sprinkled with spots of light in different shades of yellow, green, red, blue, and purest white. The effect was delightful, and even more captivating when he looked up again into the ever-moving constellation of flashing gems.

How beautiful, he thought. Then, more to the point, how valuable. And was it truly unwarded? He held out his hatpiece. It glowed green, though the uncut cabochon made a poor showing against the massed glitter from above.

Right, he thought. To work. But still he stood and stared, mouth open like a bumpkin at his first raree-show. He had to exert a mental grip on himself. *Never mind staring. Pluck one!*

He reached, put his fingers around a low-hanging emerald as big as a plum, and tugged. A second, harder pull separated the gem from its stem with a faint *pop!* The entire tree shivered, its reflected lights flittering across his upraised arm, then it subsided. Krunzle put the green gem in his hat, and reached for a pear-shaped diamond so large his thumb and fingers could not meet around its width. Again, it came free with a good tug, and again the tree shook—though not with pain, he thought. More like excitement.

It was an emotion Krunzle shared as he reached and tugged, reached and tugged, and his hat filled with splendorous riches. Should've bought a higher-crowned one, he thought. He set it down between two of the flood lamps in the top of the pot and swung his satchel around on its shoulder strap so that it hung down his front instead of at his side. Now he could pluck gems with both hands.

The satchel, like the hat, was soon filled. Krunzle had not even exhausted the low-hanging bounty of the tree. If I remove my cloak, he thought, I could pile more jewels on it and fold and tie it into a bundle. He did so, flapping the cloth to lay it on the ground. Then he made to climb upon the lip of the pot, the better to reach higher.

And found he could not. Though he willed his feet to lift, they would not. Nor would the muscles of calf and thigh flex. Krunzle looked down and saw, through the flashing of reflected spots of light, that his lower limbs, to a height of halfway between knee and hip, were wrapped around with roots as thick as his wrist. As he watched, the thin ends of the fibrous material extended themselves, winding around his thighs to reach ever higher.

Krunzle pulled against the roots' grip. Nothing happened, except that the pressure increased. He noticed, too, that he had no feeling from the knees down. Indeed, if he were not so tightly wrapped, he would surely fall over.

His hand went to the top of his buskin but the short, thick-bladed knife was clapped fast to his leg by the tree's grip. He reached instead for a thin-bladed dagger that fitted into a sheath sewn into the back of his shirt, just below the collar. A moment later, he applied the stiletto's needle point to one of the roots.

The weapon sank into the living wood, and this time the tree did more than shiver. Its trunk flexed and its branches thrashed, and a sound like a whispered groan came from somewhere within its center. Krunzle pressed harder, cutting with the razor edge just behind the point. But from near where he had wounded the root sprang a forest of tendrils that sought out the weapon and the hand that held it, wrapping themselves around the blade and his arm right up to the elbow. In panic, he sought to pull away, but the tree was faster—and, a terrifying thought, more experienced at this kind of contest—and now Krunzle was stooped over, one hand pinned to his lower leg, with only one free hand to help himself.

But it wasn't free for long. More roots shot out from the top of the pot, scattering the hat and satchel and their contents that he had left lying there. Though Krunzle struggled to avoid it, in very little time both of his arms were immobilized, and the vegetative bonds were creeping up his torso. When he strained against them, they constricted his belly and diaphragm; he was finding it hard to breathe.

So that's its game, he thought. In the jungles of the Mwangi Expanse, he knew, there lurked great serpents that dropped from the trees onto unwary passersby, wrapped them in coils of powerful flesh, and squeezed the life from them before devouring them whole. This tree must have the same ambition.

A moment later, he realized his analysis was not quite accurate. The roots ceased to exert themselves, now that they had him safely immobilized. Instead, a new tendril extended itself, this from the base of the tree's trunk, where it grew from the soil. The tubule wavered toward him, its motion reminding him of a blind worm guiding itself by scent. Its end divided into two smaller tubes, and these into two more each. Then each of the four questing tendrils showed something like a mouth, ringed with something like teeth, and—as if they had now come close enough to scent him—they shot forward and fastened themselves to his cheek.

Krunzle felt a sensation of needles being sunk into his flesh, then a sense of suction. The places where he had been struck first went cold, then numb. In the still-glittering reflections from the jewels above, he saw the pale tubules pulse and fill with red. The tree shivered again, and this time he was sure it was a signal of gratification.

Time went by; it could have been seconds, or minutes. Krunzle remained as he was, stooped and bound. Gradually, the numbness in his cheek spread to cover his face and then his neck. He examined possibilities and strategies—all led nowhere. Or, more accurately, all led to the same dreary destination: the householder coming out into his garden to enjoy the splendors of the morning and finding beneath his tree a shriveled husk that had once been Krunzle the Quick.

All strategies but one, that is. And, with no other avenue open, the thief launched himself down it with an energy born of despair.

"*Help!*" he cried. Or, again more accurately: he croaked. His mouth and throat were parched, his tongue now also beginning to suffer from the tree's numbing influence. He manufactured some spittle, swallowed, and shouted again, this time with more gusto.

No answer came, but the bonds around his abdomen constricted a little more tightly. Krunzle found his breathing reduced to short and rapid panting. "*Help!*"

From the darkness that surrounded him, he heard a smooth baritone say, "My, but you seem to be in a pickle."

The feeding tubules would not let Krunzle turn his head far enough to see who spoke. "Pickles," he said, attempting to show a light-hearted spirit in adversity, "might envy my situation."

"Indeed," said the voice, and now he heard the swish of fabric in motion. Into his field of vision, necessarily downcast as his right arm was still pinned to his right calf, came a pair of feet clad in pointed white-leather boots. The footwear was obviously of high quality, as was the white cloth of the garment that covered the wearer from the ankles up to the knees—and doubtless all the way to the neck, though Krunzle could not raise his head to confirm it. A close-set line of buttons, opals alternating with pearls, closed the garment at the front. He recognized the buttons from earlier in the day, and realized that he had heard the voice before.

For the tale Krunzle had offered to the Blackjackets had been only a partial lie. That morning, he had stopped a Kersite of imposing height and dignified mien who had been descending the steps of the Bourse into Kalistrade Square and begged the gentleman for directions. But he had not been seeking the route to the Mercenary League's recruitment center. Instead the encounter had gone like this:

Krunzle had snatched off his hat and said, "Pray, sir, will you do a stranger the kindness of telling him where he might see the finest homes in Kerse?"

The man, in a close-fitting kaftan of shining white with opal and pearl buttons, and with boots and gauntlets of supple white leather, had made to pass without answering. But whichever way he turned he found the crouching supplicant in his path. Finally, he stopped and said, "What possible use could it be to you to see the outside of what you can never hope to see the inside of? For no Kersite would ever invite such a ragged vagabond to profane his premises. Now, begone!"

But Krunzle remained in his way. "Please, sir," he said, "I wish only to see the exteriors. That will surely be enough to inspire me to work hard and trade cannily, so that someday I, too, might don the distinctive garments of your caste, and take my place among the justified prophets of Kerse."

"You?" said the Kersite. "A prophet?" His laugh was harsh. He gazed down upon the cringing Krunzle from a great height and seemed about to dismiss him with a curse—but then his eye fell upon the cabochon set in the outlander's hat ornament. His expression became as unreadable as it would have been if he had been bargaining with an equal on the floor of the Bourse. "What was it again you wanted?" he asked.

Krunzle formed his features around his most ingratiating smile. "Directions to the mansions of Kerse's foremost magnates," he said, "prophets of the highest rank and stature, to inspire me to emulate their peerless qualities."

The prophet had made a small noise in his throat. It might have been a laugh, or a swallowed snort of contempt. But he turned and pointed toward Enterprise Way, where it led south from the square and up into the hills beyond. "Follow that until you come to Diligence Circle," he said, "then turn either left or right and continue to climb. Soon you will see winding boulevards. Along these you will find what you seek. The higher you climb, the finer the properties." He paused as if a thought had just entered his mind, then said, "There is a park with a fountain where you may refresh yourself if the climb proves taxing."

Krunzle offered his fawning thanks, but the prophet had already brushed past him to hail a pair of his white-clad peers striding across the square toward the Bourse. He fell into conversation with them and paid Krunzle no more heed.

Or so it had seemed. Now the Kersite said, "So, we meet again."

Krunzle, still bent double said, "Have I had the pleasure, sir? I don't recall—"

"No more," said the prophet, in a tone that betokened no sympathy for the thief's plight. "No more, or I will go inside, go to bed, and let the servants sweep up whatever's left of you in the morning."

Krunzle weighed his options, found them depressingly few and light. "Very well," he said.

"You were looking for places to rob," said the other, "places that the gimcrack in your hat would identify as unwarded."

It was not a question, but Krunzle felt an answer was expected. The cold in his face and neck had spread to his shoulders. "Yes," he said.

"You thought you'd found one."

"Yes."

"Instead, you are being drained of your vital essence."

"Yes."

"It does not argue for your being a competent thief."

"You do not see me at my best."

"Ah! Spirit!" Krunzle saw a pointed toe tap once, twice. "Perhaps you will do."

"Do what?" asked the thief.

"I have need for a resourceful agent," said the Kersite. "Someone who can be sent on an errand with some chance of seeing the job through."

"I prefer to choose my own assignments," Krunzle said.

"This," said the prophet, "is not a negotiation. Think of it more as an interview, and put forward your best. If I decide you have the qualities I seek, I will release you and put you to work. If not . . ."

"I welcome an opportunity to demonstrate my worth!" said the thief.

"Better," said the man in white. A moment later, Krunzle heard a chime, as if the other had struck a small bell. Immediately, the tubule at his cheek detached itself and withdrew. The chime sounded again, and he felt the bonds that constrained him relax and pull away. He immediately toppled over on his side, his lower limbs senseless. Moments later he felt excruciating pain as his blood began to force itself back into ten thousand vessels from which it had been squeezed. He made an involuntary sound.

"Show fortitude," came the prophet's voice. "It is one of the attributes I require in an agent." Then came the sound of fingers peremptorily snapping and footsteps hurrying.

Krunzle suppressed a whimper. Four strong arms picked him up and carried him, still contorted and face down, out of the garden. He passed over the patio's flagstones and then over a threshold into the house. He was carried across a room, then along corridors, and finally through a door, where he was dropped onto a hardwood floor. Hands briskly searched him. The knife in his boot departed to join the stiletto that had been pulled from his numb hand in the garden. The garrote around his waist was whisked away, and the lead-weighted, leather-sheathed pacifier in his pocket also left him.

The two burly servants, lantern-jawed Kersites, rolled him over on his back and efficiently—though not gently—rubbed the circulation back into his limbs. Then they sat him on a low stool and told him to stay and say nothing. It seemed to Krunzle to be an eminently wise course of action, at least for the time being.

After a while, the man in white came in. He regarded Krunzle from an even greater height than he had in Kalistrade Square. "What," he said, "is your assessment of your situation?"

Krunzle had been thinking about it, and had come to the conclusion that a truthful answer would best serve. "You saw me in the square this morning, and thought I might be useful to you."

"Good."

"You steered me to that park where I could see the tree of jewels—"

"All fake, by the way," the Kersite interrupted. "Even now they are dissolving back into the paste from which they are formed."

Krunzle let that one go by. "You disabled your defenses so that my cabochon would not warn me off. Then you let the tree catch me."

"Yes. What else?"

Krunzle thought for a moment. "Rogues like me are hard to find in Druma," he said, after consideration. "We don't last. So whatever need you have for me has come up suddenly, and you do not wish to waste time sending outside the country for help."

The prophet smiled thinly and inclined his head. "Very good. And?"

It took but a moment for Krunzle to see it. "And, whatever the problem is, you do not want it to come to the notice of your peers, hence your decision not to involve the authorities."

The smile widened. "Excellent."

"Does that mean I get the job?"

"Not yet," said the Kersite.

There followed a series of tests—of dexterity, endurance, intellect, and moral fiber—that Krunzle found taxing, especially after losing some of his essence to the tree. He passed them all—except, of course, the ethical conundrums. But then, that was not an area in which his prospective employer wished him to excel.

At the end of it, which was also the end of the night, with the first rays of the sun warming the east-facing window, the Kersite pronounced himself satisfied.

"What, then, is the task?" Krunzle said, panting and sweating.

"My daughter, Gyllana," said the prophet, "has decamped with a Taldan, a former officer in the Mercenary League. His name is Wolsh Berbackian. They were seen heading in the direction of the Five Kingdoms. You will go after them, find them, and bring her back." A thought occurred to him and he added, "Or die trying."

Chapter Two
An Ulfen, an Osirian, and a Half-Orc . . .

The Kalistocrat's name was Ippolite Eponion. His title was meaningless to Krunzle: First Secretary to the Second Commissariote, or vice versa. But it was clear he commanded both wealth and power, the two being synonymous among the merchant-oligarchs of Druma. He also appeared to enjoy the services of a full-time wizard, a small and wizened Tian who was introduced as the Inestimable Thang-Sha, bald as bone and with a face as wrinkled as dried fruit. A wispy beard drooped from his chin and a mustache thin as a pair of rats' tails depended from the corners of his upper lip.

The wizard came when summoned from somewhere in the labyrinthine bowels of the mansion. He arrived blinking, preceded by an odor of acrid smoke, clad in a well-worn robe of watered silk figured with arcane symbols and characters in the Tien script. In one crabbed hand he carried a bulging sack of black cloth.

Bidden to examine the new hire, he first peered at Krunzle from various angles, sometimes through squinted eyes, sometimes through open, finally through one eye at a time. Next he brought out of the bag a telescoping spyglass of black crystal through which he examined the thief's irises, ear canals, nostrils, and mouth.

"He is no one else's," he told Eponion, in the sing-song manner that marked him as a Tian as much as his copper-colored skin and dark eyes, "but if you are sending him after Gyllana, you will need some means to guarantee that he remains yours once he is out of sight."

"What do you suggest?" said the merchant.

The spellcaster pulled his stub of a nose, thought for a moment, then said, "Most reliable: kill him now, reanimate him, impose Brumel's Comprehensive Geas. It acts with particular potency on the freshly undead cerebrum."

Krunzle raised a finger and opened his mouth, but Eponion forestalled him by saying, "I need him to have his wits about him. Along the path the Taldan may have left puzzles to unpick. He may encounter persons he'll need to outwit."

The Tian shrugged. He reached into the bag and withdrew what looked to Krunzle like a coil of bronze wire, thick as a finger. But then the wizard held the object in his upturned palm, breathed on it and spoke some syllables the thief could not make out, and the coil unwound to become a small snake whose close-set scales shimmered from copper to old gold. It raised itself up and stared at the wizard's face, its head weaving back and forth, its eyes a deep shade of green, as the man spoke to it, again in words that somehow failed to lodge in the thief's ears.

When the wizard had finished addressing the snake, the creature turned its head and regarded Krunzle.

The rogue thought that he had never met a reptilian gaze that seemed so knowing. He was still thinking that thought when the spellcaster's hand moved with startling speed and Krunzle felt something cold strike the front of his throat. A moment later, he felt the same sensation on the sides and back of his neck. He reached up a hand to where his short-cropped hair met the collar of his shirt and there he found both the snake's head and its tail, the creature's mouth clamped tightly down on its opposite extremity.

"That will do," said the wizard, returning to the bag what looked to be a jewel of the same shade of green as the snake's eyes. To Krunzle, he said, "Its name is Chirk. Its loyalty is unshakable, its grip unbreakable. Try it."

One of Krunzle's hands sought for the snake's neck, just behind the jaws, the other found its tail where it disappeared into the mouth. The thief gripped, pulled, twisted. Nothing happened. He squeezed with his fingers, exerting sufficient pressure to crush reptile bones, but felt only the unyielding hardness of strong metal. Then the spellcaster spoke incomprehensibly again, and suddenly the rogue could no longer breathe. Krunzle felt his blood being stymied as it attempted to reach his brain, then the room began to darken and a low rushing sound filled his ears.

"That is what will ensue whenever you depart from the path on which the master is setting you," said the wizard, "or shirk your responsibilities." As he spoke, the snake relaxed its grip. Krunzle sucked in a great breath and tried to fit a finger between his skin and Chirk, to loosen the constriction further. He did not succeed.

"And the next time you touch Chirk," said Thang-Sha, "it will char your fingers to ashes. Now," the wizard paused while his rootlike fingers compressed the middle of his lower lip, "it can be rough traveling, between here and the mountains. We had better give him faster boots." He rummaged through the bag and came up with a fat little jar whose top he unscrewed. A foul odor filled the air, but the spellslinger ignored it and scooped up a blob of the jar's waxy contents on two fingertips. He knelt and applied the stuff to the sides of Krunzle's buskins, then lifted each foot in turn to smear their soles.

"That should do it," he said, then reached again into the bag and brought out a short sword in a scabbard of scuffed brown leather. He spoke a few syllables over the weapon, then attached it to Krunzle's belt and stepped back to study the result.

The result was that the thief immediately drew the sword and applied its edge to Chirk. Two more results ensued: the weapon's blade became as limp as a girl-child's hair ribbon, collapsing to dangle over the sword's in-curved quillions; and Chirk instantly choked Krunzle to the brink of unconsciousness, only failing to proceed to full senselessness when the wizard said, "Not all the way." The spellcaster stooped to pick up the weapon and resheathed it in its scabbard.

He then addressed the thief: "The sword will serve you only in self-defense. It is, however, a well-practiced weapon; you have but to draw it and it will do the rest. As well, it will serve none but you. If it is taken from you, it will find a way to return to your grasp. But if you attack anyone, it will become as limp as you saw it a moment ago."

Eponion said, "Except Wolsh Berbackian."

"Indeed," said the wizard. He spoke to Chirk, "The sword is allowed to attack the malefactor who has seduced away Gyllana." Eponion added an amendment, and the wizard passed on the instruction, almost as an afterthought: "And anyone who offers harm to the woman."

"It is not only allowed," said the Kalistocrat, "I insist upon it. I want Berbackian's blood. Attack the dastard the moment you encounter him."

"What about," said the wizard, "the purloined item?"

"It is of small value," said Eponion.

"Still, it will do your reputation no good if you do not recover what was stolen from you."

The other man considered the point for a moment, then said, "You are right." He turned to Krunzle. "Berbackian stole an object, some sort of talisman, old and of indeterminate origin, made of base metal. Bring it back."

Thang-Sha exuded an air of quiet satisfaction. "Chirk," he said, "take note." The cold circlet about Krunzle's neck tingled for a moment.

"Wait," said the thief, his mind constructing uncomfortable scenarios. "Perhaps some of this should be left to my discretion. Suppose I come upon the debaucher and the young lady, but in the absence of the item. What if he has sold it, or lost it crossing a river? I may become embroiled in a conundrum."

Eponion said, "My daughter's safe return is your first concern; Berbackian's death a secondary, though essential, goal; the talisman a distant third in priority."

"In case of complex circumstances," said Thang-Sha, "let it be a joint decision with Chirk, then. But Chirk's shall be the final say." He looked at Eponion inquiringly. "Does that suit?"

The Kalistocrat said, "You trust the snake?"

Thang-Sha nodded. "It has been with me for many years. I have come to rely on its abilities."

"Very well. Then send him on his way."

"Wait," said Krunzle, "I am not fit for a journey. I have been up all night being fed to trees and forced to perform feats of strength and dexterity. I suggest I retire to a well-made bed for several hours, then fortify myself with a good breakfast before going down to the docks and boarding the next packet upriver."

Thang-Sha smiled an unpleasant smile. "Your plan is rejected. You will find that servants of Kalistocrats and Tian wizards address themselves to their duties with commendable briskness."

"Just so," the Kalistocrat concurred. "I tolerate no lackadaisicality. You may rest when your labors are completed. And to my satisfaction."

"Very well," said the thief, "there remains only the question of the reward for my inevitable success." He named what he considered an appropriate figure.

It was received with a routine expression of horror and disbelief from Eponion, while the wizard composed his features into a mask of sardonic amusement. "Bidding farewell to Chirk will come to seem more than enough recompense," he said. Then he seized Krunzle's shoulders and spun the rogue around. A solid push sent him moving toward the open door. "Chirk, you know the way! Instruct the boots! Now, be off!"

Krunzle felt the wizard's hand between his shoulder blades, propelling him onward. But he soon discovered why the order to depart had not been aimed at himself but at the snake and the ensorcelled buskins. Of their own accord, his boots began to rise and fall, taking his feet and legs with them, and as he traversed two hallways and passed through a door that swung open to let him out by a servants' entrance, the pace began to accelerate. Moreover, his boots took longer and longer strides. By the time he came to a side gate in the wall, he was moving at a rapid lope.

Out on the street, the buskins turned themselves toward Lake Encarthan and soon their wearer was leaping downhill fast enough for the wind of his passage to bring tears to his eyes. Chirk, satisfied for the time being, loosened its grip enough for Krunzle to breathe freely. The rogue tugged his belt around until the sword no longer banged his left knee with every other prodigious step, and adjusted himself to his new circumstances.

He came down Enterprise Way and into Kalistrade Square, the glistening pavements of the great open space dark and empty. By now he was covering fifteen feet with each step, at a speed to be envied by thoroughbreds. He shot past the pillared Bourse with its grand statue of the Prophet Kalistrade seated on a jewel-studded throne, cleared the Fountain of Plenty in a single leap, and zipped through the filigreed ivory of the Admonitory Arch too quickly to appreciate its carved panels showing allegorical figures engaged in buying, selling, accounting, and hoarding under Kalistrade's benevolent gaze.

Past the arch, his boots took him toward the wide Promenade that ran along the shore of the bay, then turned him eastward toward where the river that the Kersites called Profit's Flow ended its journey from the Five Kings Mountains. The night was overcast, a full moon shining somewhere above the clouds, casting a diffuse light over the gray waters of Lake Encarthan that stretched smooth into the distance. The lake resembled a sheet of unpolished pewter.

"Hey!" cried a startled voice as Krunzle's fast-leaping progress took him past a Blackjacket guard post overlooking the boat basin where barges from upriver tied up. The thief heard an order to halt, then the sound of boots pounding the promenade's pavement. But the pursuit soon fell behind, and within moments, he had gone past the barge harbor and reached the spot where Kerse's city wall came down to the point at which the river met the lake.

There was another Mercenary League post here. The men-at-arms, alerted by the shouts and bootfalls, were already out and ready. Krunzle could see only vague shapes, like shadows against the gray stone of the wall—then someone kindled a torch into a blaze of red-yellow flame, and someone else lit a second fire from the first. He heard a shout, in a tone of command, and now he was leaping toward a circle of light in which he could see the points of halberds, four of them, charged and leveled at him.

"Boots?" he said, then, "Chirk?" He didn't know what answer he expected. In any case, he received none. The ensorcelled buskins carried him relentlessly on, the metal snake dozed around his neck, and four Blackjackets waited for him to come out of the murk and into their torchlight so they could spit him like a roasted capon.

There stood the Rivergate, its heavy portcullis of iron-braced timbers blocking the opening. And before that, a ramp leading down to the water, at its top the Mercenary League's fastboat on its wheeled dolly, standing ready to be put into the water to deal with any mischief in the harbor. And beyond the boat, the halberds: six of them now, and two more torches lit and put up high in the sconces to either side of the guard post's door.

"Wait!" said Krunzle, to anyone who cared to listen. But no one did. As he reached the top of the ramp and came into view of the rank of Blackjackets—he saw the surprise on their faces—the boots swerved him downward. In two strides he was at the foot of the incline, and the buskins came together just long enough for both of them to lift him into the air.

His flight followed a long arc out over the water and he had sense enough to take a deep breath and put his arms out in front of him so that his hands cut the water of the bay and made a hole for the rest of him to dive into. He went deep, his boots kicking powerfully, and the water was black. Krunzle could not tell which way was up, down, or sideways. A stream of bubbles escaped from his mouth, his lips pushed back and aside by the speed of his passage.

The pressure in his ears increased—*I'm going deeper!*—then his still-outstretched hands encountered a deep layer of slime and saturated soil. A moment later, he felt something hard slide along his back, and realized it was the fastboat's keel even as the shock caused him to open his mouth and gasp. But the bay's cold water got no farther than the back of his throat, because the bronze snake instantly tightened its grip around his neck. The constriction made Krunzle think his head was going to pop open, but not a drop of liquid reached his lungs.

And now the pressure eased, as did the metal noose around his throat. The boots kicked again and the thief shot knee-high out of the Profit's Flow, to splash down again.

"What's that?" came a voice from somewhere behind him. Krunzle rolled over onto his back, the buskins now thrashing the water, propelling him powerfully upstream against the flow of the current, and saw the portcullis backlit by torches. Two Blackjackets were at the bottom of the ramp, extending their lights over the water. One of them said something to the other, but by then Krunzle was already out of earshot, the top of his head parting the river like a poorly designed ship's bow.

He did not know how long he traveled in this way, though he grew increasingly cold as the mountain-fed river chilled his limbs. He was carried past Kerse's eastern suburbs, past the straggle of sheds and wharves along the river's shore. The few and scattered lights gave way to blackness and he knew he had reached the semicircular belt of farmland that cupped the city against the bay. A little farther on, the boots steered for the bank and brought him to the foot of an incline of rough earth—some farmer's boat launch, the rogue thought.

He crawled, soaked and shivering, up the muddy slope, the buskins pushing him until he rose, staggering, to his feet. Immediately, he was moving swiftly through the darkness again, the cold night air rushing by and chilling him to the marrow. "I need to stop and warm myself," he said, but neither snake nor buskins heeded him.

During one leap, he tried to raise a leg so that he could pull off its boot, but the leather clung to his foot like a sodden limpet. Chirk gave him a warning squeeze. Shuddering, teeth rattling against each other, the thief wrapped his wet arms around his wet torso and endured the chill as best he could. Somewhere along the way, he lapsed into a dull-minded doze, which eventually became sleep.

He returned to awareness to find himself leaping along a dirt-and-gravel road that followed the river's winding path. On its other side, the track was bordered by fields alternating with patches of mixed forest. He saw no signs of habitation except a fortified farm on the other side of Profit's Flow, its fields running down to the distant shore of the river. It was soon behind him.

The sun was better than a hand's-breadth above the distant mountains to the east, and growing warm enough to take some of the chill from his limbs. His clothes were mostly dry from the constant rush of air past and through them, but he was still bone cold. And hungry. His evening meal of bread and cheese and olives was but a memory.

"I must eat," he said. "Take me to where I can find nourishment." Not that he had any funds to buy it. His last coins had gone the way of his knives and garrote. He would have to improvise, but on such occasions he seldom came up wanting.

His statements were not acknowledged, unless the buskins were already doing all that could be done to put him within reach of food. He folded his arms and watched the land and river rush by. Off to his left, high above the northern horizon, something large was flying in a lazy circle. After a couple of circuits, it broke its cycle and angled toward him.

"Chirk," he said, but he needed say no more. The boots lengthened their stride and put on more speed. The thing in the sky began to fall behind, then it wheeled and soared on a thermal current, rising to resume its patient circling.

The sun was now two hands high, the morning well warmed. Ahead, Krunzle saw that the river curved to follow a narrowing valley. He had been passing open pastures on his landward side, backed by steep, pine-forested hills. But where the river bent, the trees came down almost to the water's edge, leaving only the strip of road and a few feet of bank. He noted, too, that the river also temporarily lost its freedom—someone had built a lock here, for the convenience of the flat-bottomed barges that hauled freight between Kerse and Highhelm.

Krunzle's spirits rose. A lock should mean a lock-keeper. A lock-keeper meant a cottage, and a cottage meant a pantry. His mouth watered. As if they had a mind of their own that ran in concourse with the thief's, his buskins began to slacken their pace. His leaps became bounds, became steps, and all at once he was walking along the road at a pedestrian's pace.

The road entered the long curve. Krunzle craned his head to see farther round the bend, looking for the smoke of a chimney. Now, the lock's downstream gate was in full view; a few steps later, he could see the upstream works. But no cottage, not even a booth. The bargemen must have to turn the windlasses for themselves.

His mouth dried, and his spirits laid themselves back down where they had been languishing. Then he saw movement: out of the woods stepped three men—no, two men, he soon corrected himself; the third was surely a half-orc—who ranged themselves across the track, the big one in the middle.

Krunzle looked left, right, behind. No help in sight. "Time to run," he said, because he could see that the trio did not wait for him with empty hands. But the boots kept marching him onward. They stepped forthrightly up to the three bandits—for Krunzle knew an ambush when he saw one, having participated in several, and from both sides of the dichotomy. He tried one more time to turn and flee, but the buskins were as if nailed to the ground.

The man to his left was lean and wiry, an Osirian by the look of him—a first impression confirmed when he spoke in the languid accent of that southern land. "Traveler!" he cried, in a tone that said he was glad to see Krunzle. "Well met this morning!" He gestured companionably with the short recurved bow in his left hand; a black-fletched arrow was already nocked to the string of twisted sinew, held against the bow's leather-wrapped grip by the Osirian's forefinger.

Krunzle looked to the one on the right—surely an Ulfen, by his long-limbs, braided yellow hair, and leather-bound leggings. The man said nothing, only smiled to reveal teeth much the same shade as his braids as he resettled the long-bladed sword that rested, unsheathed, against one shoulder.

The half-orc, for that was what the middle one unquestionably was, also said nothing—as was to be expected. The thief knew that half-orcs preferred to make their statements nonverbally, though in a way that rarely left the recipients in any uncertainty as to the meaning. He was leaning on a hip-high—chest-high if compared to Krunzle—cudgel of fire-hardened ironwood into which were set palm-sized fragments of pale chert, chipped to a razor edge.

"I have nothing," Krunzle said.

The Osirian's thin lips turned down in a moue of disappointment. "Now, here we are, just at the very beginning of our acquaintanceship, and already you mar its companionable spirit with a fib." He raised the bow so that the arrow pointed at Chirk. "I see a rather nice torc around your neck. Is it gold?" He peered at the snake. "No, perhaps not, but the workmanship appears exquisite. Tian?"

"I do not possess the thing," said Krunzle. "It possesses me. Still, it makes a fascinating tale, which I would gladly trade for breakfast."

The Osirian now looked at the traveler as if Krunzle had revealed himself as a teller of poor jokes. The Ulfen spat and flexed his shoulders so that the sword's blade bounced against the muscle. The hulk in the middle of the road said and did nothing, but his hard, dark eyes did not depart from Krunzle's face, and his expression left the thief in no doubt as to whether or not he had won the half-orc's affections.

"Unfortunately," said the one with the bow, now moving his right hand to lace its fingertips on either side of the arrow's nock and drawing the string slowly back, "we have only enough for ourselves. Sheshakk, here,"—his head inclined to indicate the huge figure on his left—"is blessed with a healthy appetite."

Krunzle could not help letting his eyes go to the half-orc, who now opened his lips to reveal teeth like tombstones. The thief had an inkling of what Sheshakk would do with his body, once the others had removed anything of value. At the same time, the traveler's right hand had gone behind his back, where the short sword still hung, clear of his knees. The weapon seemed to press itself into his palm—no, Krunzle thought, there was no seeming about it: the smooth wood of the grip fitted itself exactly to his hand. He felt a tremor pass from the sword to his arm, as if he had laid his hand upon the neck of a warhorse just as it heard the horns blow the charge.

Before he could think another thought, the sword was in his hand, and his arm was out in front of him. Though he was famished and sleep-bereft— and more than a little worried about the outcome of the next few moments—the weapon's point did not quaver.

The Osirian made a tsking sound, drew back his arrow, and let fly. They were so close that Krunzle would have taken a bet that he could spit and hit the man's shoes. There was no time to duck; there was barely enough time to flinch. But even as the thief was helplessly twisting his head away from the missile's flight, the sword twitched in his hand. Krunzle saw a blur of motion, followed it to his right, and saw that the black flights of the arrow were now half-embedded in the Ulfen swordster's throat.

The man's mouth opened, but he had neither air enough nor time for a last word. His knees bent, and he fell to them, the blood-smeared arrow sticking out of the back of his neck. Then he toppled face-forward, the long-bladed sword beating him to the ground with a metallic clatter.

The Osirian's eyes had gone wide, but already his features were settling back into what was probably a life-long skepticism. He dropped the bow and drew a curved dagger from the back of his belt, at the same time saying, "Sheshakk."

He needed to say no more. The half-orc was already lifting his dark cudgel, the bludgeon coming up in a two-handed grip and with surprising speed. Krunzle's instinct was to dodge back, but his boots had another plan. He found himself leaving the ground in a prodigious leap—he hadn't even bent his knees—that took him toward his monstrous assailant.

He narrowly missed coming within the arc of the descending cudgel, then he was somersaulting over Sheshakk's boulder-sized head. The sword exerted some arcane leverage on him in midair, so that his arm swung down and the blade passed cleanly through the short, muscle-corded neck. The half-orc's head went backward while the momentum of the cudgel's swing carried the body forward, so that the decapitated corpse and its missing part were separated by several feet—a situation that almost guaranteed the half-orc was rendered harmless.

Krunzle landed on his feet beside the Osirian. The sword flicked out, brushed aside the curved dagger even as the bandit tried to bring it up in a belly-opening slice, then spitted the man. The point passed through the Osirian's breastbone as if it were made of cheese, and burst through his spine in a spray of blood.

The dark eyes stared into Krunzle's with mild resentment, as if the thief had pulled some cheap trick, then they gazed at nothing. The sword withdrew itself from the dead man, then pulled Krunzle's arm down so that it could wipe itself clean on the Osirian's cotton shirt, and finally guided him to slide its blade back into its scabbard.

The thief recovered his equanimity with the speed for which he was renowned among those few who could claim more than a passing acquaintance. He bent over the Osirian's corpse, rummaged within the bloody shirt, and felt his hand touch a drawstring purse. Something within the soft leather clinked, but as Krunzle reached to seize it he was yanked away. The buskins were striding once more along the road.

"Wait!" he cried, but the pace only speeded up. "They might have had something to eat! I may have to outwit this Berbackian fellow. I will be of no use if I am faint from hunger!" The boots took two more steps, then slowed. Krunzle pressed his advantage. "The Osirian had money. What if I have to pay for information? Or take passage upriver? If you make me swim all the way to Highhelm, I will arrive in no state of usefulness."

The buskins stopped. Krunzle turned, and now his boots behaved liked ordinary footwear. Something spoke in his head—no, he did not hear an actual voice, but experienced a diffuse sense of communication having been effected: he could return to the site of the ambush and forage for anything that would contribute to the mission.

"Good," he said, and started back toward the three corpses. He was aware that his legs shook and trembled, and wondered if it were a consequence of shock, or simple fatigue. Perhaps both.

Then he posed another internal question: *Who spoke without speaking in my mind? Was it you, Chirk?* A moment later, he knew that it was so. *The buskins and the sword, have they their own voices?* Again, a moment passed, and he knew that the bronze snake was to be his only interlocutor. *I will do my utmost to make ours a happy partnership*, he thought. An instant later the knowledge came to him that Chirk could hear more than his surface thoughts. Krunzle swore within the privacy of his mind and received in reply a constriction of his breathing. *You control my actions*, he returned. *Allow me at least my feelings.*

For a moment, he felt that judgment was suspended. Then the snake eased its grip.

Good, he thought.

The span of their odd conversation had brought him back to the site of the ambush. He went first to the dead Osirian and the pouch, fished it out and emptied its contents into his palm: one small gold coin, worn almost faceless, a few rounds of silver from various nations' mints, and the rest in copper.

He went next to the Ulfen, and found a goat-hide wallet on a string around his neck, the outside of the purse still covered in the animal's parti-colored hair. Inside he found coins of silver and base metal, but no gold. Under his beard, however, the swordsman had worn a broad leather collar in the front of which was set a heavy silver amulet of barbaric design—probably marking the dead man as a devotee of one of the rage-loving war gods to which the northmen made blood sacrifice.

Sheshakk had worn nothing but a pair of stinking leather leggings which, when Krunzle looked more closely, might have been fashioned from tanned human skin. He saw neither purse nor pockets, but did spot a lump where something had been roughly sewn into the waist. He went and got the Osirian's dagger, relieving the corpse of the weapon's sheath for good measure, and came back to the headless half-orc's body. When he applied the dagger's finely honed edge to the protrusion, the leather split and out popped a rough nugget of pure gold, the size of the top joint of the thief's thumb.

"Thank you, Sheshakk," he said, and was rewarded with a curl of the lip from the half-orc's head, still oozing blood a small distance away. Krunzle stepped carefully around it and went into the woods where he soon found the trio's rough camp: a lean-to for the two men, and a pile of bracken for the semi-human; some knuckle bones marked for gambling; and a woven basket with a tight-fitted lid that proved to contain some half-stale bread and dried meat. There was also a keg that held a pint of musty ale.

From farther back among the trees came a fouler, stronger smell. Krunzle went to take a look and found a dead man sprawled on his back, his head driven down into his shoulders and the top of his skull smashed to jelly. His leather jerkin had been ripped from hem to neck, and his exposed belly was torn open. It was difficult to see through the cloud of flies, but the thief thought the liver and heart were missing.

It was not unheard of for half-orcs to eat human flesh. If he had not had the sword and boots, Krunzle thought, he would have joined Sheshakk's larder. On the other hand, if he had not been snared by Eponion, he would not have fallen into the bandits' ambush in the first place. He decided to call it a draw and went back to the camp, collared the bread, jerky, and ale, and sat down to eat.

When he rose a few minutes later, his legs no longer felt like overboiled vegetables. He poked about the camp, saw nothing more to command his attention, and relieved himself in the bushes. Then he went to the river to wash his hands and came back to scoop up the basket with what remained of the provender. The purse, filled with coins and the nugget, was already tucked in his shirt. But when he reached for the dagger in its sheath, he felt a warning tingle at his neck.

It is a valuable weapon, he thought. *I could sell it in the first town we come to.* A moment passed, and then he knew that his rationale was not accepted. He would have no other weapon than the one the Tian spellslinger had given him.

Still, it was a good sword. He would not have survived the encounter with the bandits without it. The thief saw no profit in grumbling, but he did so anyway, on general principle. Heedless, the snake told the buskins to come back to life. Moments later they were carrying him, with increasing stride and speed, once more onto the river road and onward.

Chapter Three
Room Thirteen

He saw no other traffic on the road that morning, though he did pass a flotilla of barges moving upriver, poled slowly against the current by hard-muscled crewmen. A company of Taldan archers stood with their bows strung and in armor, half of them in the prow and half at the stern. They watched Krunzle from the moment he came into their sight until the moment he was out of view. He knew he must make a comical sight, leaping along in twenty-foot bounds, but not one of the archers showed a smile.

Not a land for the light-hearted, he thought. He had seen no villages or hamlets since he had come back to consciousness. Here and there, set well back from the river, had been fortified farms, the buildings tightly grouped, showing the outer world no windows wider than an arrow slit, and with high walls of upright, pointed timbers closing the gaps. Before the gate of one of these thorps the farmer and his retainers had erected a gibbet from which a crow-pecked corpse hung by its ankles. A hand-lettered sign was tied by a rope to the body's middle. Krunzle could not read it as he flashed by on the other side of the river, but he did not doubt that it would say *Thus to all reivers* in the local script.

Here and there, he came to places at which streams ran down from the hills to join the river. No bridges had been built—probably the Kalistocrats of Kerse saw no profit in doing so—but where the water was too deep or fast to ford, flat-topped boulders had been strung across to make stepping stones.

As he flew past a couple of these confluences, Krunzle saw on the shore the remains of sluice boxes and bucket chains where gold-hunters had shoveled stream-bed gravel onto screen-bottomed boxes while their workmates hauled water to flush grains of gold out of the detritus and down through the mesh to where the iron pan waited below. When the local gold was all taken, the miners would move upriver to the next place where dust—and perhaps even a nugget— pooled in the stream's sediments. They took their pans, leather buckets, and close-woven screens, and left the boxes to rot on the stream banks.

Sluice-mining was an effective means to quick riches, the traveler knew, if you happened upon a deposit of slush-sand and gravel that had been accumulating washed-down gold since the gods first made the world. Otherwise, it was just another way to break your back and your spirits. The thief preferred to let others find the riches, consolidate them neatly, then look the other way while Krunzle the Quick scooped them into his pouch.

Thus he would not have been tempted to poke about in the disused mining camps he saw on the banks of the inrushing streams, even if his boots were not carrying him ever onward. And thus he was more than a little surprised when, having leapt from stone to stone across one of these tributaries, his buskins did not carry him farther along the river road; instead, they turned west to follow a smaller trail that ran along the new watercourse and into the woods.

He formed words in his mind: *Chirk, where are we going?* Soon the knowledge came, as if it had always been his, that Berbackian and the seduced Gyllana were known to have taken passage on a barge to this spot; they had disembarked and mounted the horses they had brought with them, then followed the stream, whose name was the Piddoch, toward the hills western.

Not to Highhelm then? Krunzle asked. The answer he received was vague. He saw a mental image of the Tian wizard crouching over a bowl of heavy oil, peering at its surface through a lens held over one eye by a network of straps fitted over his hairless head. Again and again, he stirred the oil with a rod of gray metal, then examined the result through the eyepiece. The wizard's mouth frowned in a perfect bow.

He lost them, Krunzle thought. *They had some means to cover their tracks against his scrying.* Chirk let him know that Eponion, like any well-set-up merchant, had the means to keep his movements out of the sight of competitors—knowledge being so often the difference between a handsome profit or a devastating loss. Gyllana, it seemed, had appropriated whatever magical apparatus her father used to defeat scryers; the wizard, being familiar with the object in question, could obtain some partial success in piercing its barrier—but only enough to lead the pursuit to a certain point along the elopers' path. That point lay not far ahead; after they got there, it would be up to Krunzle to use his abilities to pick up the trail and follow it.

What else did she appropriate? he asked the snake. *A spell to blast any pursuer into scintillating fragments? An invocation to summon up some infernal creature, all tooth and talon, to carry me down to Hell, rip me three new orifices, then spend eternity finding inventive ways to plug them?*

Almost, there came an answer, but the thought died in Krunzle's mind even as it was forming. He suspected that Chirk had been about to reveal something, then had decided against it. Instead came an assurance that nothing Gyllana carried would do the thief harm. Berbackian, on the other hand, could be a problem.

You had better tell me about him.

A picture formed inside his head: a tall, broad-shouldered Blackjacket, with dark, curly hair and blue eyes, the latter showing intelligence and a questing spirit. The smile on the man's mouth was one of ironic amusement, with an underlying hint of cruelty. To Krunzle, he looked the kind who would spot the course, clearly and early, that led to his own best advantage; and, to secure his ends, he would show no hesitation in doing whatever was required.

A potentially formidable opponent, the thief thought, and was glad he had the ensorcelled weapon. That led to another thought: *The spell that empowers the sword, has it limits? Will it wear off?*

He was again told that he need not worry. It was not an entirely satisfactory answer, but continuing to question brought him no other—and when Chirk wearied of it, Krunzle suddenly found it hard to breathe. *All right, then, what about the girl?*

A moment later, he saw her in his mind's eye: a slimmer, shorter—though not that much more feminine—version of her merchant father. She was pretty enough, if you didn't mind an underlying sullen cast to her expression, and definitely female enough, especially if you liked them on the plump side.

Krunzle did not expect to like her under any circumstances, nor did he expect her to like him. He was, after all, intent on bringing her back to her father's house, a prospect she could not be expected to relish. He might have to drug her, bind her, certainly keep close tabs on her until they got back to Kerse. She would, doubtless, resent him. He was sure he would be able to endure the burden of her opprobrium.

The land into which he was moving was a series of wooded terraces between ridges that climbed toward the hills that he could no longer see through the dense woods. The flat land on some of the terraces was marshy, the stream all but lost in a morass of tussocks and sodden peat. Here someone had laid a corduroy road of timbers staked into the wet ground. At one point, as he tripped lightly over the serried logs, he saw up ahead what looked to be a mound of vegetation stir itself and move slowly toward the roadway. But the boots had him speeding by long before the swamp creature could organize its slow vegetative processes to catch him. Soon after, the trail began to climb again, the stream tumbling along beside him.

He could only vaguely position himself. He was moving roughly west. The Profit's Flow was behind him. Kerse was somewhere off to the northeast, and the town of Macridi—where the Great Goldpan River joined with Profit's Flow—was probably southeast through the deep forest. What was ahead was a mystery; even Chirk had no image to show him.

At noon, Chirk acceded to a request to stop so that he could relieve himself again. The thief sat beside the Piddoch and chewed the last of the bandits' dried meat. The bread was hard, but softened when he soaked it in water. The snake had not let him bring the ale keg, but it did allow him to pick a few handfuls of tart beebleberries that grew along the bank.

Then Krunzle was bounding through the woods once more, the hills rising more steeply now. Some hours later, he came out of the trees at the top of a ridge and saw below him a shallow, wooded valley through which the Piddoch ran. On its far side rose a crumbling escarpment—a slope of boulders and scree probably thrown down during the long-ago eruption of Droskar's Crag. Through this the river had cut a narrow gorge that continued to deepen as the water passed into the valley. At the mouth of this canyon was a wide space denuded of timber. He thought he saw buildings, but before he could examine the view, the buskins moved him down the slope and he was back into the trees.

Evening was setting in when Krunzle bounded out of the woods and into a sea of stumps and mud that ran up to where the escarpment was split by the gorge. On this side of the river, which ran fast here, was a huddle of cabins, shacks, and sprawling frame buildings. Though the raw planks from which the structures had been built could be no more than a few months old— some of them were still oozing sap—the place had the look of a camp that had been knocked together and was already falling apart.

Boom town, Krunzle thought. He would have liked to have stood and surveyed the place before plunging down into it. Chirk and his boots had other plans. But halfway down the slope he directed a sharp thought at the snake: *It would be best if I idled into town like any other goldbug drifter, instead of by prodigious leaps that attract the attention of everyone on the main street. I don't want to have to spend my time fending off attempts to steal my boots.*

Chirk did not reply, but the boots lost their energy and the thief descended the rest of the way to town at a normal pace. At the outskirts, where there were more tents than shacks, he came across a placard hung on a post. It read *Ulm's Delve* in bold red paint, roughly daubed. Beneath it: *No thieves, filchers, bun-passers, vagrants, or holy-fakers.* And below that: *By Order, Boss Ulm.* As an afterthought, someone had painted in blue near the bottom: *Ladies Welcome.*

Krunzle passed on into the town, finding that it had one long central street that paralleled the course of the gorge, with several shorter avenues cutting in from either side. The principal thoroughfare was lined with two-story establishments catering to the needs of gold-hunters: taverns, hotels, brothels, tool-and-equipment vendors, one bathhouse, and an assay office. He saw no sign that suggested an Ulm's Delve constabulary, nor that Kerse or Macridi extended any official presence.

Wide open, he thought. A walk along the crowded main street soon confirmed his impression. He rubbed shoulders with persons from half the nations of the Inner Sea, and saw no fewer than six dwarves. Most of those who braved the street were muddy to the knees, and many of them carried the implements of their calling. In fact, Krunzle thought, anyone who cornered the local trade in pickaxes and shovels could retire after a year.

Two blocks into town, he came upon more imposing buildings—in the sense that their fronts had at least been painted and the signs that identified the goods and services to be bought within featured less imaginative spelling—and he left the street for one of the wooden sidewalks that ran along the fronts of the enterprises. He stopped outside the largest, whose wall bore signs advertising it as a genteel hostelry and tavern catering to the discerning.

This, he said to Chirk, *is where Gyllana would stay, if she had to stay in this sinkhole. Here is where I will make my first inquiries.* The snake did not disagree, and he pushed open one of the swinging double doors and entered.

The lobby was what he would have expected: a front desk, a staircase leading to rooms upstairs, and a wide archway to one side through which came a hubbub of many voices talking at once, a continual clinking of glasses and metal tankards, and a fug of sweat, smoke, and fermented drink. He turned away from that distraction and approached the man behind the desk, who was just lighting an oil lamp.

"A room," Krunzle said, "with a bath." Chirk tingled warningly, but when the thief thought, *I may need somewhere to put her,* the snake subsided.

The man behind the desk, a Keleshite with slicked-back hair and a brocaded vest, regarded him without favor and hooked a thumb toward a sign on the wall that advertised the hostelry's rates. The cost of a room for a night would have paid the weekly rent on a comfortable apartment in Kerse.

Krunzle brought out the bandits' purse and shook out the single gold coin. The clerk looked at it and shook his head. The traveler put back the gold piece and dug deeper in the pouch. Then he placed Sheshakk's nugget on the unpolished wood of the counter. The clerk's eyebrows went up and he cast a guarded look at the thief.

Krunzle said, "Will that do?"

The functionary offered him a smile, then scooped the lump of gold from the wood and into a drawer. "Indeed," he said.

"For how long?"

"Oh," said the clerk, "you'll get yourself a good long stay for that one."

"Fine. Let me know when I've reached the mid-point of what it will buy."

"Certainly."

"Now I want to see my room. I'll want hot water brought up for a bath right away, then I want to see the dinner menu."

"Of course." The clerk selected a key from half a dozen hanging from a rack behind him, then shouted a name. The owner of the name, an elderly, bearded, stooped fellow of indeterminate nationality, came out of a booth set into the wall. "Take this gentleman to room thirteen," the man behind the desk said.

The oldster blinked and his mouth fell open. "Thirteen?" he said.

"Thirteen," said the clerk, his tone harsh. To Krunzle he said, "Buldrus's wits rarely assemble all at the same time. Pay him no heed." Then he gave the old man the key and said, "Get along now."

Krunzle followed the bent back up the stairs and down a hallway to its very end. The fellow fitted the key into the lock and the thief was glad to see that both the door and the fastener looked sturdy. The room, when he was let into it, was also fitted with stout iron bars across the single window.

"I need fear no nocturnal incursions here," he said to Buldrus, slipping him one of the copper coins.

"If you say so," said the old man. He left, closing the door behind him.

Krunzle went to the window and surveyed the view outside. He saw only the blank, unpainted, wooden wall of a building opposite, separated from the hotel by a narrow alley that was unlit and dim as the last of the daylight faded. A parcel of men came bustling out of a ground-level door and moved with deliberate haste up the alley toward the main street. He paid them no great heed, though he noticed that all of them were strongly built and none of them wore the mud-spattered clothes that would have marked them as miners.

He turned to inspect the room and found it adequate, though not large. Then he noticed that there was no tub for his bath. He looked for the key and, not finding it, realized that the elderly loon must have taken it with him. He crossed to the door to pull it open, but was surprised to find it locked against him.

At that moment, Chirk stirred—not tingled, not constricted—against the flesh of his neck, as if something had caused the snake to shiver. Krunzle gave a passing thought to the question of whether or not snakes *could* shiver—he would have doubted it—but his main concern was the locked portal. He pounded on the wood, cried "Hello! I'm locked in!", heard no response, and thumped and yelled again, rattling the brass door opener with the hand that wasn't pounding the very solid panel.

Then the metal turned in his hand, the door flew inward, and he was face-to-face with a heavy-jawed man whose bristle-short hair revealed several scars on his scalp that complemented the ones on his face. *A brawler* was Krunzle's first thought. *And a mean one.*

Behind the man were two others who showed the signs of similar histories—a red-bearded Ulfen and a wide-bodied Taldan—and behind them, watching the thief from over their shoulders, hung a thin, cadaverous face with an expression of wariness coupled with suspended judgment.

Krunzle stepped back, his hand going automatically to the hilt of his sword.

"Clear the way," said the man at the back, his mind now clearly made up. The bruisers stepped efficiently out of his path, revealing a skeletally thin Chelaxian in an ankle-length robe of silk dyed deep blue. The man brought together the fingertips of both hands in a particular manner and quickly intoned seven syllables, three on a rising inflection, three more on a descending, the last as a shout.

Immediately, the sword fell from Krunzle's hand, but before he could even hear it strike the floorboards, his world went blindingly white, then equally blindingly dark—though, by then, he was unaware of anything.

"Where'd you get it?" said a voice. A moment later, a hard hand rocked Krunzle's face sideways with a stinging slap that rattled his eyeballs in their sockets.

"Wha?" he said. "Whu?" He struggled to rise. Somehow, he knew he was sitting, even though he had only now emerged from the blackness. His legs would not obey him, nor would his arms when he gripped the chair's arms and sought to push himself upright. He was tied tightly at wrist and ankle. For good measure, a stout rope also bound him to the back of the chair.

"Hit him again," said the voice. It came from behind and to one side and sounded as harsh as dirt rattling on a coffin lid.

Krunzle turned his head in that direction and said "Wait," just in time for the hard hand to connect once more with his cheek and temple. This time, he definitely felt it. Whoever was hitting him was hitting him hard—striking right through the target, as the thief's old instructor in unarmed combat had taught him all those years ago at the rogues' guild in Elidir.

"Awake, now, are we?" said the voice. Its owner circled around from behind the chair to come into view. Krunzle saw a heavy-set man of middle years whose features were dominated by a great lump of a nose, which was itself dominated by a huge brown wart from which three black bristles sprang. He had the kind of mouth that can form only an unappetizing smile, because the only situation that would prompt a smile would be the exercise of the cruelty the thief saw in the man's eyes.

"The nugget," said the grating voice. "Where did you get it?" A yellow patch appeared at the bottom of Krunzle's blurred vision. He blinked away the tears the slap had brought to his eyes and focused: it looked to be the nugget he'd taken off Sheshakk's corpse.

"Off a dead half-orc," he said, and realized as he spoke that his tongue was bleeding on one side. He must have bitten it during their efforts to awaken him. He spat a little blood in the direction of his interrogator, but most of it ended up on his own shirt.

Another slap spun his head around. He focused on the other man in the room—an Ulfen, this one with red hair and beard, both in braids, and a big belly that strained his coarsely woven wool shirt. He had been one of those who had come to the door of Room Thirteen. Now the man with the wart brought the gold back into view. He held it so that Krunzle could see what he hadn't noticed before: stamped into one end of the lump of raw gold was a sigil of a butterfly. He thought he recognized it as the sign of the goddess Desna, the deity most appealed to by gamblers.

"Tell the truth," Wartnose said, "and you might live to see daylight."

"I took it off a half-orc," the thief said again. "His name was Sheshakk and he was working with an Osirian and an Ulfen. I didn't have time to get their names."

The redhead raised his arm for another slap, but the wart-nosed man stopped him with a gesture. He squatted down now so he was at eye level with Krunzle. "You killed Sheshakk?" he said, "not to mention Boabdil, Imrit, and Ernulf?"

The red-bearded man spoke. "Hard to believe. Unless he snuck in while they were sleeping and cut their throats." He spat on the floor. "He looks the throat-cutting type."

"Cut Sheshakk's throat and you'd only annoy him," said the squatting man. He rubbed his nose wart and studied the thief.

Krunzle had been counting on the fingers of one swollen hand. "You said four names. I killed only three. A fourth man was in the bushes. He'd been dead a couple of days."

Wartnose stood, stiffly, massaged his lower back and looked at the Ulfen. "I know what you're thinking," he said.

Redbeard had the uncomfortable look of a man who has been proved right when his boss has been proved wrong—a boss who is not likely to take it well. "It's all history now," he said, and looked anywhere but at his employer.

"Tell me what happened," Wartnose said to Krunzle.

The thief recounted only the essential elements of the tale; full details would not help him. "They braced me at the river. The Osirian mistakenly shot the Ulfen. In the confusion, I was able to take off the half-orc's head. Then I ran the bowman through before he could nock another arrow."

Wartnose studied him for what seemed a long time. Then he shook his head as if to throw off an unproductive chain of thought. "It sounds . . . far-fetched," he said. "Yet here you are, and here is Boabdil's lucky nugget, which he would never give up willingly."

Krunzle cast his memory back to the camp. "Was he a gambler?" he said. "I saw a set of knuckle bones by their fire."

Wartnose received the information as if it fitted into a slot in his mind. "What else?"

"The corpse in the bushes, his head was crushed— I'd say by the half-orc's bludgeon—and his belly was ripped open."

Wartnose's eyes moved left, right, and landed on Redbeard. "There it is," he said.

"What?" said the Ulfen.

Wartnose sighed. "Why must I always be surrounded by animated lumps of earth?" he said. He addressed himself instead to Krunzle. "The picture is clear: They settle beside the river to wait for the barge and collect the landing fee from any passengers coming to town. They're bored so they throw knuckle bones. Boabdil relies on his lucky nugget, but this day its power is running thin. He loses to Sheshakk, but refuses to pay.

"Sheshakk is not bright, but he has a strong sense of his own entitlement. He demands the nugget. Boabdil, in a strategic blunder, swallows the gold. Sheshakk acts as a half-orc would and recovers the nugget by the shortest possible sequence of events."

"He also," Krunzle said, "appeared to have eaten the man's heart and liver."

"Well, there you go," said Wartnose, "Sheshakk was never one to waste an opportunity for a meal." He tugged at his warty proboscis, causing the traveler to wonder if years of such mistreatment had rendered it so large and unlovely. "Then you happen along, they decide to see if you can make their day profitable— but you end up killing all of them." He pulled again at his nose. "That's the part that's hard to square with the other factors. You must admit that you do not present as an accomplished warrior. Imrit and Ernulf were capable; Sheshakk was a force of nature. Why are you here, and they not?"

"I may be able to answer that," said a new voice. The door to the room was out of Krunzle's restricted, chair-bound view, but now he heard it close as another man entered. Into view came the bone-thin man who had been behind the bruisers sent to collect the thief from Room Thirteen.

"How?" said Wartnose.

"His sword is wrapped in a powerful charm, as are his boots." As the newcomer said this, Krunzle realized that his numb feet were in stockings. "And let me have a look . . ." The thin man squatted as his employer had done, his bony knees creaking and popping, and stroked a long finger tipped by a pointed nail along the ring of bronze around the thief's neck. He withdrew the digit sharply, with a hiss of intaken breath, as if he had touched hot metal, though to Krunzle the snake felt as it always did.

"Tian?" he said, rising with more crackles and snaps from his joints.

Krunzle said, "The man who put it on me was."

"And who was that?" Wartnose wanted to know.

"Again" said the thief, "we did not exchange names and honorifics."

"For that tone," said the man in charge, "you get another slap. Brundelaf?"

Brundelaf the redbeard stepped quickly forward, as if glad of a chance to play a useful part, and delivered another hard, open-handed blow to Krunzle's cheek. The traveler felt a tooth loosen in its socket.

"What are you doing here?" Wartnose said. "Who sent you?"

Krunzle's inclination again was to tell the essential truth. But he found himself unable to speak, as Chirk chose this moment to tighten about his neck. In the thief's mind, an understanding formed: telling the tale of Eponion, Berbackian, and Gyllana would not be helpful to his situation; indeed, Chirk would see that attempting to do so would be immediately fateful.

Agreed, he answered, within the privacy of his own cerebrum. *But what do I tell them?*

A moment later, the answer came, and he spoke.

"No one sent me. I was indentured to a Tian merchant who thought I would make a useful caravan guard."

"Why would he think that?" said Wartnose.

The story came from the back of his mind. "Because I had come into his service after being captured during a raid on one of his convoys." He showed them a chagrined face. "The plan—my plan—was a good one, but my second-in-command was the nervous sort. He brought his section of our company out onto the road too soon.

"We still tried to make a go of it, but timing is everything in the bandit trade. The merchant had time to activate his defenses—one of which was a wizard who was quite capable when he was not under the influence of flayleaf."

"What is flayleaf?" said Wartnose.

Krunzle felt the answer forming in his mind, but was forestalled by the cadaverous man. "You might know it by some other name. It is a drug that supposedly opens the senses to other planes, but I've heard that it can be habituating."

"So," Krunzle continued, "the mage happened to be sober that afternoon. He laid us low with a blast of purple light. Those of us not killed outright were captured and added to the slave coffle at the rear of the baggage train. But the merchant conceived a different plan for me: I was to scout ahead and uncover any other dangers on the road. The wizard put something on my boots and did something to my sword that made it invincible in defense—though useless in attack—then put this thing about my neck to keep me biddable."

His interrogator's eyes narrowed. "Yet here you are, with no Tian merchant in sight. How do you explain that?"

The response was coalescing in the thief's brain even as the question was put. "I cannot be sure," he said. "I noticed that the farther in advance of the caravan I got, the less grew the snake's power. I suspect that the wizard mishandled the incantation that bound it to him—although I soon learned not to try to take it off. I thought eventually I would find a mage who could do it for me."

Wartnose looked at the skeletal man. "Could you?"

The other stroked his bony chin. At first he seemed of two minds, then he signaled a negative. "Perhaps with a year to study the matter. I know the principles of Tian magic but am far from familiar with the technical details. I can tell you without a doubt, however, that there is power at the heart of this. Room Thirteen could only damp down its control of the boots and sword, and I have known first-degree spells to fade to insignificance under the influence of the charms built into the walls and floor of that chamber."

"Hmm," said Wartnose. "Let us sum this up. Absent his sword and boots, this one,"—he indicated the traveler—"is nothing but another ditch-haunting throat-cutter. The whatever-it-is about his neck empowers the boots and sword, which are nothing without its strength. So, obviously, it would not serve us to bring them back together. How about if we just kill him?"

The skeletal mage thought about it. "Unwise, I should say. It seems to be bound to him now. Remove him from the mix and it might begin to act independently."

"That worries you?" said Wartnose.

"Inasmuch as I cannot get a close read on its capabilities, I would prefer to see it remain where it is. It would give me an opportunity to study it."

"And how," said his employer, "would I profit from that?"

The thin man bent to examine the snake again. "I have a sense," he said, "that there is more power here than meets the mage's eye. Indeed, I suspect that the entity in question is disguising its true nature."

"Entity?" said Wartnose. He rounded on the man in the chair. "Is that thing around your neck alive?"

The thief didn't need Chirk's prompting. "I am a simple wayfarer," he said. "Wizards' tricks are beyond my understanding."

"Here's what I suggest," said the thin man. "Keep him well away from his boots and sword. Put him down with the chain gang. He can earn his keep moving baskets of ore. In the meantime, I'll pore through my books and consult a colleague or two."

"And, at the end?" Wartnose said.

"I make no promises, but that object around his neck may give you more rock-cracking power than a battalion of Skanderbrogs." He bent and peered again at Chirk. "Assuming, that is, that we can harness it."

Krunzle wondered what a Skanderbrog was, but the rest of the conversation's import was clear to him: he was going to be kept alive while the mage studied Chirk; he was also going to be put to work—never a prospect that held great appeal—in some kind of mining project. He directed a thought to the snake— *This sits well with you?*—and received the mental equivalent of a shrug.

Meanwhile, his bonds were cut and for the second time in as many days his extremities felt the agony of his blood reoccupying its old haunts. Redbeard opened the door and shouted a name. The scar-pated brawler the thief had last seen in the door to Room Thirteen came and seized him by one arm while the Ulfen took the other. He was hustled across a room and out into the alley he had last seen from above. He offered a protest about the state of his feet, which earned him a quick, short jab to the jaw—a professional's blow—from the brawler. After that, he knew nothing for a while.

Chapter Four
A Promising Young Troll

When he awoke this time, he was at least unbound. He was lying on his back on a wooden floor in a dark place. But he knew he was not alone from the hubbub of voices and motion around him. Something startling had happened—no, frightening, he thought as his senses fully reassembled themselves and reported for duty—and a crowd of people were reacting to it by putting as much distance between themselves and the something as their circumstances allowed.

But their circumstances were not liberal; the mob had not gone far away, though the panicky cries and curses suggested they would have liked to. Krunzle also suspected that, given the chance, the unseen melee of forms struggling against each other in the darkness would have welcomed the opportunity to bathe—surely, nobody wanted to reek of filth, sweat, rotten meat, and untreated sores. And over it, a strong stink of charred meat.

His head ached, but at least it was clear. He sat up, and as he did so he heard from behind him the tramping of hard-soled boots on planks, accompanied by a faint light that grew stronger. He turned his head and, seeing vertical stripes of light, realized that they were gaps between the timbers of a heavy door. Someone was approaching the other side, carrying a light.

A rattle of iron keys, then the turning of an unoiled lock, and now the door was pushed in. A big man armed with a club bent to peer under the low lintel of the doorway, extending the oil lamp into the room. "What's all the ruckus?" he said.

He didn't seem to have directed the question at Krunzle, and the thief used the presence of the light to look about him. He was sitting on the floor of a large room, its walls made of squared-off logs. The room contained three or four score men—ragged, filthy, scrofulous-looking men—who were crowded in a group against the far wall, their eyes large in the lamplight.

The eyes were frightened and focused on Krunzle—except he now saw that the mob's collective gaze kept going to something on the floor between him and them. Something man-sized and man-shaped that, when the fellow with the lamp came into the room, casting more illumination on the scene, was revealed to be a man. Or at least most of one. And what was left of him was dead.

The man with the club stepped past the thief and bent to examine the body. Krunzle took the opportunity to rise. He thought about making a break through the open door, but decided he was far too wobbly on his feet. And for all he knew, in the blackness that seemed to be outside this jail—for ragged men, a strong door, and a man with a key and a club all said jail to Krunzle—he'd run straight over the lip of the gorge.

The corpse was that of a heavily muscled man with a scarred face and no hands or forearms. Above where his elbows should have been were charred stumps, still smoking. His eyes were wide open, as was his mouth, creating an impression that his final emotion had been huge and painful surprise.

The jailer made a noise of confirmation, straightened, and poked the club gingerly in Krunzle's direction. "You," he said, "back off. Over in that corner, and stay there." When the traveler raised both hands in a gesture of non-confrontation and did as he was bid, the man with the club pointed at a couple of the ragamuffins and said, "You two, haul this out and dump it in Skanderbrog's trough."

The indicated pair crept forward, took the corpse's ankles, and began to drag it toward the door. "Wait," said the jailer, then stooped to rifle the body's rags, which Krunzle noted were in better condition than any of those worn by the other men in the cell. Having found and pocketed a few items, the man with the club said, "Carry on."

He remained in the room, eyeing Krunzle warily, until the corpse detail returned. Then he pointed the club at the thief again, said, "No more trouble," and left, taking the lamp with him.

Krunzle heard the key turn in the lock again. Before the light went, he had seen rags and sacking on the floor near him. He scooped these into a pile, then lay down. Over on the other side of the room, he heard stirrings and mutterings and a few curses as the crowd of ragged men composed themselves for what remained of the night.

None of them came too near Krunzle, for which the traveler was grateful. Their stench was not to his liking. He raised a hand to carefully waggle his jaw, poked with his tongue at the loosened tooth, and contemplated the general ache in his skull. He had known worse.

He needed sleep. Tomorrow would bring more information about his predicament, and perhaps some means of improving it. His last thought was to wonder again what Skanderbrog was.

Krunzle, along with the other slaves, was roused at dawn by the clanging of an iron bar on an iron triangle hung outside the strongroom. The door was flung open by another man with a club, and the slaves roused themselves from where they had slept on the floor and rushed outside. The thief rose and followed.

He found himself on a broad platform made of planks, close to the edge of the gorge. The ragged men were clustered around a big cauldron near the door to the barracks. They'd taken rough wooden bowls and were dipping them into the big pot and slurping the contents. More tough-looking men with cudgels—some of them had coiled whips at their belts—stood around, some of them telling the ragged men to hurry up and finish.

Krunzle went to the pile of bowls, found one that was not too encrusted with dried remnants of previous meals, and moved toward the cauldron. He could not help but notice that those in his path—or even well wide of it—moved out of his way. Even the bruisers seemed chary of coming too close to him.

He dipped the bowl into the stuff in the pot—some kind of pasty gruel afloat with chunks of spoiled vegetables—and brought it to his lips. It tasted like pig swill, the kind given to swine who were not highly prized by their owner. But he reasoned that the day was not likely to offer better nourishment, and he remembered someone saying last night that he would be "moving baskets of ore." That was not work to be undertaken on an empty stomach.

He saw the red-bearded Ulfen who had beaten him at Wartnose's behest come down from the town and speak a word with a big-shouldered guard who looked to be in charge. The thief recognized this one too: he had been one of the men who had come to take him from Room Thirteen. Now Redbeard went back the way he had come and the head guard cast his gaze over the workers, until he found the one he was looking for. "Raimeau!" he called. "You show the new man what to do!"

A gangling young man with long locks of prematurely gray hair got up from where he'd been eating, drained the final few drops of gruel from his bowl, then wiped its wet inner side with a finger to lick off the absolutely last remnants. He tossed the bowl onto the heap of others and came very slowly toward the traveler, his hands extended in a gesture that said he hoped for no trouble.

Krunzle noticed that Raimeau's eyes went from his to the thing around his neck and back again. The traveler put the facts together. To the young man he said, "You have no need to worry about this,"—he moved a hand to indicate Chirk—"as long as you leave it alone."

"Have no fear," said the other. "Seeing what happened to Chenax was instruction enough for me."

"Chenax was the man with no hands?"

"He was, though he had a very hard pair of fists before he met you, and had no qualms about using them."

At that moment, a whistle blew and the slaves moved toward the edge of the platform. "Work?" said the thief.

"Work," said Raimeau. "We'll be hauling baskets of ore from the face up to the crusher. Watch where you put your feet, because there are no railings on the ledge or the scaffolding. One misstep, and you'll be joining Skanderbrog for dinner. Like Chenax is about to do for breakfast."

The thief focused on the immediate. "Are Chenax's shoes still available?" He indicated his stockinged feet. "Mining is no work for the unshod."

"They will be if Skanderbrog hasn't had breakfast yet. He usually doesn't bother to peel his fruit."

Skanderbrog, it turned out, was a name—a name that had been given to a juvenile male troll by his mother, who after nursing him through childhood and teaching him the rudiments of trollery, had handed young Skanderbrog the forequarter of a deer and sent him down from the mountains to see if he could establish a territory for himself and get on with life. But Skanderbrog had been unable to find a niche that was not already occupied by larger and more experienced trolls. Starving, he had come down to forage on the outskirts of Ulm's Delve. After eating a couple of unsuccessful gold-panners—they made poor meals, being half-starved themselves, living off leaves and roots while striving for the elusive gleam in the pan— he had been trapped in a pit that Wartnose's mage had caused to be dug and lined with charms.

The man with the wart on his nose was, as the thief might have expected, the same Boss Ulm by whose order Ulm's Delve barred "thieves, filchers, bun-passers, vagrants, and holy-fakers." The skeletally thin wizard he employed was Mordach the Prudent, and the red-bearded Ulfen was Brundelaf, the outfit's chief enforcer. He even knew the name of the brawler who had clipped him: Little Fost, he was called— apparently there was a larger version somewhere in the world. The thief thought he would as lief as not be spared the experience of making Big Fost's acquaintance.

Raimeau was both the knowledgeable type and the sort who liked to tell what he knew. As they descended the scaffolding then stepped off the trestle-work to where a broad ledge had been cut in the rock face, he filled Krunzle in on the history of Ulm's Delve. By the time they had wrested a pair of sturdy shoes from the feet of dead, handless Chenax, laid in a broad wooden trough at one end of the ledge, near a cave sealed behind a grillwork of black metal, the thief was well briefed.

Boss Ulm had established himself quite solidly here in the Rumples, as this stretch of hilly country was called. Hearing of the gold strike and the rush of goldbugs into the region, he had come with his henchmen to establish the first saloon, brothel, and hardware emporium—in tents at first, though a sawmill was one of his earliest accomplishments, so that he could put up more enduring structures.

Once the instant town was booming, and Brundelaf and Little Fost and the others had eliminated any doubts as to who was in charge, Ulm had begun to think larger thoughts. He had hired Mordach the Prudent and set him the task of locating the source of the alluvial gold that had the prospectors lining the river's banks, panning and sluicing. The mage had cast his runesticks and questioned a number of subterranean beings he managed to summon and bind. Finally, he had marked a spot halfway up the south side of Starkriven Gorge, as the sheer canyon upriver from the town was called.

Ulm had established a claim to the gorge by the simple expedient of sending his bullyboys to throw out the handful of gold-hunters who were trying to work the gravel beneath the swift-running water at its bottom. He then moved the infant town to the edge of the chasm and began to develop a mine.

Mines require miners. These Ulm acquired by the simplest and least costly of measures: he promulgated several ordinances, signed by himself as de facto Reeve of Ulm's Delve. He knew that gold camps attract more than goldbugs; they attract several categories of persons who are skilled in separating prospectors from their pokes of dust and the occasional nugget. Boss Ulm made many of these activities illegal—the penalty for engaging in such banned enterprises was to be sentenced to an indefinite span of labor in the mine or the sawmill. He soon had a sizable, though resentful, work force.

Ulm had them build a trestle-work of timbers from the gorge's bottom to its top, and cut a wide ledge at the level where the seam of gold within the rock came closest to the rock face. Some of his enslaved card sharps, cutpurses, badger-gamers, and sandbaggers were set to hacking their way through to the gold, while others carried baskets of split rock to the surface, piling up the ore where Ulm had put more of his prisoners—there seemed to be an unending supply—to building him a crushing mill.

In the early days, the work had gone slowly, but the pace speeded up considerably when Mordach was able to bring Skanderbrog—in massive leg fetters of hammered iron—into the picture. Accommodating the troll required extra shoring up of the scaffolding, the cutting into the rock of a cell barred with a thick grill of charmed iron—the cell outside which Chenax waited to make his final contribution to Boss Ulm's wealth—and the manufacture of a huge hammer and chisel scaled to the young monster's size. But the investment was worth it. After a couple of the least-motivated workers were delegated to become troll-fodder, in full view of the rest of the work force, the mine's productivity increased severalfold.

Krunzle was on the ledge with Raimeau, trying on the dead man's shoes—they almost fit—when the whistle blew again. "We should leave here," the other man said. "Skanderbrog's coming out." As he spoke, a creak of metal on metal announced that the iron grillwork covering the opening at the end of the ledge was being winched upward on unseen cables. The thief needed no more encouragement but went quickly back the way they had come.

The young troll emerged into the morning light, blinking. Krunzle could see that he was not full grown: his undertusks thrust up no more than a few inches and he was barely twice the thief's height, even allowing for the stooped, bent-kneed stance that was common to his species. But his months of enslavement to Boss Ulm, each day spent swinging a hammer with a head as big as a man's torso to drive a long, thick chisel into resisting rock, had put even more muscle onto Skanderbrog's arms and shoulders than most mature trolls ever achieved. Trolls were generally averse to hard labor, preferring to make their livings by leaping from concealment onto passersby of whatever species. After overwhelming their prey with sudden, massive violence, they would sit down immediately to eat them raw. Trolls actually preferred cooked food, but most were too lazy to bother gathering fuel and going through the process of kindling a fire.

Skanderbrog's attention was drawn to the trough. He picked up Chenax in both his talon-tipped hands and brought his long snout down to sniff the body's charred arm-stumps. He clearly found the scent unpleasant, and delicately pulled Chenax's upper limbs from their sockets, much like a man twisting the wings off a cooked fowl, and threw them into the gorge.

The iron entrance to his cave closed behind him. He ignored it, and hunkered down on his haunches. A single twist of his wrist and Chenax's head popped off in his hand. He tossed the morsel into his mouth and Krunzle heard it crunch between the wide molars. Skanderbrog chewed, it seemed to the traveler, quite thoughtfully for a troll, his gaze moving across the crowd of slaves ranged over the flat and inclined surfaces of the scaffolding. He focused most clearly, however, on Mordach the mage, who had come down from above, along with a crew of torch-bearing men from Boss Ulm's cadre of enforcers.

While Skanderbrog made short work of the rest of Chenax, spitting out a metal belt buckle before swallowing the last of his meal, the men formed a double line of fire across the ledge between the troll and any possibility of his escape up or down the trestle-work. Mordach took up a position behind the twin rows of lit torches, raised his hands skyward, so that his sleeves fell back from his stick-thin arms, and shouted several harsh syllables.

The troll reacted as if he had experienced a sudden toothache. He shook his head, spittle flying from his black lips and prominent bottom tusks, and got to his feet. The look he gave the mage and the torchmen would have rendered Krunzle in instant need of a toilet, preferably one behind a locked and troll-proof door, but the men did not flinch. One or two of them even jeered and made rude noises with their tongues and lips.

Skanderbrog took only three steps, then paused where a sheet of canvas covered something against the gouged rock of the cliff face. He bent and threw back the heavy fabric as if it were the lightest cloth; beneath were his hammer and chisel. Mordach sent another string of syllables his way, and the young troll took up the tools and faced the rock. He set the chisel's edge into a crack, drew back the hammer, and slammed it forward. The collision gave off an almost musical *chink*, and a chunk of rock separated from the cliff and fell at Skanderbrog's feet. He swiveled, stooped, and bashed the hammer against the lump of stone, smashing it into fragments. Then he turned, straightened, put the chisel back against the wall, and repeated the process.

The torchmen parted enough for Mordach to step through to the fore. The troll eyed him askance but continued to cut rock from the cliff face and reduce it to smaller pieces. The mage's arm moved in a sweeping motion aimed at the ledge, and a rune carved into the nail of his index finger glowed with a light that made Krunzle's eyes ache, even at a distance. A smoking line appeared on the floor of the ledge just short of the growing pile of rock fragments. The troll paused in his work, sniffed at the air above the line, and growled. Then he went back to work.

Mordach and the torch-bearers departed, climbing the scaffolding's steps back up to the town, though not before the wizard favored Krunzle with a considering gaze. When the steps were cleared, the overseers hurried the slaves to form two parallel lines from the ledge up to the top of the gorge. Baskets were passed down from above until every man had one. The thief and his minder were pressed into line, becoming two links in what would become a continuous double chain to move baskets up and down the scaffolding.

Now a slave with a long-handled iron rake stepped up to Skanderbrog's growing pile of broken stone. Gingerly, the man extended the tool and pulled some rock across the line, which had now ceased to smoke but remained plain on the ledge's surface. As the rake's heavy tines grated on the stone, the troll paused in his labors and turned his head slightly toward the sound. Immediately, another slave, whose only function appeared to be to watch Skanderbrog, hissed a warning. The rake man stepped back. But the troll only growled again, then with a grunt, swung the hammer against the chisel head. The first man in the basket chain scooped rock into his basket then passed it to the slave beside him, who passed it in turn to the next man.

And so went the morning. For the first hour, Krunzle was in the upward-moving chain, taking a loaded basket from his left and passing it to his right. It took about half a minute for a basket to be loaded with Skanderbrog's output, so that every thirty seconds he had to bear a load for a few moments. At first, it wasn't hard, but as the minutes piled up, his shoulders and lower back began to ache, and his forearms to cramp. Raimeau was opposite him in the second chain, passing empty baskets downward to where the troll kept making fresh material for them to shift.

After an hour, a whistle blew and the two chains changed jobs. Krunzle welcomed the relief. But all too soon, it seemed, the whistle sounded again, and he was back to the hard life. By now the sun was well up, and the rock face caught and reflected its heat. Sweat ran down the thief's face and chest, soaked his shirt to his back, made his eyes sting with its salt. He reminded himself that he had sworn never to engage in brute labor—a vow he had seldom broken, and then only at the order of a magistrate who could command guardsmen with whips and truncheons to enforce their sentences.

The whistle blew again, and Krunzle was back to passing empty panniers. "Do we get lunch?" he said to Raimeau, working opposite him.

"More gruel," was the answer. The man next to Raimeau made a face. "Sometimes with a cat or a few rats in it."

Krunzle grunted. It was time to find a new occupation. But he was surprised at the idea that emerged from the back of his mind—until he realized that the thought had not been his, but Chirk's.

Are you insane? he thought back at the snake. *Even here I am too close to the troll.*

But the thought formed: after lunch, the snake wanted him to take the place of the man with the rake.

Why? But in a moment, he knew the reason. Chirk wanted to have a conversation with Skanderbrog. *You are insane*, Krunzle thought. *No one ever benefited from a conversation with a troll, unless it was the troll—a little diversion before dinner.*

The word formed in his mind: *Nonetheless.*

No, returned the thief, *and that is final.*

But it wasn't. Chirk showed him pictures: Mordach the Prudent dissolving the thief in a vat of acid, then draining it away to retrieve the unharmed bronze serpent from among his smoldering bones; Mordach sliding Krunzle into a blue-flamed furnace, then raking through the ashes for the again-unharmed Chirk; Mordach coating the traveler with a sticky, sweet syrup and staking him down between two great anthills, returning later to—

Enough! said Krunzle. *He will do one of these things?*

A moment later he knew that Mordach was delayed only because he had not yet decided which of these methodologies would create a maximum reduction of Krunzle with a minimum effect upon the object around his neck. The mage was known, after all, as "the Prudent."

Lunch was gruel and rotten pumpkin. Krunzle found a few flakes of gray meat in his, and swallowed them without comment. The work had given him an appetite as well as an acute awareness of several muscle groups that he had always taken for granted. He cataloged his aches and pains and swore to himself that Boss Ulm would one day render up an accounting for each and every one of them.

While they were eating, Mordach the Prudent returned and, with the torchmen to shield him, renewed the strength of the boundary spell he had cast that morning. Then he went back to town, throwing Krunzle a considering gaze as he passed.

The whistle blew and the thief said to Raimeau, "Come, and quickly." They descended the rough wooden steps as lightly as could be allowed by Krunzle's ill-fitting shoes and the prospect of plunging to a deadly battering on the rocks below. By the time the basket lines were reformed, he was standing near the mage's deadline—still visible, though no longer smoldering—with the rake in hand. Raimeau was beside him, wearing a look of deep uncertainty when he wasn't casting fearful sideways glances at the troll, the monster sitting with his back against the wall, glowering at them and the rest of the uncooperative world.

The man who had used the rake before said, "Give me that." To add emphasis, he scooped up a fist-sized rock and cocked his arm.

But it seemed to the traveler that the man did not have the full conviction that the implied threat required. *Chirk?* he thought.

Instead of an answer from the recesses of his mind, Krunzle saw the man lower his arm. The chunk of rock rattled among others in a basket, and the fellow—and his assistant, though not without a muttered threat to Raimeau—joined the basket chain.

The gray-haired man was regarding the thief with even more trepidation than when they had first met. "What?" said Krunzle, turning to where Skanderbrog was levering himself to his splay-toed feet and taking up his tools again.

"You don't know?" said Raimeau, keeping his voice low.

"Assume I don't." Krunzle raked a pile of rock toward the man whose job it was to fill the baskets.

"The snake," his partner whispered. "It glowed, kind of purple, but when you look at it too long black spots start floating before your eyes. It did that when Chenax tried to take it."

"Oh, that," said Krunzle, "of course. I'm familiar with the effect."

"Get to work!" The shout came from above, where one of Ulm's bullyboys was pushing his way down the steps between the lines of basketmen, and reaching for a whip coiled at his belt. Krunzle turned and began to rake rock.

Skanderbrog hacked at the cliff face as if it were his direst enemy. The muscles of his shoulders and arms bulged and flexed as he swung the hammer that

83

seemed to weigh no more than a switch of willow. Raimeau watched the troll closely, speaking a warning whenever the creature gave over attacking the wall of rock and turned to smash the boulders at his feet into pebbles. For that phase of the operations, the thief and his helper stood well back.

Even so, a flying shard opened Krunzle's cheek. He felt the sting, then a warm trickle making its way down through the dust on his face. The troll looked up from his work, snuffling, his nostrils dilated. He stared at Krunzle, and for a few seconds the traveler knew what it was to be a rabbit undergoing inspection by a fox. Though he was well beyond the mage's line, still he took a step backward.

As he did so, words formed in the back of his mind. He pushed them back where they had come from, saying, *I don't think so. One of my longstanding rules is not to draw the attention of man-eating monsters. It has served me well so far and—*

A jolt of pain shot up from the base of Krunzle's spine to rattle his skull. He felt an even larger one forming where the first had begun, like a thundercloud boiling up on the horizon.

Well, if you insist, he thought. Ideas began to form in his mind, a strategy for gaining the troll's cooperation. Krunzle watched the sequence of thoughts unravel, then said, in his inner voice, *No.*

A jolt of pain shot up from his spine again. He spasmed, hissing, so that Raimeau looked at him in alarm. The thief ignored the man and the troll, which had also glanced his way, and said to Chirk, *I did not say 'no' to the project, but only to your approach.*

He was surprised to hear a voice, soft and sibilant, speak in his head. *It makes sense,* came the reply. *The creature must hate Ulm and Mordach. A chance to take revenge—*

Krunzle cut off the voice. *You are collecting crumbs, ignoring the cake.*

How so?

Let me show you. He received no response and took the silence for acquiescence. Aloud, he spoke to the troll in a carrying whisper: "Skanderbrog! Do you enjoy your work?"

The creature was back at work on the rock face. Krunzle saw it regarding him from the corner of one eye while the hammer and chisel continued to gouge out chunks of gold-bearing ore. Over the clink of iron on iron, he heard a deep-throated growl. "You mock me?" Skanderbrog said.

"Don't mock him," said Raimeau. A full-body shiver had taken possession of Krunzle's helper. "He doesn't like being mocked."

"I cannot pass the line," said the troll, "but these can." He nudged the pile of broken rocks with the end of the chisel.

"It's true," said Raimeau. "Boss Ulm had a half-orc overseer named Horkak who used to stand just clear of Mordach's line. He would mimic Skanderbrog's labors and make uncomplimentary comparisons. One day, the troll picked up a piece of ore and threw it at him. The boundary spell heated the stone so greatly that it exploded in Horkak's face. He fell into the gorge and broke on the rocks."

"Horkak tasted bad," Skanderbrog said. "Too much gristle." He turned his head to look Krunzle up and down. "You will be more tender."

The thief would have gladly ended the conversation at that point, but Chirk was insistent. "I do not mock,"

Krunzle said. "I wondered if you had had enough of working for Boss Ulm. If you might want to move on."

Skanderbrog addressed himself to the rock face. "I do not like to work," he said. "But before I was captured, I starved. I ate frogs and dug for worms. I tried to make a place for myself in a cave on the edge of Grunchum's territory, but he drove me away. The same happened when I went into the land of his neighbor, Brugga. Here, at least I eat well and do not sleep on wet leaves."

Krunzle smiled to himself as he raked the cracked ore toward the men who filled the baskets. "Still," he said, "it's no life for a promising young troll."

The hammer rang on the chisel. Another great wedge of rock fell at Skanderbrog's feet. "It is true; I am not content," he said. "But I am resigned to my fate."

Krunzle let a few moments pass, then he said, "What kind of weapon does Grunchum wield? Or Brugga?"

Skanderbrog turned to smash the wedge of gray stone. He cocked his head, remembering. "They are traditionalists," he said, "and favor the long cudgel. They are not particularly adept, but they make up for it in sheer power."

"Do they eat well? As well as you have been eating this past little while?"

It was obviously not a question that had occurred to the troll, if indeed questions ever did. "Now that I think of it," Skanderbrog said, "probably not. The odd deer. Or a bear when they're still in winter sleep."

"And would either of them have developed the kind of muscles that now adorn your upper body?" Krunzle said.

Again, the troll took a long moment while the dull teeth of his mentality engaged the issue. "Grunchum was big-bellied, but his legs were spindly for a troll.

Brugga looked as if he had had a good winter. But he's getting long in the tooth."

Krunzle nodded. "So would either of them expect to be confronted by a well-fed, hard-shouldered young challenger armed with an iron-headed hammer? Not to mention a sharp iron spike that he could throw like a spear?"

The troll paused, the hammer poised. He held the chisel out at arm's length and studied it. "I would have to think about that," he said. He set the iron spike into a crevice, and brought the hammer down. Splinters of rock flew.

"You might also think," Krunzle said, "about how comfortable a territory an enterprising troll might make by combining both Grunchum's and Brugga's. You did say they were neighbors?"

Skanderbrog had gone back to cutting more rock from the cliff. He did not answer, but his expression was as thoughtful as his kind could manage.

We'll let it cook for a while, Krunzle told Chirk.

Where did you learn about trolls? the snake said.

I know nothing about trolls in particular, said the traveler, *but I know what it is to be young and seeking for a place in an uncooperative world. Don't you?*

Chirk was a while in responding. *My history,* it said at length, *is different from yours.*

Yet we are both bound to another's service, aren't we?

The snake was even longer in giving an answer, so that the traveler thought he would receive none. Finally, he heard, *You should know that I am not as easily gulled as a troll.*

Chapter Five
A Headache for Mordach

After a supper of more gruel, this time with cobs of stale, moldy bread to dip into it, the slaves were put away for the night. All except Krunzle. Red-bearded Brundelaf stopped him as he was about to enter the noisome lock-up. "Wait," he said, before efficiently binding the traveler's hands behind him and pushing him in the direction of the town.

When they reached the main street Krunzle expected to be ushered toward the back room of the saloon, where Boss Ulm had questioned him the night before. He hoped not; he was not at all sanguine that his tale of being a caravan scout would have held up under any kind of concentrated mulling. And the wart-nosed man looked the kind who would worry at a nagging suspicion until it was chewed to rags.

But when they had crossed the mud-puddled thoroughfare, Brundelaf did not compel him toward where light and noise spilled from the drinking establishment's doors and windows. Instead, the prisoner was shoved in the opposite direction. They walked uphill for two blocks, then came to a narrow, three-story building that featured only a few small windows, well barred, and a flat roof with a railing all around it. When the Ulfen pounded on the stout, iron-studded door, it opened soundlessly and without any visible agency. The redhead suppressed a shiver and, putting a hand between Krunzle's shoulder blades, propelled him through the door. The barrier closed silently behind the rogue, and he heard the sound of a lock engaging.

He was in a lamplit foyer, a spiral staircase to his left and a hallway leading into darkness at the back of the house. From above came the voice of Mordach the Prudent, beckoning him upstairs. Krunzle climbed. The second floor was one large room, scarcely lit by a brazier filled with glowing charcoal. One wall was lined with shelved books, many of them ancient and tattered, some of them scrolls of dried animal hide or coarsely made papyrus. Nearby hung an isinglass in a carved frame.

In the center of the room stood a workbench littered with alembics and retorts, and instruments of metal and other materials whose shapes and purposes, given the lack of light, remained a matter for conjecture. He did see, however, his buskins, sword, and scabbard, pinned down by what looked like thin gold wires. All three objects twitched as his gaze fell upon them, as if they were straining to break free of their bonds. He thought about trying to recover them himself, but a tingle in his neck told him that Chirk did not favor such a strategy, and in this place Krunzle was ready to take the snake's advice.

As the traveler continued up the spiral stairs, something in a cage hanging in the far corner of the room turned large, lambent eyes toward him, the twin golden circles disappearing then reappearing as the unknown creature lethargically blinked. Before he left its sight, he heard a hiss that carried a note of disappointment and a sound like an attempted fluttering of confined wings.

The top floor was Mordach's living quarters. The walls were unpierced by windows and the domed ceiling was asplash with stars. The room itself was a starkly ascetic space containing only a narrow bed, a bare table and a hard chair against one wall. The center of the chamber was dominated by a complexly patterned rug that covered most of the floor. The staircase ended at one corner of the carpet; the wizard was waiting at the corner diagonally opposite. "Approach," he said.

The thief did so. But as he stepped onto the rug, a mist sprang up behind him and to his sides; it thickened rapidly, until there was nothing in the world but the carpet, the wizard, and Krunzle. Even the raucous sounds of Ulm's Delve at night faded to silence. The captive had the impression of being in a much larger space than the area of the woven cloth, and the room's low ceiling seemed to have receded into infinity.

Mordach also had changed; in this place, he was somehow larger, more prepossessing. "Now," he said, "let us have a proper talk."

"I am happy to do so," said the traveler. "The conversation of the men with whom I spent the day lacked sophistication. As well, we were often short of breath, the work being strenuous."

The mage's smile showed an absence of amusement. "Save your blandishments," he said. "I saw Chenax's corpse before Skanderbrog got at it, and had the arms recovered from where the troll threw them."

There did not seem any useful answer Krunzle could make to this. He remained silent but contrived an expression that conveyed his interest in anything further the wizard might wish to say.

Mordach said, "The tale you told, of caravans and such, has lost much of its savor."

Again, the thief said nothing. The tale had, after all, been Chirk's; he did not feel a need to defend it. Besides, he was waiting to see if the snake would offer anything in its place. But though he waited, nothing came. Nonetheless, he felt a presence in the back pastures of his mind, and he had now become familiar enough with the relationship between himself and his keeper to recognize that he was not on his own in this encounter. He had the impression that Chirk was listening to what the wizard had to say—indeed, that he was waiting to hear something.

Mordach approached. More accurately, Krunzle would have said he *loomed*; he did not so much come closer as grow larger. "In this place," the mage said, one bony hand circling to indicate the space within the mist, "I need not fear the fate of Chenax—"

Krunzle felt the presence of Chirk grow stronger, and words came to him that he spoke aloud: "Still, you would do well not to touch."

Mordach's face showed a weighing of options, then he said, "At this point, you are probably correct. I think I am beginning to gain some idea as to what I'm dealing with. And, with your boots and sword under restraint, you are not likely to try to leave town. As well, without them I believe you are not much of a threat."

Nothing came to Krunzle. The snake was back to listening. Now the wizard, too, seemed to be waiting to see if the captive would make a response. The silence grew. Finally, the traveler shrugged—it was not as eloquent a gesture with his hands bound behind him—and said, "Well, if that's all, I've had a long day . . ."

"Do you know," Mordach said, "that every region, indeed every era, of the recondite arts has its own . . . shall we say, odor?"

"It is not the kind of information in which I usually take an interest," Krunzle said.

"Really?" said the mage. "It's one that has always been of interest to me."

Mordach interlaced his fingers, all except the two index, whose tips he brought together then touched reflectively to the groove above his upper lip. After a moment he withdrew them and said, "I cannot closely inspect your serpentine torc, but I am conscious of its scent. It is different from that of your boots and sword—garden-variety Tian, by the way." The wizard paused as if expecting a reply. Again, silence took charge of the interval. Finally, he said, "I confess, I do not recognize the smell that emanates from the snake—and that, in and of itself, is highly interesting."

"As I told you," Krunzle said, "such is not within my competence."

Mordach brushed this aside. "The most interesting thing, however, is that I have scented the same odor on someone else's goods." He fixed the traveler with a serious gaze, but Krunzle had the strong impression that Mordach was trying to look *through* his eyes to something deeper within the thief's being. "And quite recently."

Krunzle was suddenly aware that Chirk was fully alert. Words now came from the back of his mind. "Really?" he said. "And what does this coincidence tell you?"

Now there was a kind of amusement in the wizard's thin-lipped smile. "Ah," he said. "It speaks." He waited for a response, watching Krunzle closely, and when Chirk offered nothing more, he said, "I would like to offer you a partnership—at least an association—once I have separated you from this"—he indicated Krunzle—"beast of burden."

Still, Chirk had nothing to say. Krunzle thought it was time he joined the conversation. "I don't know what you're talking about—"

"Silence, you!" said the mage, and in this strange place, his voice carried an almost physical force. "I am not talking to the dancing bear, but to the one who plays the tune!"

"Where is the other object?" said Krunzle, though the words came from the back of his mind. "And the person who carries it?"

"He was at the hotel," said Mordach. "He checked in this afternoon—Room Eight—with a woman. Though by now she should be moved to Room Thirteen." He frowned again. "It was on her that I scented the unrecognizable odor, but she did not possess the object that is its source. Unfortunately, he who carries it made an arrangement with Ulm, before he consulted me, and now the man has left town. He did so, however, on a horse bought here. My isinglass, tuned to that steed, can tell me where he goes."

"Interesting, indeed," Chirk said, through Krunzle.

"Then a partnership? I am better able to take you to the man than your present carrier," said the mage.

Krunzle would have welcomed the chance to be free of the snake around his neck, assuming Mordach could remove it. But Chirk had a different appreciation of the situation. "I need to weigh some competing aspects," he found himself saying, on behalf of the snake. "Let us talk about this tomorrow night."

Mordach shook his skull-like head. "That may be too late. The man may separate himself from the horse. Tomorrow morning."

Chirk had Krunzle say, "Too soon. I need to consult—" then checked himself, as if he had said too much.

A real smile, though not a pleasant one, now showed on the mage's lean face. "Ah," he said, "something to think about."

"In the afternoon," Krunzle suggested. "I could use an early conclusion of the workday."

"Very well," said Mordach.

"Then we're agreed."

The skeletal mage seemed to move back—either that or he grew smaller—then the mists disappeared, and they were back in the third-floor room. Mordach made a vague shooing motion, then crossed to the table where an open book lay. He lit a lamp and stood reading whatever he found there, his brows compressed in thought. After a moment, he looked up, as if surprised to see the thief still there. "We are done," he said. "Begone!"

Krunzle shrugged again and turned to descend the spiral staircase, wishing he had a hand free to grasp the railing. The thing in the cage hissed at him again as he passed the second floor, and when he reached ground level, the door unlocked itself and swung wide. Brundelaf was waiting outside. The Ulfen checked his bonds and pushed him back along the way they had come.

In the partial privacy of his head, Krunzle said, *What was all that about?* He got no answer. *Gyllana is at the hotel? Berbackian is riding south?* Again, no response. *We were supposed to follow them. Instead we got here first.*

Silence in his head. He thought about it, not caring if the snake could see his thoughts fitting themselves together—and fit together they did, into a shape he did not find pleasing. *None of this was an accident!* he said. *You planned it. You wanted me to be taken up by Boss Ulm and put to hard labor. I hate labor of any kind, and hard labor most of all! And that wizard wants to feed me to ants or dissolve me in acid!*

Chirk said nothing. Krunzle considered his options. What if he told Brundelaf to take him back to Mordach's right now? What if he told what he knew, little though it was? He waited to see if the bronze circle around his neck would constrict and choke him.

It did something else instead. Krunzle had many a time heard the expression "every bone in his body ached." Now he knew what it felt like. For only a couple of seconds, every bone in his body screamed, reporting that it was being stressed to a point just short of snapping. He stopped, all his muscles rigid, then collapsed to the ground, limp as boiled asparagus.

Oh, he said to the snake in his mind, *in that case, we'll go with your plan.*

Good, came the response.

"What's the matter with you?" Brundelaf said.

"A sudden pain in the neck," he told the Ulfen.

"You're just not used to hard work."

"I'm sure that's the explanation. Would you help me up?"

The redbeard's assistance consisted of kicking the captive in the buttocks with a hard-toed boot. The technique was surprisingly effective, and the thief was shortly back on track to the lockup.

In the morning, rock chips flew as Skanderbrog alternately chiseled and smashed. Krunzle raked and said nothing, but he saw the troll watching him again from the corner of his eye. A couple of times, he also noticed the creature heft the hammer in a different grip, swinging it in an upward motion before returning to the regular stroke. Once, too, the troll took the chisel in his right hand and made a tentative throwing motion. Then he went back to work, his low brow wrinkled.

As they neared noon, Krunzle paused to wipe the sweat from his eyes and said, "Well?"

The troll looked at him sideways. "I have been thinking about it. You may be right, but . . ." He gestured to the scorched line that ran across the ledge. "I tried to cross that once. It burned me. Inside."

Krunzle could sympathize. Magically induced pain was worse than the ordinary. But Chirk had its own agenda. The words formed in the traveler's mind and he spoke them. "I have heard that some spells do not last beyond the caster's life."

"I don't know about magic. My mother said I should avoid it."

"Good advice," said the thief. "Still, that's what I've heard."

The troll continued working, but his brow wrinkled again with unaccustomed mental effort. "So the fire line dies when Mordach dies?"

Krunzle listened for Chirk's answer, then said, "So it seems."

The troll smashed rock and Krunzle raked. "And the leg chains?"

"The chisel and hammer should take care of them."

"Hmm," Skanderbrog said, and chiseled another boulder-sized fragment out of the cliff. He smashed it to pieces and set the chisel against a crack. "But he watches me. He has other spells at his fingertips, and I am not fast."

"Suppose," Krunzle said, "something distracted him?"

Skanderbrog drove the hammer forward. "What kind of something?"

"Any kind of something, just when he was about to renew the boundary spell." The troll labored on, but his brow was now profoundly wrinkled. "And suppose," the traveler said, "you were ready when that moment came."

Skanderbrog stopped work, looked at the tools in his hand, then switched the chisel to his right and hefted it like a spear.

"There you go," said the thief.

The creature's brow cleared. He repositioned the tools and drove the chisel into the rock face again. They worked in silence for a while. Then Skanderbrog said, "Why do you want to help me? My mother said not to trust men." He gestured with the hammer to indicate his circumstances. "She was right."

"By helping you, I help myself," said Krunzle, and did not need Chirk's prompting to extend the argument. "If you are not smashing rock, I do not need to be raking it."

The troll took that in and after a while moved his tusked head up and down.

"Mordach always comes to renew the spell during lunch?" the traveler asked.

Again the troll nodded.

"Well, then," said Krunzle, and went back to raking.

They were up on the wooden platform, eating gruel. Mordach and his torchmen came down from the town to descend the scaffold's steps to where the troll squatted on the ledge, chewing on a leg that was left over from breakfast—two goldbug partners had gotten into an altercation over the details of their claim, and one had decided that if words couldn't settle the issue, a pickaxe would. His partner, however, had served for years as a mercenary before being struck by gold fever; he had undercut the pickaxe argument with their camp's bread knife.

As Mordach and his party crossed the platform, the wizard threw Krunzle a knowing smile that the thief took as a sign of the man's confidence that all was working out as it should. The traveler returned him a gesture freighted with a recognition that loss was an unwelcome but frequent element of existence. Mordach's smile broadened and he went down the steps after his torchbearers. Krunzle drifted over to the edge of the platform to watch.

He found himself above and a little behind Mordach and lowered himself to sit on the edge of the platform, his gruel bowl in his hands. The bowls came in several shapes and different types of wood, and today Krunzle had chosen a large specimen, carved from a heavy hardwood. As the torchmen ranged themselves in two ranks and Mordach stepped up behind them, the traveler drained the last of his gruel and wiped the inner surface clean with a finger, which he then put in his mouth.

Skanderbrog had finished with the leg bone and laid it down beside him, next to the long, iron chisel. He watched the wizard as Mordach raised his arms, opened his mouth, and prepared to utter the first word of the incantation. Then events moved quickly: instead of an ancient and arcane syllable, the mage emitted a loud, "Ow!" and clasped both hands to his pate, which had just received a ringing blow from a heavy wooden bowl flung from above.

Even before the impact, the young troll had closed his hand around the long spike of iron, and as the bowl struck Mordach's head he was rising to his feet, drawing back his arm. He took one step forward and let fly. He did not have a clear target, the torchmen being in the way, but he compensated for the lack by putting sufficient force behind the missile to drive it clear through the man in front and into the wizard.

The boundary spell tried to do its best as the iron hurtled through it, charging the chisel with the last burst of energy from its morning casting. The missile thus shone white hot as it burned its way through the torchman and was still a deep red when it transfixed Mordach. It entered the wizard at a downward angle and burst through his back. Gore hissed and steamed from the still fiery metal.

Now Skanderbrog moved forward, cautiously at first, his left hand extended until the claws on its fingertips touched the air above the line. Nothing happened. A smile drew back the troll's black lips. His right hand reached down and closed around the haft of the great hammer, and he lifted it and drove it down so that the head's forward edge struck the links of iron that connected his ankle fetters. The chain parted like soft cheese.

The torchbearers had already turned and rushed for the steps, crowding and jostling each other. One plunged screaming into the gorge below. Skanderbrog came after them, pausing at the wizard's body to retrieve the chisel, which had turned cold again. He transferred the chisel to the same hand that held the hammer, giving himself a free hand so that he could reach down and twist Mordach's head from his body. This he tossed into his mouth and, chewing happily, he pushed his way up the steps, scattering the least agile of the torchmen to their deaths.

The scaffolding creaked under the troll's weight but he came up onto the platform, a weapon in each hand. He looked about him. The slaves and overseers were fleeing into the town, fighting each other for precedence in the narrow alley that led to the main street. Skanderbrog watched them go, then his head moved from side to side, eyes going here and there among the buildings.

"You're looking for Boss Ulm, aren't you?" said Krunzle. He didn't need the snake to tell him that. Raimeau was hiding behind him, ready to run if the troll turned out to be as ungrateful as their kind often were.

"Yes. Which house is his?"

"I can show you, if you'll do me a favor first."

"Will it take long?"

"A matter," said the thief, "of moments."

And so it turned out to be. They pressed up the narrow alley to the main street, then crossed over to another passageway that ran between the hotel and Boss Ulm's saloon. "See that barred window up there?" the thief said. "If you would just reach up and yank the bars out for me . . ." The troll reached and the iron grill clattered to the ground. "Thank you," said Krunzle, as a terrified scream came from Room Thirteen, "and now, as for Boss Ulm—"

The screaming from above continued as the thief turned toward a noise that came from the other side of the alley. He saw that a door had opened, the one that Ulm's bullyboys had come through the night their employer had sent them to bring Krunzle for interrogation. Now out of the door came a head. A head that bore a huge nose. A nose that bore a huge wart. "Well," Krunzle said, "speak of the—"

Skanderbrog growled—not the frustrated growl of a juvenile held prisoner and forced to work, but the full-throated, belly-deep rumble of an angry, free troll who is just about to take his long-contemplated revenge. Boss Ulm's face paled, so that the wart stood out like a housefly landed on a linen tablecloth, and he ducked back inside, slamming the door after him.

The troll did not bother with the door—it would never have accommodated him—but raised his hammer and brought it down with a splintering crash against the planks of the saloon's outer wall. A wide gap appeared and he stepped through, his voice booming, "Ulm!"

Now the screaming from above was counterpointed by even more from the saloon. Krunzle took a moment to peek through the opening. Skanderbrog was smashing his way through room after room, breaching walls and scattering tables, Ulm fleeing before him but being slowed down by the need to open doors, and by the terrified patrons, many of whom tried to flee in contradictory directions. The saloon's main room was ringed by a balcony behind which stood the smaller, private upper rooms. Their doors were now flying open, disgorging a sudden flood of partially clad persons of both sexes, who quickly sized up the situation and departed by whatever routes would take them away from Skanderbrog.

The troll continued on his single-minded pursuit of the saloon's proprietor, wielding his hammer and chisel to sweep any and all from his way, finally jabbing the spike through the shoulder of the town's boss, pinning Ulm to a window frame just as he had thrown up the sash and was about to escape.

Skanderbrog dropped the hammer and picked up Ulm by one ankle, held him dangling, squirming and pleading. An oil lamp had broken in one corner, igniting a fire. Displaying a fortitude unusual for his kind—as most trolls' fear of fire usually overcame their desire for cooked meat—Skanderbrog carried his former captor over to the pool of flames, kicking some broken chairs and tables toward it to build up the blaze.

He hunkered down beside the fire and pulled the long chisel from Ulm's shoulder. He regarded the tool and the man for a moment, then made his decision. Carefully and slowly, he inserted the length of iron into his captive. Ulm's screams went on for a surprisingly long time. When they finished, Skanderbrog suspended the spitted corpse over the fire. Ulm's clothes and hair caught fire, and the troll fanned with one huge hand to waft away the fumes as he moved safely back out of reach of the flickering flames, watching intently as his former master popped and crackled in the worst death a troll could imagine.

Krunzle turned away. Raimeau, he was surprised to find, had remained with him. "Now what?" the gray-haired man said.

The thief pointed to the unbarred window of Room Thirteen. "Give me a boost," he said.

Chapter Six
Thief Meets Maiden

Krunzle's first impression was of three dark circles arranged in a downward-pointing isosceles triangle: the two upper circles were Gyllana's eyes; the lower her open mouth, which was emitting a continuous low moan, the end of a long scream that was running out of air. The triangle motif was repeated below her chin as well, since she was stark naked.

The thief, standing in the space where the barred window used to be, looked around the room. As Mordach had said, there was no sign of a former Mercenary League officer, unless the seducer Berbackian had left his paramour to fend for herself and taken shelter under the unmade bed, from which the young woman had leapt upon hearing the commotion outside.

"Where is he?" he said. Gyllana continued her moan, then broke off to take a breath—Krunzle assumed to begin anew from the top. He stepped forward and interrupted the cycle by seizing her shoulders and shaking her vigorously until she said, "Wait, stop!"

The traveler did not release her. "Where is Wolsh Berbackian?" he said.

The fear had not left her eyes, but he saw it joined now by calculation. "What do you know of Berbackian?" she said.

"All I need to. I have been sent to bring you home, and to deliver justice to Berbackian wherever I find him."

She looked him over. For a naked damsel who had moments before been screaming in terror, she recovered with admirable speed, Krunzle thought.

"My father sent you?" she said.

"He did." Krunzle saw no reason to go into details of motivation. He stooped to look under the bed, saw no Berbackian, and decided that was a sufficient search. "Get dressed, and we will go."

Her eyes went past him. "There is a troll—"

"He is busy roasting Boss Ulm for lunch."

"That may not occupy him long," she said, "and I have heard that the creatures have formidable appetites."

"Don't worry about Skanderbrog. He and I have an understanding." She looked at him curiously. The traveler felt himself being weighed up, and recognized that the young woman was cut from the same timber as her father. "Do not," he said, "think that you can manage me for your own interests. Be assured that I will always be one too many for you. Now, where are your clothes? I wish to return you to your father forthwith."

"Stop staring at my bosom and my . . . elsewhere," she said, striving for the tone with which she no doubt addressed the servitors in her father's house. "My clothes are in another room. Ulm's bravos took me out of bed just as I was and threw me in here. The door is sealed by an incantation."

"Mordach's?" Krunzle said.

"Does it matter whose?" she said. "Are you a more powerful mage? If so, you disguise it well." Two red spots had appeared on her cheeks. "Will you stop staring at me?"

Krunzle redirected his gaze, at the same time crossing to the door. He turned its knob and pulled it open. The hallway beyond was empty. "Which room?" he said, and when she told him he went there and came back with the woman's clothing he found piled on a chair. He threw them to her.

"Turn your back while I dress," she said.

He didn't like the look in her eye. "And have you brain me with a chamber pot? Pfah! If you don't wish me to see your bubs and underthatch, cover them. And wear stout shoes; I mean to travel quickly."

She pulled a shift over head then reached for a pair of knit stockings and sat on the bed to pull them on. "Think again," she said. "We are not going back to Kerse."

"I would prefer your cooperation," said the thief, "but I am prepared to apply coercion."

"We are not going back," she said, shimmying into the garment known as a chlamys with which Kersite women of means clothed their upper bodies, "because I don't want to, and—"

"Your wishes do not interest me. I am—"

"*And*," she repeated, "because you'd only be sent back again."

Krunzle had been about to press on with his statement of intent, but the calm assurance with which she voiced her last words compelled his attention. "Why?" he said.

She had stood up and was stepping into a long, pleated skirt of sturdy cloth. She tugged it straight around her waist and buckled its sewn-in belt, then gave him a mocking smile. "You don't really believe that Ippolite Eponion, Second Secretary to the First Commissariote, has gone to the trouble of sending a trace-sniffer all this way to find me, out of a fatherly concern for my virtue?"

Krunzle listened to the tone of her voice. If she was lying, she was very good at it. "Don't I?" he said. "Why not?"

She had sat again to put on her boots, and regarded him from beneath raised and precisely plucked eyebrows as her fingers skillfully did up the row of little buttons. "He wants me back," she said, passing on to the other boot, "so that I will marry the man he has picked out for me."

"And you don't care for the fellow?"

"The circumstances are no concern of yours." She stood up and studied herself in the mirror over the dresser, and seemed to find the image acceptable. "What my father cares about is his reputation. Berbackian has got the better of him, by taking something that should have been under his control. He will not be satisfied until Wolsh is dead. Nor, for that matter, will I."

Chirk placed a thought in Krunzle's mind. The thief said, "There was also mention of an object purloined by Wolsh Berbackian, an old talisman. I am to recover it also."

She smiled the same thin smile that he had seen on her father's face. It was no more appetizing on hers. "He took it with him."

"And where is he?"

"I haven't seen him," she said, "since before two of Boss Ulm's big mutton-thumpers came and took me out of our room and put me in this one." She chewed on her inner lip a moment, thinking, then said, "Berbackian said he had to go consult with a man who knew something about the . . ."—here she fluttered a hand to pass over the undisclosed item whose return her father desired—"and that he'd be back directly. But Ulm's plug-uglies said that I had been sold to their employer, and that I would either be held for ransom or auctioned off to the highest bidder."

"Who was the man?" The way she looked at him told Krunzle that she was weighing up whether or not it was in her interest to tell him. "You are not going anywhere without me," he said. "But if I believe I can trust you, you will at least travel without your hands bound behind you and a lead rope around your neck."

Her eyes flashed, but she quickly regained control. "What if I stumbled? How would I catch myself?"

"Exactly," he said. "You would be too busy avoiding a misstep to plot an escape, one that perhaps would involve inflicting painful injuries upon your escort." She scowled but he showed her an implacable mien. "Now," he said, "whom did Berbackian go to see?"

"It was Mordach."

"Ah," said Krunzle.

"You know him?"

"I did. He will not be able to aid us."

"Why not?"

Krunzle gestured through the hole where the window used to be and the gaps Skanderbrog had made in the outer and inner walls of Boss Ulm's saloon. Through the smoke they could see the young troll, hunkered down against the still-standing far wall and chewing on the charred torso of his former captor.

"The troll overcame the wizard?" she said, disbelief in her voice.

"The creature had," the thief said, "some timely assistance."

A light dawned for Gyllana. "Hence," she said, "your understanding." Krunzle made a gesture of confirmation. "You are not," she said, looking him over again, "as witless as you appear."

The traveler resisted the urge to offer a cutting rejoinder. "Tell me this," he said, "do you think that Berbackian was primarily interested in your . . . shall we say, feminine attributes? Or was his attention more on the unnamed item that so moves your father, and that has not been seen since your lover abandoned you to the mercies of Boss Ulm?"

She bridled at the implication, but the rancor was brief. The thief realized that the young woman was capable of a dry-eyed, even cold-blooded, assessment of her situation. "That," she said, "is a question I will put to Berbackian at the earliest opportunity."

Krunzle turned again to watch Skanderbrog devouring the former despot of Ulm's Delve and saw that the troll was chewing through the large muscle on one of Ulm's seared thighs. "We should leave now," he said. "I propose that we go together to Mordach's house and see what we can discover of your romantical Blackjacket—not to mention certain goods of mine that I last saw there."

"Agreed," she said. They went out through the hotel and onto the main street, now deserted. At the sound of their bootheels striking the boardwalk, Raimeau came out of the alley. Krunzle was surprised that the gray-haired young man had waited for them, with a troll in the vicinity.

They turned in the direction of the wizard's house, which meant they had to pass the half-wrecked building in which Skanderbrog squatted, gnawing the last bits of meat from Ulm's yellowy femur. He looked up as the trio went by and Krunzle offered him a parting wave. Skanderbrog returned him a nod and a long look that appeared again unusually thoughtful for a troll.

What do you think? Krunzle asked Chirk when they stood outside Mordach's locked door. He received an answer, not in words, but in an understanding that Mordach had not bothered with wards and barriers but had employed only alarms that would have summoned him to the scene. Krunzle gathered that the wizard had enjoyed dealing with intruders personally. Thus a thief's skills were all that were required to gain entrance. *Huh,* Krunzle thought back, *not a lot to say now? Why did I not hear anything from you when I was having that revealing discussion with the woman I was supposed to rescue?*

To this, he did not receive any answer at all, and it was his own thought processes—well honed on the deviousness of humankind—that cut swiftly to the correct conclusion: *You knew it all the time! You knew there was more to it than a simple bring-back-my-daughter!* He thought again. *Thang-Sha!* he said to the snake. *He was the one who put you on my neck, and it was he who was most interested in the talisman!*

Again, Chirk kept its own counsel. Krunzle's mood turned darker. It was bad enough to be captured and set to unwonted effort, not to mention having his life and limbs—to all of which he was deeply attached—put at risk. But to be treated as one unworthy to be told the true nature of the game! To be made what the sham-shifters of the rogues' guild at Elidir called a nonregard, a can-carrier, a gullibloon, a galumph! That was off the board! That was a dire insult to his rank and stature! It made an already bad situation worse, and worst of all was to have to swallow the sharp-edged fact that he had not seen it first!

He swore, a chain of bitter words emitted through clenched teeth.

"What's the matter?" said the woman. "Can you not gain entrance?" She studied the wizard's door. "It looks sturdy enough, but unless I misjudge your character, you have encountered more—"

Krunzle spun on one heel, the other lashing out to connect with the portal just above the lock. Wood splintered with a loud *crack!* and the door swung inward. He stepped within. First things first, he said to himself, and spent a moment mastering his anger. Then to the others he said, "Wait here. Mordach's spells will have faded, but if he kept a ravenous basilisk to greet uninvited guests, it will still act according to its nature."

To Chirk, he thought, *The boots and sword are here somewhere.* He did not have to think further before he heard a sound of breakage from the floor above, then the weapon and its scabbard came sailing smoothly down the spiral staircase, trailing gold wires that dissolved into air as the sword pressed its hilt into his hand like a faithful hound offering its head for a pat. The boots came behind, descending the stairs as lightly as if they were on a dancer's feet. They stopped before the thief, turned about, and stood as if awaiting his pleasure. He quickly shook off Chenax's shoes and slid his feet into the familiar old buskins.

He turned back to the others and saw that Raimeau's eyes had widened, while the young woman had taken events in stride. She looked about her with faint interest. Krunzle said, "Do not be fooled by appearances. This place may still offer danger. I will search the downstairs for any risks, then lead the way upstairs. Wait."

They did. He was soon back, having found no basilisks lurking in the house's kitchen and pantry. "Upstairs. I will go first." He received no arguments, Raimeau swallowing audibly before nodding; Gyllana shrugging with her finely arched brows. To Chirk he thought, *If there's anything you can tell me that will help, now would be a good time.* He received no answers from that source either, but did experience a sense that nothing threatening waited above. *Not even Berbackian?* he thought. The snake sent him in response two successive pictures: first both rooms upstairs, one after another, both empty; then the second-story chamber alone, with something glowing on the wall.

Krunzle went up the stairs, the sword extended before him, just in case there was something else the entity coiled around his neck was not telling him. He found the second floor untenanted, except by the thing in the cage; again, it hissed at him from its corner, but this time the sound was mournful.

The workbench was littered as before—Mordach had not been a tidy spellcaster—but added to the clutter now was a heavy tome, its pages of yellowed parchment bound in black leather that was cracked from age. It lay splayed open to a page of handwritten text in a cursive script Krunzle did not recognize. He paid it no heed, but saw that his wallet and his hat with its useful panache were on the floor beneath the bench. He was surprised to find the wallet not quite empty—Mordach had left its mundane contents undisturbed. He tucked it away in his shirt. The gem in his hatpiece should have been glowing, given all the magic-infused material in the house. But it was inert, dead, probably drained of its power by the wizard. Still, the feel of his hat once more on his head gave Krunzle a curious satisfaction—he and the battered object had been through much—and he turned with interest to locate the item that Chirk had caused to glow in his mind's eye.

But the snake called him back to the bench and the book that lay open there. *Read it,* said the voice in his head.

I cannot, said the thief.

Just cast your eyes over it, starting at the top right and going left, then right at the next line, and so on. Krunzle did so, marking his progress with a fingertip underlining the text until he had made his way down the page all the way to the bottom. Chirk then had him continue overleaf, and he scanned a few more lines of the undulating script. Below the text was a line drawing in black ink of what looked to be a conically shaped mountain. A segment of the mountain had been cut away to reveal a many-sided object nestled within its base. More of the sinuous writing accompanied the illustration. Krunzle moved his eyes over it, as ordered, and experienced an echo of emotion from the place where his keeper's consciousness intersected his own.

This has meaning to you? he asked the snake after a while.

Yes.

And what is the meaning?

I don't know yet.

Is there anything else we should be doing here? As he spoke he turned to the spot on the wall that Chirk had made glow in the mental image downstairs, and recognized the oval of dull glass framed in polished wood that he had glimpsed in passing on his first visit. Now he approached it and saw that into the wood frame was carved a frieze of intertwined characters and symbols. Krunzle knew some of the figures, and knew also what the object was.

An isinglass, he thought. *A scryer's tool.*

Indeed, came Chirk's reply. *Now do this*—in his mind Krunzle saw an image of his own left hand reaching out to place two fingers on two of the symbols—*then this*—now his right hand touched three characters, one after the other, on the opposite side of the frame.

He did as bid, and immediately a scene formed in the glass, the last subject the isinglass had been charged with locating. He saw a strongly built man in doublet, cape, britches, and knee-boots, all of a dark hue, riding a powerful black horse along a twisting trail. Ahead, the land rose into hills. Beyond, the terrain climbed higher, into snow-capped mountains.

Gyllana had come to stand behind him. He was conscious of her scent: cloves and some attar of lush blossoms. She breathed a word in his ear: "Wolsh!" Then another, a very strong word that reflected poorly on the Blackjacket's character—and some would have said on her own, since it was not the kind of word that Kersite ladies of good family were expected even to know, and certainly not to utter in mixed company.

"He's run off and left you," said Krunzle.

"He'll wish he hadn't."

"What has he stolen?"

She regarded him archly. "My father did not tell you?"

"He may have mentioned it," said the thief, "but at the time my mind was on matters of more consequence."

"Hah!" she said, and "Ho!"

"You disbelieve me?"

"I'm sure you must be used to it."

A loud crash came, not too distant, followed by more screams. Raimeau looked worriedly in the direction the sound had come from. "Skanderbrog has finished lunch," he said.

"A good time to depart," said Krunzle. He tugged his hat down firmly and headed for the staircase. But again he was brought up sharp by an imperious voice in his head. *The isinglass. Bring it.*

"Read this, bring that, befriend a troll," he muttered as he went back to lift the oval of wood and dull glass from the wall. He touched it gingerly, half-expecting it to punish him with some shock or sizzle, but it was inert. He handed it to Raimeau, saying, "Carry this," and turned to leave.

The lanky man took the object but did not follow. He said, "We should free the thing in the cage."

Krunzle saw no reason to disguise his exasperation at the succession of burdens being placed upon him. "Why? So it can wrap its leathery wings about us and drain our blood? Or satisfy whatever other foul appetites might move it?"

The creature in question emitted a resentful hoot.

Gyllana moved closer to the cage. "It seems harmless," she said.

"Remind me," the thief said, "to tell you about a fellow I knew whose last words were exactly those you just spoke. It is a tale rich in tragedy and irony." He strode toward the staircase, saying over his shoulder, "Much like my life."

Behind him, he heard the woman and the man cooperating to detach the cage from its hook, but heard no screams of agony or fright as he went down and out onto the main street. They joined him moments later, and set the cage on the ground. Raimeau found a stick and used it to work the catch, until the barred door fell open. The thing inside blinked its huge amber-colored eyes as if the light hurt them, but worked its way through the opening. It gave another hoot, this one sounding like a question, then unfurled a pair of complexly folded wings into a surprisingly wide span, launched itself into the air, and flew slowly up the street, gradually gaining height. At the end of the block, it wheeled to the right, caught a thermal, and rose into the upper air.

Krunzle had not bothered to watch it go, once he saw that it was not about to throw itself at him. He looked downslope, into the town—or what remained of it. Boss Ulm's saloon and bordello were now blazing, throwing up a thick column of dense smoke that flattened as it climbed into the still air. Sparks and flaming debris filtered down from the black mushroom, and smaller, secondary fires were kindling themselves on shingle roofs and in the curtains of open windows.

Krunzle thought the town could have been saved from a general conflagration if Boss Ulm had ever invested in a fire-wagon, and if anyone cared enough about Ulm's Delve to remain in the vicinity of a well-muscled young troll who was going from building to building, swinging his hammer at any architectural feature that caught his eye. It seemed to Krunzle that the troll was experimenting with different methods of using the tool. As the three outside the wizard's house watched, Skanderbrog swung the hammer to his left, then allowed its momentum to spin him around in a full circle, his feet leaving the ground, his arm straightening, so that the great iron head came swinging around with even more force. The effect of the maneuver was to snap with one blow a pair of heavy posts that supported the second-floor balcony of an establishment whose facade-wide frame advertised it as Madam Proserpe's Palace of Pleasure.

The balcony collapsed, taking most of the building's front with it. The troll moved on to the next structure which, fortunately for Krunzle and his companions, was downhill. He spied a water barrel and flung the chisel right through it, following up with a leap and a diagonal hammer strike that splintered the oak staves like kindling. Krunzle almost felt sympathy for Grunchum and Brugga, the trolls that had denied Skanderbrog a place to lay his head in what trolls considered comfort.

In the farther distance, where the edge of town met the stump field, the mud road was packed with former residents of Ulm's Delve. The more fortunate were fleeing on horseback or in wagons; a few pushed wheelbarrows or pulled carts piled with their possessions; some carried packs or shouldered duffel bags; many fled with nothing more than the clothes on their backs, though perhaps there was a poke of gold dust or a nugget secreted on their persons.

But one thing they all had in common: they were consigning Ulm's Delve to memory. And, between Skanderbrog's hammer and the fire, soon that would be all that remained of the gold camp. Krunzle watched the progress of the troll and the multitude for a moment, then turned and looked uphill. In that direction, the town's buildings petered out, as did the road. There was a trail that paralleled the gold stream along the gorge and into the canyon that the river had cut through the slope of boulders and smaller stones.

"That way," said the thief. He saw no other refugees going in the same direction. He sniffed the air and caught a familiar scent. "Horses. Let's find them."

Behind the buildings on the west side of the street they found a corral with a half-dozen horses in it, all of them wild-eyed from the smell of smoke—and probably, thought Krunzle, of excited troll. Their owners must have been downhill when Skanderbrog came up out of the gorge, and had not thought it worthwhile to risk passing the troll twice to collect their mounts and flee northward with the rest of the population. Another horse can be found anywhere, but once a person's head has become troll candy, no replacement is available.

They found tack and saddles in a storage shed and spent some time calming and readying the horses. Gyllana turned out to be an asset at this, far more so than Raimeau, whom she had to help. Krunzle used a familiar technique, rendering his mount more afraid of him at close range than of fire and troll at a distance. He climbed into the saddle, saw the woman already mounted and calming down the sorrel mare she had chosen. Raimeau was hopping one-legged in a circle, his black gelding going around in the same direction. At some point, the string of the isinglass that he had slung over his shoulder snapped, and the glass shattered as it struck the hard earth.

Krunzle felt a flash of irritation from the back corridors of his mind. *No use trying to follow Berbackian?* he thought.

It will just be more difficult, said the snake. *Now let us move.*

Gyllana nudged her horse over to Raimeau's skittish animal and blocked its motion long enough for the gray-haired man to step up and swing a long leg over. He looked down at the splinters of glass and said, "I'm sorry."

Krunzle had chosen a deep-chested roan. He kneed it toward the corral's gate, reached down and lifted up the loop of hide rope that fastened the opening to a post. He nudged his horse out, carrying his end of the gate a short distance, then dropped the rope as the three riderless animals pushed forward and forced the barrier wide open. They raced away toward the boulder-strewn slope south of town, and the three travelers let their mounts follow. In moments, they were clear of what had been Ulm's Delve and were climbing among the rocks, the stream tumbling down beside their right hands.

At a place where the streamside trail curved in a way that would cut off their view of the gold camp, Krunzle reined in and looked back. The wooden buildings, many of them smashed by Skanderbrog, were well alight, the flames leaping from roof to roof and from one debris pile to another. Smoke rose thick and high, and the sound of the conflagration had progressed from a crackle to a roar.

Raimeau pulled up behind Krunzle and craned his neck to look. He voiced a single syllable expressive of wonder tinged with dismay, then turned back to the thief. "I guess that's that," he said.

"A good guess," said Krunzle.

Gyllana was bringing up the rear. She did not bother to look back. "Berbackian," she said, "is not lollygagging and ogling the scenery. Let us get a move on."

"Let me make sure of the troll's route," said the thief. His gaze moved over the smoke-obscured landscape. After a while he saw Skanderbrog, chisel and hammer in hand, making his way through the stump field. The troll was heading east at a measured pace. "Good enough," said Krunzle. He dug his heels into the horse's ribs and took the curve in the southbound trail.

The canyon wound upward, following the course of the river, until it gradually widened and finally debouched upon a plateau. The three travelers paused to scan the ground ahead, but saw nothing to give immediate concern. The terrain here was flat grassland, dotted with pockets of scrub and gorse, with only a gentle upward slope trending toward another set of hills and then a range of mountains. Some of the peaks had a disturbingly conical shape to them.

"Volcanoes," Raimeau said, when Krunzle pointed this out. "There are several up this way."

"Are they active or dormant?" the thief asked. He peered and was glad to see no plumes of smoke or ash, but knew that an absence of either was no guarantee.

"It is best to assume they are all active," said the gray-haired man. "Volcanoes are remarkably heedless of the interests of passersby. When they go, they go without a by-your-leave."

Krunzle swore again. One of the peaks in the drawing Chirk had had him study was conical. To Raimeau he said, "Are you knowledgeable about such things?"

"I spent most of my life at sea," the other said, "much of it on a ship whose captain kept a library. He let me read widely."

Gyllana urged her mare forward. "We should get along. We can tell our life stories later, around the campfire."

"I'm sure yours is riveting," said Krunzle, but he went where she led, Raimeau again bringing up the rear.

They rode through the afternoon, following the beaten-earth trail across the grassland. In places, it would fork and then Chirk would urge Krunzle to left or right. By the time evening's shadows were stretching out, they came to a broad hollow with a wide, shallow lake covering its bottom, the edges lined with reeds. The trail skirted the shore on the water's east side and took them past several spots where travelers had camped and built fires. At one of these that offered a sheltering stand of trees, a ready-made fire-ring, and some lengths of logs arranged for sitting, Krunzle said, "This looks like a place to stop for the night."

Raimeau stepped down from his horse, produced a small folding knife, and explained its provenance: "Mordach's. I thought it would come in handy." He went among the trees and came back with a sapling, spent a couple of minutes working on it, then strode down to the reedy shallows carrying a rough-and-ready fishing spear. More in hope than expectation, Krunzle gathered dry wood for a cooking fire.

Gyllana led the horses to where the grass was thick and loosened their cinches. She was back in a moment, chose a log and seated herself to watch as the thief built a pyramid of twigs and branches then applied his fire-starter. When a cheerful blaze began to dispel the dusk, he took a seat opposite her and sat with his arms folded. It was the first chance he'd had to study the Kersite at his leisure.

The firelight was kind to her, softening the harshness of her ambient expression. Her eyes even shone a little, he thought, and though she was more than a touch plumper than the girls he usually favored, he would not have to violate his standards to—

"Not a chance," she said.

"I beg your pardon?"

The eyes were not shining now. They were as hard as river-polished rocks. "You may have spent much of your life until this moment among the near-sighted or the simply dim," she said, "leading you to believe that your face disguises your thoughts. Prepare to receive unwelcome news: you are as easily read as a schoolchild's primer."

"And you are baldly spoken." Krunzle looked away. Raimeau was stirring among the reeds.

"And here are fresh tidings," the woman continued. "I would no more couple with you than with Skanderbrog, although I am sure he would bring more style and imagination to the wooing."

"You do not like me," Krunzle said.

"I was scarcely aware of you," she said, "until a moment ago when I saw that you had the temerity to appraise me. I thought it best to acquaint you early with your chance of success, which is somewhat less than the likelihood that your companion will return from the lake bringing a frog who began life as a prince. Indeed, a frog, even one entirely unensorcelled, would have a better chance than you."

"You really do not like me," said Krunzle. When her only response was to look pointedly in another direction, he continued, "Well, I am none too fond of you. I have been sent to collect you against my will, and could I but release myself from the grip of this object about my neck I would show you just how deep my disesteem can run." As he spoke, his anger grew, and his sense of being unfairly put upon. He rose to his feet. "I have been half-drowned, set to fight bloodthirsty bandits, chivvied and run off my feet, enslaved and forced to back-breaking labor and the inveigling of a troll. And now I am further impelled upon a chase to bring back your errant lover, who seems to have dropped you at his earliest convenience—"

Now she was on her feet as well. "Why, you impertinent, grimy little—"

"There," said Raimeau, throwing down a brace of fish, each as long as his forearm. "That should feed us. Now what's all the fuss?"

The sight of the fine, fat fish focused Krunzle's attention on his stomach. His mouth watered, thickening his voice as he said, "How did you manage that?"

The lanky man shrugged. "You just have to give the fish what they want."

"And what do fish want?" Gyllana said.

Raimeau smiled. "Same as us: dinner. There are caterpillars feeding on the reeds. The fish come in and bump against their underwater stems, hoping to dislodge a fat one. I simply plucked a few worms, dropped them to float and wriggle on the surface, and speared the fish as they rose to the bait." He knelt down, unfolded his knife, and began to clean the first of the catch. Soon after, the two fish were spitted and mounted on twigs stuck in the rocks on either side of the fire.

"Smartly done," said Gyllana. "It's good to know there's someone here I can rely on. Besides myself," she added, reaching into a pocket of her long skirt and bringing out two loaves of bread, long and thin, but fresh. "Mordach won't miss these either."

Raimeau attended to the meal-making, apportioning the bread and fish equally. When they were seated around the fire in a rough triangle with himself between Krunzle and the Kersite woman, he said,

"May I suggest that we all try to get along? This is not the most hospitable part of the country. There are more men than dwarves, and some of the runts resent their relative decline in status since the days of Tar Taargadth."

"You've had much to do with dwarves?" Gyllana said, wiping a scrap of golden flesh from the corner of her mouth.

"At one time, more than I cared to," said the gray-haired man, "but most of what I know of them comes from Captain Hdolf's copy of Uthorpe's *History of the Five Kingdoms*. I read it twice."

The woman looked over at Krunzle, who was making sure no morsel of the meal escaped his needs. "What of you, errand-runner? Do you know much of where we are heading? Or anything, for that matter?"

The thief returned her a level gaze. "I know who I am and what I can do," he said. "I find that usually suffices." He arranged a piece of fish on a crumb of bread and popped both into his mouth.

"I would be interested to hear your life story," Raimeau said. "I have been impressed by your accomplishments since we were thrown together in the barracks."

Krunzle smiled expansively. "Well," he said, "it all began in a palace in Taldor. I was—"

"Is this the one where the princess is enamored of the lieutenant of the guard, but her lordly father refuses the union?"

"I believe," said Krunzle, "that you are referring to your own situation."

"Indeed. Except that mine has elements of truth in it."

"And mine does not?" Krunzle said. "You say this before you have even heard it?"

"I do not need to hear a crow squawk to know it will not make music."

"Hmmph!" said the thief, and gave his attention back to the meal.

"What about you?" the woman said into the ensuing silence. She was looking at Raimeau.

"Me?" The man made a self-deprecating face and accompanied the expression with a lift and fall of his shoulders. "There's not much to tell."

"But at least it will likely be the truth," Gyllana said. "How did you come to fall into the clutches of Boss Ulm?"

Raimeau used his last chunk of bread to wipe the fish grease from his fingers, then swallowed the softened mass. "I suppose," he said, "it was because I always think things are going to work out for the best."

"And," said Krunzle, "do they?"

"No. But I often learn interesting lessons."

"Tell," said Gyllana.

Chapter Seven
The Regulate of Grimsburrow

Raimeau's family were ship's chandlers in Almas, providing provisions and necessities to the galleys, roundships, and caravels that carried cargo and passengers into and out of the port city. His father, a stern and unbending groat-squeezer, decreed that his son should succeed him in the business and instructed him in the elements of successful chandlering: haggling, ledger-keeping, inventory control, and the techniques of keeping rotten meat and weevil-rife hardtack from revealing its true condition until the ship it was sold to was far out at sea.

But the growing boy was ever drawn to the places where seamen gathered to tell their tales of golden cities and salubrious lands, there beyond the horizon. He longed to see swaying maidens on a white-sanded beach, smell spice trees on the offshore breeze, watch the sun sink like a golden coin into the wine-dark sea. His father made every effort to beat the dream from him, but it had sunk its hooks deep into his heart, from which they could not be wrenched free without breaking it. At the age of thirteen, he followed the captain of the tall ship *Nereus* up its gangway and pleaded to be taken on as a ship's flunky.

Captain Hdolf questioned him and soon realized that Raimeau's training as an apprentice chandler would make him more useful than the average young lubber fresh off the strand with a romantic's yen for the sea. He started him out as a purser's assistant and general dogsbody, and saw to it that the crew did not make him suffer most of the ill use that is the usual lot of boys who run away to sea. The captain soon saw promise in the youngster and took time to teach him navigation and ship handling, allowing him the run of his onboard library.

By the end of five years, the boy had become a competent master's mate and might have looked forward to commanding his own ship, had not the *Nereus* fallen afoul of Okeno slave-takers while becalmed south of the Isle of Kortos. The sea-reivers came out from behind a headland in two fast-moving galleys and boarded the motionless ship from both sides. At the sight of the yellow sails and the decks thick with armed men, the outnumbered sailors gave up in the hope of receiving mercy, but that was a commodity the slavers did not stock—especially when, as in the case of the *Nereus*, the cargo was only wheat, with marble carried as ballast, neither of them readily transferable to galleys that were already packed with men.

The passengers and any crewmen who looked as if they might have something worth taking were tortured until they yielded their goods. The sturdiest of the men were clapped into irons and marched down to the galleys' benches and chained to oars. The women aboard suffered the inevitable horrors until the pirates were sated, then they were taken on board one of the galleys, along with those men who were marketable;

the vessel backed oars, turned, and sped off toward Absalom and its slave market.

Raimeau, having grown tall and well-knit, was one of those now pulling an oar for Absalom, hearing all around him the sobs and lamentations of those who had, in an afternoon, gone from being sailors and passengers to become cargo. But his pity was not for them, nor yet for himself, but for the sight of Captain Hdolf's abused body, twisting at the end of a rope from the top yardarm of the mizzenmast—the Okeno pirates' signature.

"I was taken to the slave market at Absalom and sold to the iron mines of the Fog Peaks," he told the man and woman seated with him at the fire, "where I spent ten years digging iron ore. The overseers were all dwarves—and not the better sort—and they drove us like beasts. My hair turned gray before its time."

"Yet you survived ten years," said Gyllana. "Not many do."

Raimeau's face took on an inward cast and his eyes saw something the others did not. "I was sustained," he said, "by a dream that came to me often as I lay in the filth and rags we slept on."

Krunzle's attention was caught. "A dream? Of wealth, perhaps? Is that what brought you to Ulm's Delve?"

The other man made a negating gesture. "Not wealth, no. It is hard to describe. It was merely a sense—a kind of knowing—that I was destined to accomplish some worthy deed, that I would be kept alive to do so."

"And have you accomplished your destined deed?" said the thief. "Was carrying rock for Boss Ulm the cause of your existence?"

"Don't mock him," said the woman. "He has come out alive after ten years in the mines. Could you have done as much?"

"I have endured such trials as would make strong men tremble," Krunzle said, gesturing with a fishbone, "ordeals to strike terror into the—" He broke off, ducking sideways, as she threw a piscine vertebra at his head. He reached for a leftover length of kindling and raised it to repay the compliment, while she defied and dared him with eyes that showed white all around their rims. But at that moment Chirk intervened with a warning constriction, and the thief let the missile drop to the ground, unsped.

So there you are, he directed a thought toward his inner mind. *I was wondering if you had fallen asleep.*

I do not sleep, came the answer, *but I have been thinking.*

Whereas I, thought Krunzle, *have been managing trolls and rescuing damsels—all on my own.*

I was available, if needed. Now hush while I hear what the man has to say.

While Krunzle and the snake had been conversing inwardly, Gyllana had asked Raimeau to tell more of his quest. The gray-haired man was saying, "The dream called me to Ulm's Delve. I hired on as a teamster on a wagon train bringing supplies to the town, then stayed to try my hand in the gold streams. But a man trespassed on my claim and when I protested to Boss Ulm, I was charged with boisterous conduct and sentenced to the basket chain."

"I would be careful of following that dream any farther," said the thief. "Perhaps it does not mean you well."

"Let him—" Gyllana began, but Raimeau quieted her with a soft gesture.

"I have pondered on it," he said, "and I admit that I cannot say, one way or another, whether the dream is a helper . . ."—he moved both hands, palms up, as if weighing two identical objects—"or a taskmaster." Now he put both hands together and linked their fingers.

"But I can say that without the dream, my bones would be crumbling to dust under the slag heaps of the Fog Peaks. So, whenever it calls me to action, I step up and step out. And I go forward, hopeful that the future deed around which my life is shaped will indeed be worthy."

The man's words resonated with Krunzle, enough so that for a moment he forgot to maintain the air of supercilious detachment that was his usual guise. The woman, being the product of generations of breeding among Kerse's most astute hagglers, saw the flicker of unguarded sentiment and immediately knew it for what it was. It drew her attention the way the mere twitch of a mouse's whiskers across the entire width of a kitchen floor will catch the eye of a cat.

"Don't tell me," she said, a sly smile tugging at the corners of her lips, "that our vagabond rogue is also dream-drawn to some grand arena, where you will doubtless astonish the world with—"

Again, Raimeau raised his hand and she subsided. The gray-haired man turned his quiet eyes on her and said, "It is, as you yourself have said, not a thing to be made mock of." His gaze went to Krunzle and he said, "Was it a dream that brought you to Ulm's Delve?"

The thief framed in his mind a retort that would end the line of inquiry, but before it could reach his lips, he heard the snake's voice from the back of his head: *Tell him the truth. I wish to hear it, too.*

Krunzle blinked once. *It offends my principles,* he said inwardly, *not to mention the practicalities of self-preservation.* "When two know your business, that is already one too many" is a thieves' maxim in which I put my faith.

Nevertheless, said Chirk, adding a faint reminder of the pain that slept in the base of the traveler's spine and could be awakened in a roaring instant.

131

"Well," said the woman, "are you formulating some new saga with which to astonish us? I would have thought you had a raft of them to choose from."

"No," said Krunzle, "the truth: I, too, have had a kind of dream. Nothing precise, no burning words in the night. But a sense, or just an inclination, that my destiny lay in a certain direction—east and south. Over the years, my travels have taken me many places, yet always in the end I find myself trending back that way."

Raimeau was interested. "And have you come to understand what that destiny might be?"

"Not yet." It felt odd to the thief to be speaking candidly, as if he had discovered an unusual ability he had not known he possessed. "But I feel it has something to do with wealth. And perhaps stature."

He expected Gyllana to make sport of his declaration, but she did not. Instead, she sat, thoughtful, her eyes on the fire. It was Raimeau who spoke. "And you, madonna, have you also experienced some sense of destiny?"

She turned her gaze on him. "A dream?" She shook her head. "No, I am a daughter of a Kalistocrat of Kerse. I deal in plans and projections. I dream no dreams." Her face grew hard and she threw the last of the fishbones into the fire. "But Berbackian did."

They took turns watching that night, and kept the fire well lit, with long brands laid into it that could be snatched up and thrust in the maw of anything that came out of the darkness. Nothing did, though Krunzle, taking the second watch, heard something snuffling and huffing under the shadows of the trees. He shouted and threw a stick in that direction and heard it leave.

Gyllana took the last shift and woke him when the first gray of dawn limned the tops of the mountains, still far off to the south. They had nothing to break their fast but water from the lake, and soon they were once more following the trail across the grassy plateau. They rode in silence for an hour, then Raimeau, again bringing up the rear, said, "It came to me again last night."

"You dreamed?" said Gyllana, riding ahead of him.

"I did. And it was full and strong."

Krunzle looked back at the two of them. The other man's face was serene; the woman's was pensive. She returned the thief's gaze and said, "What about you?"

"I had enough to contend with, keeping off the feral beasts drawn to your snores," he told her. "But since we have taken up the subject again, I remind you that you have heard our tales but have not told us your own— only that you are not here in pursuit of a dream."

"I am in pursuit of a cad," she said, "a liar and a deceiver."

"Three?" said Krunzle. "This may take longer than I thought. Come now, what of this Berbackian? I may have to face him, sword in hand. Tell me."

She formed her mouth into a moue of distaste, but said after a moment, "I suppose you will hear the whole sordid story from someone; better it was from me." She made a wordless sound as she collected her thoughts, then continued. "He is from Taldor, I think of good family—he may have been lying, but his manners and mode of speech bespoke some breeding—and he was well schooled in warlike arts. He applied to the Mercenary League and was commissioned an ensign, and soon promoted to undercaptain."

She had met him when his platoon was assigned to guard duty at the Temple of Kalistrade. Her father had been one of that month's seven deacons and she had gone with Eponion to carry his paraphernalia for the noon observance.

"We were having a dispute, my father and I. He had—informally, mind you—committed me in matrimony to Euphobios, the alum tycoon—"

"Alum?" said Raimeau.

"It is a mineral that, ground into powder, fixes colors in the dyeing process. Without it, there would be no red cloth, no purple, blue, yellow, whatever. He who controls the supply of alum controls the entire cloth industry of the Inner Sea."

"Ah," said the lanky man.

"My father deals in high-value commodities: silks and satins, jewels and precious substances. Marrying me to Euphobios would have strengthened his position in the cloth trade. Euphobios, for his part, liked the idea of allying his interests with my father's shipping line."

"But you wanted the strapping young Berbackian, instead of the old alum king," said Krunzle.

"Fool!" said Gyllana. "Euphobios, though older, is a well-made man. And what has wanting to do with marriage? I thought my father should get us out of the betrothal because there were rumors that a huge deposit of alum, hitherto unsuspected, had been discovered in the Aspodell Mountains. When it comes on the market, Euphobios will be selling pencils in Kalistrade Square."

Now it was Krunzle's turn to say, "Ah."

"Berbackian was to be nothing but a fling, an escapade carefully managed. Instead—" She broke off and swallowed, her face flushing. "Instead, I found myself acting like a schoolgirl. I don't know what came over me."

Chirk was nudging the thief from within. "Did he perhaps," the thief said, "use a spell or a potion?"

It was as if the idea had never occurred to the woman, but now having been voiced, she saw the shape of it clearly. "Why did I not think of that?"

Prompted by the snake, Krunzle said, "I have heard that there are some incantations that protect themselves from discovery in just that manner."

Gyllana's face resumed its customary expression of concentrated calculation. "It's possible," she said after a long stillness. "Though he would not have needed to use such means to interest me. He is a well set-up fellow, and knows which end of the boat to . . ." She paused, thinking. "But he was always wanting to look through my father's knick-knacks, especially the—"

No one had interrupted her. She had caught herself thinking out loud in company and stopped herself. But Krunzle wanted to hear the rest of the thought—and so did Chirk. "Go on," the thief said.

"It is none of your business."

"I think it is. Thang-Sha was particularly interested in an object that he said was of base metal, a talisman of some kind. I am not to come back without it."

"I thought you were here to rescue me!"

"It is a double assignment."

She gave him a hard look, but he could see her thinking it through and coming to a conclusion. "Thang-Sha was interested, you say? Curious. He appeared on the scene at about the same time that Berbackian took the talisman. There was some discussion between him and my father, about retaining him for unspecified purposes, but it seemed that the talk always came around to that odd little object. And before I knew it, my father was demanding that I recover it. His pride was at stake."

She had no more to say, and with the day growing warmer and all of them unfed since the night before and unwatered since dawn, neither of the men felt like broaching another topic. They rode on in silence, the ground gradually rising in a series of broad terraces, like waves of earth frozen in an instant and grown over with long, wheat-colored grass.

Then they climbed to the top of one of these great ripples and saw, sheltered from the wind below, a road of packed earth and gravel, running roughly north to south. Into its surface was worn a pair of ruts as wide apart as Krunzle was tall. Where the trail met the thoroughfare, the woman dismounted and studied the ground. "There," she said, pointing to a hoofprint in the softer earth at the edge of the road. The horse that had made it had been shod, and into the shoe had been pressed a row of diamonds alternating with circles. She lifted up the hoof of her own horse and said, "That's the work of the Ulm's Delve smith. Berbackian went that way."

She remounted and set her horse south along the road, Krunzle and Raimeau following. The gray-haired man studied the road as they went, and after a moment said to the thief, "The wagons that made these ruts were iron-rimmed, and the beasts that pulled them were iron-shod. I've seen them before."

"And by the look on your face," said Krunzle, "you'd rather not see them again."

"Runts," said Raimeau, as if the word filled his mouth with sourness.

"Dwarves," said the thief. "I've nothing against them, myself."

"Known many?"

"Not really."

"You're about to," said Raimeau. He gestured with his chin up the road.

Krunzle looked. Gyllana had already reined in. The road rose in a gentle slope not far ahead of them until it topped a small rise. Over that crest, trotting toward them at a ground-eating quickstep, with twenty spears straight up like a hedgehog on alert and twenty shields slung over their backs, a clanking glitter of weapons hung from leather harnesses over their chainmail, came a half-platoon of dwarves.

A whistle blew several notes, and without breaking stride, the four ranks of five became two ranks of ten, stretching the width of the road. It blew again, and the pace changed from trot to march, the shields came around to cover their fronts, and now the spearpoints no longer pointed at the sky. From within a wall of iron-studded, leather-covered oak, they bristled at the three travelers.

"Halt!" came a harsh voice from within the formation. The dwarves took two more synchronized steps then stopped. The spears remained poised. The travelers had already reined in their horses, though Krunzle's was skittish. For a long moment, nothing happened. Then the shield wall briefly parted to emit a dwarf who seemed nearly as wide as he was tall. He wore a waist-length beard of grizzled black through which glinted two gold medallions pinned to the chest of his knee-brushing mail shirt. On the front of his conical helmet was a device like a brazen axe, burnished to a high gloss.

He surveyed the three on horseback and Krunzle had the strong sense that they were not making the best of impressions. Then the dwarf said, "You are on the territory of the Regulate! You've no right to be here! So account for yourselves, and be quick about it!"

The thief opened his mouth, but a warning tremor from the snake about his neck checked him. In any case, whatever he would have said would not have been heard over Gyllana's sharp retort, whereby she identified herself by name and by her affiliation to Ippolite Eponion, Second Secretary to the First Commissariote. "And that," she said, "gives me the right to plant my foot on any piece of Druma that I choose. About these two,"—she gestured to include Krunzle and Raimeau—"I need say no more than that they are my escorts. Now, if you will clear the way . . ."

The dwarf commander was not cowed. "Have you any means of identifying yourselves?" he said, and the eyes between the rim of his helmet and the upper reaches of his waist-length black beard swept over the three of them. "This one with the bronze torc around his neck has the look of a rogue born and bred, and yon stick insect of a man has the smell of the mines about him, or I miss my guess. A canny dwarf has to ask himself what kind of Kalistocrat's daughter associates with such riffraff."

"My companions are my own affair," said the Kersite woman. "Now, move aside, or you will find yourself answering to the Kalistocracy's representative at Highhelm."

The dwarf's lips moved beneath their covering of hair. Krunzle thought the motion might have been a sneer. The commander snapped his stubby fingers and said, "That for the Kalistocracy and all the rest of your kind. You stand not in Druma but within the bounds of the Regulate of Grimsburrow, and—"

"Never heard of it," said Gyllana.

"And," the dwarf went on, "I am Drosket, son of Drosket, squad leader first-echelon in the Regulate's duly sworn militia, with full powers to question, detain, and dispose of all interlopers, intruders, vagrants, and desperadoes."

"What is this Regulate?" the woman said. "Another one of these petty communes you dwarves are always slapping together? Where you sit around and drink to your ancient glories and drone those mournful dirges you call poetry?"

"Petty commune, is it?" The dwarf stepped forward and seized the mare's reins at the bit. "We are full two thousand dwarves of probity and good character, and the militia includes a thousand of us, spear-dwarves and axe-dwarves, every one of us battle-worthy and sworn to uphold—"

He broke off there as Gyllana's heels struck her horse's ribs and the animal jolted forward, half-dragging Drosket along the road. But since the animal had been facing the double rank of spears, it did not go far, and the squad leader was able to regain his footing and some shreds of his dignity.

"The trouble with dwarves," the woman was saying, "is that they think every conversation is an occasion for oratory. Here's what we'll do: You will escort us to your Regulate and there I will speak with whomever is in authority. Then we shall go about our business." She gestured with the back of one hand, indicating that they should now proceed up the road in the direction from which the dwarves had come.

Drosket applied two hands to the reins. "We will not!" he said. Krunzle saw that the narrow band of flesh between brows and beard was now a deep shade of red. Drosket looked up at the Kalistocrat's daughter with a glare that, by rights, ought to have knocked her from the saddle. "We have a mission to fulfill."

"Then fulfill it. Don't let us hold you up."

Krunzle had heard that dwarves tore at their braided beards when frustrated. Now he learned that it was a comical sight, but that it was not a good idea for an onlooker to let his amusement show.

"That one!" Drosket shouted. "Glyff! Fekret! Get him off his horse!"

Two dwarves at one end of the double rank dropped their spears and shields and ran toward the thief. One of them seized Krunzle's right ankle and knee while the other ducked under the thief's skittish horse and came up on the other side to slip the man's foot from the stirrup. A tug and a push and Krunzle was on the road, the wind knocked out of him by a short, sharp jab to his middle as he toppled. There was no need for more violence to subdue him and take his sword belt away, but the two dwarves gave him the benefit of their fists and boots anyway.

Bruised, bleeding, and struggling to restore his lungs to their normal function, he was hauled upright—though only as far as his knees—and held before Drosket. The squad leader leaned closer, his eyes asquint under the black thickets of their brows, and inspected the thief as he might an unwelcome pustule reflected in a mirror. "Your name," he said, "and your business."

"Leave him be," said Raimeau. Krunzle heard a tremor in his voice, but underneath it was determination.

Drosket looked up. "Another one needs a lesson, is it?" But his gaze came back to the man before him, and the thief saw the dwarf's gaze drop to the metal snake around his throat. *Oh please,* he thought, *please, grab hold of it. You and your two little friends.*

"That looks good enough to be dwarf work," said the squad leader. "From the old time, when we were at our best."

"And shall be again," growled Glyff or Fekret, whichever one of them was the possessor of a red beard and a grip that had caused Krunzle's left arm to go numb.

"Did you take it from some noble dwarven warrior's tomb?" Drosket said, leaning in even closer to transfer some of his spittle to Krunzle's person. Then he delivered a short, sharp jab of his own—the thief was beginning to think it might be a standard dwarven greeting—that prevented the man from making any other answer than a gargled gasp.

Inwardly, however, he was pleading with his assailant to lay hands on Chirk. He could already envision Drosket, son of Drosket, staggering back, holding up the stumps of his smoldering arms in pain and terror, with Glyff and Fekret thrown down and writhing in agony from unspecified, though serious, injuries.

The squad leader reached. There was a *crack!* and a blue flash, but when the black-bearded dwarf recoiled he had suffered nothing more than a singeing of one fingertip, which he now shook, cursing, then popped in his mouth. The two holding Krunzle did no more than jump, startled, before renewing their circulation-stopping grips.

What are you? the thief asked the snake. *Tired?*

It is my choice, said Chirk. *And I choose . . . leniency.*

There was no time for further conversation. Drosket had removed the burned digit from his mouth. Now, from the shifting arrangement of the whiskers around his lips, Krunzle had the impression that the dwarf was smiling. It was not a smile for a thief to take comfort in.

"Tricks, is it?" Drosket said. "I know a trick or two myself." He drew a short axe whose haft fitted into a loop on his harness, and said to Glyff and Fekret, "Hold him. Hold him well."

It turned out that two dwarves could hold very well, indeed. Krunzle could not move. Within his mind, he called, *Chirk!* He heard no answer, though he was aware of the presence of the snake. *Do something!*

"No!" shouted Raimeau.

Krunzle looked over his shoulder, saw the thin man sling a leg over the front of his saddle and slide off his horse. As he landed, he drew from his pocket and opened the clasp knife he had taken from Mordach's house. He advanced upon the dwarves, the little blade before him in a trembling hand, his face full of fear. But he kept coming.

Droset, the axe poised in a two-handed grip above his head, froze. His little eyes first shifted to the gray-haired man, then they grew large; his mouth opened so wide that it could actually be seen among the whiskers that framed it on all sides. Raimeau, quivering, took another step.

And now the squad leader emitted a barking sound, then another, and then a third just like the first two. Similar sounds came from either side of Krunzle, and from the spear-dwarves still ranged across the road, and he realized that he must be hearing the sound of dwarves laughing. It sounded like loose bricks rolling downhill in a steel barrel, but it was better than the sound of an axe splitting his skull, which he had moments before expected to be, for the briefest of times, the last sound he would ever hear.

The two holding him had even loosened their grips. He shook himself free of their grasp and stood up. The dwarves were still convulsed with mirth. Droset was doubled over, one hand touching the ground to keep himself from falling.

They were only trying to frighten you, said the voice in Krunzle's mind.

They succeeded, no thanks to you.

Besides, I wanted to see—

Chirk cut itself off in mid-thought. *See what?* the thief said. He got no answer from the snake, but his own reasoning supplied one. *It was you. You made Raimeau come to my aid, didn't you? Even though he's frightened of dwarves.*

Again, there was no answer. But that meant there was also no contradiction. Krunzle thought a harsh word at the voice in his mind, but then his attention was called once more to the dwarves.

"All right," said Drosket, straightening up, "we've had some good sport. Now back to business."

"Your business, not ours," said Gyllana. "We'll be on our way."

The squad leader made no move to stop her, but stop her he did when he said, "You'd be after that fine, strapping Taldan in a Blackjacket uniform—well, elements of one—would you not?"

"You've seen him?" the woman said.

The dwarf was putting his axe back into its loop. "We see everyone who comes into the Regulate. We stop them and pass the time of day." He paused to send Glyff and Fekret back into ranks. "Sometimes we send them on their way. Sometimes we send them on *our* way."

In Krunzle's mind, Chirk said, *He wants something.* The traveler returned a brief thought: *Of course he does.* Aloud, the thief said, "And before you tell us which of those sendings applied to former Undercaptain Berbackian, you'd like us to tell you something."

"Ah," said Drosket, turning to the thief, "not as thick as you look. Though that would be a trick."

"Let us forgo the pleasantries," Krunzle said. "We've just come from the north, from Ulm's Delve. You'd like to know the news from that direction."

The dwarf eyed him from the corner of his eye, paused to spit in a neutral direction, then said, "That could be."

"You'll have seen the smoke."

"There was a smudge on the horizon, and a glow last night."

"Well, then," said the thief. He glanced up at Gyllana. She said, "You're doing fine. Continue."

"Here's the offer," Krunzle told the dwarf, holding up one finger, "we tell you everything you want to know about Ulm's Delve, and you tell us the last known whereabouts and direction of travel of the Blackjacket. Plus," he continued, adding a second finger to the first before the dwarf could answer, "three days' food and drink from your rations. And,"—a third finger—"a gold coin for me. To make up for the ill treatment."

Droveset snorted, something else that dwarves did well. "You are out of your addled—"

"It might be very significant news," Krunzle cut him off. "A squad leader who was first to hear of it, a squad leader who then played his hand right cannily, might well see another medal out of it." He paused to let that sink in. "Perhaps even promotion."

Droveset said nothing but looked at Krunzle in a considering way, as a man might look at a goose that had just offered to lay him a golden egg. It would have to have been a very large goose, since the dwarf had to look up at the man, but he felt that the analogy was sound. Finally, he said, "No gold coin."

"Then a silver piece."

"For your dignity?" said the dwarf, and Krunzle thought there was probably an amused sneer hiding somewhere in the thicket of whiskers. "How about a sincere apology?"

"I would rather have the coin."

"Then you will have neither. But I will give you the food and drink. A supply wagon follows."

"And my sword?"

"Yes."

"And the word on Berbackian?"

"That, too."

They agreed that the dwarves would transfer the provisions. Then Krunzle would tell them the news. Then the dwarves would tell them the whereabouts of Berbackian. Raimeau was assigned the task of collecting the bundles of bread and hard cheese and four canteens of the dark ale that seemed to be the preferred drink of dwarf soldiers in the Regulate. The lanky man moved as if in a half-dream, like a sleeper who comes awake to find himself walking about, far from his bed.

When the supplies were stowed in their saddlebags and the three travelers had remounted their horses, Krunzle recounted the events of the preceding day. He was inclined, as he often was in telling a tale, to amplify his part in the business; but when the words formed in his mind, he found his throat briefly constricted and the snake's voice in his mind, saying, *Dwarves hate a boastful human. Tell it without embellishment.*

And so the thief told of the escape of Skanderbrog, the deaths of Boss Ulm and Mordach the Prudent, the burning of the town, and the flight of the populace.

Drosket listened with close attention, but the recounting of Skanderbrog's role in the destruction of the gold camp took him by surprise. "A troll, you say?"

"A young one that Ulm and Mordach enslaved."

"Not orcs?"

Krunzle blinked. "Orcs? In these parts?"

"There have been signs," said the dwarf.

"What kind of signs?"

The dwarf cast his gaze upward and shook his head. "Well, what would you think? Nothing makes a mess like an orc, and a gaggle of them make a fine mess indeed. Step in it and you'll never forget the experience." But now Drosket paused to think, and after a moment he said, "Ulm, Mordach, dead?"

"Very."

"You saw this with your own eyes?"

The thief signaled an affirmative. "And most of his bullyboys. They were in the saloon when the troll made his entrance."

Drosket's eyes had grown bright beneath the overhanging thicket of his brows. "What of the gold?"

"The people who fled would have had their pokes on them."

"But the refined stuff," the dwarf said. "The ingots in the stronghouse by the furnace?"

Why didn't I think of that? Krunzle said to himself, and was answered by a metal snake that told him to pay attention to the business at hand. He told Drosket, "There would have been no time to load wagons and hitch up mules. Everyone was running before the fire caught them. Or Skanderbrog."

No one could have called Drosket, son of Drosket, an indecisive dwarf. "Right!" he said, and turned to his double squad, producing a silver whistle that hung on a thong beneath his beard. He blew a single blast, then shouted, "Sling shields! Form up, column of twos! Glyff, detail two dwarves to accompany these three to headquarters, and go with them. Report what they've told us."

"What about—" Krunzle began.

The dwarf squad leader paid no attention, but continued to issue orders to his subordinate. "We will go and take possession of the mine. Send the supply wagon after us. Tell the senior crown that we will need reinforcements at the earliest, and transport to bring back the gold. Tell him we will hold the place against all comers, for the glory of the Regulate and the rebirth of dwarven honor!"

The last was said in a shout, and the dwarves, now formed up in a narrow column, roared back with a cheer and a triple clash of spears shafts on shields. Drosket went to stand beside the leading pair and raised an arm. "Column," he shouted, "at the quickstep—"

Krunzle kneed his horse in front of the dwarves. "What about Berbackian?"

Drosket didn't even glance his way. "Detained, questioned, released," he said. "Said he was carrying dispatches from the Kalistocracy for the Lumber Consortium officials in Falcon's Hollow. Last seen heading south." Then he blew the whistle in three short blasts.

On the third note, the dwarf column, less Glyff—who had turned out to be the red-bearded one—and his two leave-behinds, stepped forward at a fast walk. Krunzle moved his horse out of their way and watched them go. One of the dwarves was counting out the paces, the rest of them chiming in on every fourth beat. After a hundred, they broke into a trot. The thief had heard it said that, in the old days, dwarven armies could cover fifty miles a day, in full armor, even through mountainous terrain, at this half-walking, half-running pace. Seeing Drosket's double squad pounding down the rutted road, he thought, was like looking back across the centuries.

"Let's go," said Gyllana. When Krunzle turned, he saw that the three dwarves detailed to return to their headquarters were already trotting back the way they had come, and the woman was spurring her horse after them. Raimeau, still looking a little dazed, was waiting for Krunzle to follow.

The traveler kicked his horse into motion and the two men caught up with the Kalistocrat's daughter. They rode in silence for a while, then she said to the thief, "You handled that well. The negotiation, I mean."

"I try to rise to the occasion," Krunzle said.

"I was surprised"—her voice held a note of reflection—"that you did not make more of your role in the death of Ulm's Delve. Raimeau tells me that it was you who set the troll on his path of destruction."

"Well," said the thief, "as I say, there comes an occasion, and I rise to it."

She formed her mouth into a kind of shrug. "Perhaps I misjudged you."

"You would not be the first," he said. "Why, if I say so myself, I am known up and down the lands of the Inner Sea for my—"

"Then again," she said, "perhaps not."

Chapter Eight
The Noble Head

A half hour's ride in the wake of the three dwarves brought them to the end of the gently sloping plateau. Abruptly, the land began to rise, and now the rutted road had to switchback its way up steeper inclines. As they climbed, the grass gave way to heather and clumps of gorse, punctuated here and there by moss-covered boulders of black rock, veined with lighter minerals. They seemed to have been scattered at random, but when Krunzle commented to that effect, Raimeau informed him that the rocks had probably been flung from the mouth of Mount Sinatuk the last time the volcano had erupted.

"When was that?" the thief said.

"No one knows," said the gray-haired man.

"And when is it likely to go off again?"

Raimeau spread his hands. "Who can say?"

Not long after they began to climb, they met the dwarf troop's supply wagon, loaded with boxes and barrels and the dwarves' personal kit, and pulled by six of the short-legged but powerful ponies that had long ago been bred down to a size that dwarves could handle.

Glyff and his two dwarves recovered their gear from the wagon while conducting a brief colloquy with the four dwarves who manned it. The vehicle then set off the way the travelers had come, the driver whipping the ponies up to a trot. While the three escorts put on their packs, Krunzle used the opportunity to ask how far they had to travel before they reached their destination.

"For us, unencumbered, no more than an hour," said Glyff. He was an almost exact copy of Drosket, though not quite as wide and without the gray streaks in his beard. "With you to slow us down, nearly two."

"We have had no breakfast," said Gyllana. "We would like to rest and eat some of these rations." She patted the saddlebag in front of her leg.

"Eat as you ride," said Glyff. "Our news must reach the senior crown forthwith."

"Then you go on ahead, and we will catch you up," said Krunzle.

The dwarf emitted a sound that suggested his throat was congested with gravel. "You'll do no such thing!" he said, unslinging his spear. "You'll move on, or you'll be moved!"

The other two had followed Glyff's lead. The thief said, "Are we then under arrest?"

"You are under escort. If you'd like to try for under arrest, just keep blathering." Glyff looked at Gyllana as he said, "Though you'd find it hard to eat your brekkie with your hands tied behind your backs."

"Well," said the woman, "that makes it clear." She pulled a cob of bread wrapped in waxed paper out of the saddlebag and bit off a piece. Her knees put the mare in motion.

The road zigged and zagged its way up a series of increasingly steep slopes, topping ridges and descending only a short distance before it began to climb again. The mountains were much nearer now. After noon, they came to an almost perpendicular cliff and turned left along its base. Krunzle kept expecting to see the road enter a canyon and continue to climb. Instead, he was surprised to come around an outcrop at the foot of the precipice and see the wagon ruts ahead disappear into a gateway cut into the living rock.

Twin gates of heavy dark timber, studded and hinged with black iron and three times the thief's height, stood open. Beside them, turning toward them as they came into view, was another squad of spear-dwarves whose leader bore on his helmet the same long-hafted axe, though his was in tin.

Glyff stood at attention before this worthy and spoke to him too softly for Krunzle to hear. But there was no mistaking the import of their discussion. The three travelers were swiftly surrounded and told to dismount, but no attempt was made to take away the thief's short sword; he had the impression that the mail-shirted dwarves, not one of them possessing fewer than two weapons besides a spear, did not consider him a threat. *Probably not even a nuisance*, he thought in Chirk's direction, but received only the mental equivalent of a distracted grunt.

"Up," said Glyff, indicating the gateway with a motion of his helmeted head.

Leading his horse, Krunzle went to look through the opening. He saw a flight of steps leading upward into darkness. Far up, a dim light was set in the wall, then another, even farther. "The horses can't do that," he said.

One of the gate guards took the reins from his hands. "They go by the ascender," he said.

"The ascender?" said Gyllana.

"Good dwarven engineering," said Glyff. "Pulleys and counterweights. Now get climbing. We've a report to make."

The woman raised her eyebrows, but the dwarves were in no mind for a protracted discussion. The horses were led off and the three travelers were pressed by spear shafts toward the stairs. Krunzle thought the dwarves would have been just as happy to use spear points as encouragement. They started climbing, step upon step, and soon the daylight was gone and their way was lit by dim lights set at long intervals in the upper walls of the sloping tunnel.

His eyes grew accustomed to the gloom, and after a hundred steps or so it registered with him that the steps were precisely cut, perfectly even in height and width. The walls and ceiling of the tunnel, too, were smooth. The lights, now that he looked at one in passing, were not the low, flickering flames he had assumed them to be, but some kind of luminescent substance set in polished crystal and fitted into niches in the rock.

Dwarven construction of such quality almost always meant it was the work of hands long since turned to dust. The skills that had allowed dwarves to erect Highhelm and the other Sky Citadels, and their descendants to build the original cities and towns of the Five Kingdoms, had since declined. Dwarves still set many of the standards by which Golarion measured excellence in the mechanic's arts, but great chasm-spanning arched bridges, counterweighted fortress gates that opened to a finger's pressure, aqueducts that fed a myriad of fonts and fountains, palaces and mansions whose marble walls looked as light as if they were made from spun confectioner's sugar, war engines that could throw a hundredweight stone a thousand paces with the accuracy of a marksman—those were the products of a bygone age.

Yet this work—this tunnel, these steps, these lights—was no more than a year or two old. Every edge was sharp, undulled by time. The crystal of the lights had not clouded. A millennium of footsteps had not worn shallow grooves down the middle of the steps.

"Raimeau," Krunzle said, speaking softly so that the dwarves ahead and behind them would not hear, "you know your history. Does this look like dwarven work to you?"

But before the lanky man could answer, Glyff said, over his shoulder, "I heard that."

"He means no offense," Raimeau said.

The dwarf blew out an expressive breath. "What you're seeing is what dwarves are capable of, now that the Regulate has come. For thousands of years we have slipped below the bar our ancestors set. Now we have stood up."

Who would notice? Krunzle was tempted to say, but was wise enough not to. "What is this Regulate?" he asked.

"You'll see, soon enough," said the dwarf. "And you'll mind your manners."

"I believe," the thief said to Raimeau, "that I just might."

By then, Krunzle's calves and thighs were already beginning to complain. Ten minutes later, as the stairs went ever upward, the complaints became silent shrieks and moans of agony. He was both curious and chagrined to note that neither the gray-haired man nor the Kalistocrat's daughter showed signs of anything more than grim discomfort. He supposed Raimeau had spent years carrying backbreaking loads up and down the endless steps of the iron mines; for him, to climb unburdened must be like skip-tra-la-la through the park. The woman, too, was lighter than the thief, and had probably enjoyed a lifetime of strength-building exercise kicking undesirables from her path.

Chirk, he said inwardly, *can you not activate the boots?*

The snake's voice came back after a moment, like that of a man called away from a pressing involvement: *What is the problem?*

You can rummage through my mind. Listen to what my legs say.

The voice made a wordless sound indicative of a failure to be impressed. But a moment later, Krunzle felt the boots come to life. They lifted and set down his feet without further contributions from his pain-racked leg muscles.

Thank you, he said. There was no response. He felt the snake withdrawing from their connection. *Wait,* he called after it, *what are you up to, that keeps you so occupied? And, more important, what does if portend for me?*

I am thinking, said Chirk. *Thinking and remembering. As for what it means to you, why should that mean anything to me?*

Because our destinies are, at least for a time, wedded together. My fate may have some bearing on your own.

The thief had never heard a snake laugh, and now that he did—a dry chuckle deep in his mind—he knew he wouldn't mind never having to hear it again. *For a time, indeed,* said the thing around his neck. *You have no idea how little a time it would be to me, even if I hugged your neck until you were the oldest of your kind.*

You're a long-lived snake, then? asked Krunzle.

I am only now beginning to remember what I was, Chirk said, *and I have not even begun to recall how I came to be as I am. But, yes, I am long-lived, because the memories that now come to me, thin and weak as the ghosts of ghosts, are glimpses of a world far gone.*

I am less interested in your past than in our mutual present and future, thought Krunzle. *I still have Berbackian to catch, along with whatever he has stolen from the Kalistocrat. And before that, I have to deal with whomever runs the show at the top of these endless stairs. I may need your help.*

You will do fine, said the snake. *Only those of strong spirit are called.*

Called? Krunzle couldn't find a way to laugh scornfully in his mind. He contented himself with a sarcastic *Ha, ha!* and added, *Eponion didn't choose me. He stumbled over me in Kalistrade Square and seized the opportunity.*

I was not referring to Ippolite Eponion, Chirk said.

No? Then to whom did you refer?

If I knew that, the voice in his mind said, *I would know much more besides. Like why, and where, not to mention several significant whats. But I do know that there has been culling, and there have been responses to the call.*

This was not the kind of thing Krunzle wanted to hear from a creature that had been set over him as whip-master on an already unwelcome quest. He told the snake so, and was advised that his preferences had been duly noted. Unsaid was the implication that they had been just as duly discarded.

The thief said, *I just want to find this Blackjacket, recover whatever it was he took, and bring it and Gyllana back to Kerse. There might even be a reward. Either way, that's all I ever agreed to do.*

I don't recall you agreeing to anything, said the voice in his mind. *I was myself only half-awake, but I clearly remember that your side of the discussion mostly involved*

*choking and some silent cursing. In any case, though
you may demand of life that it offer you only simple and
uncomplicated challenges, life is not obligated to comply.*

Listen—

No. I am otherwise and more gainfully occupied.

But—

You would have more immediate and pressing concerns,
Chirk said, *if I deactivated your boots.*

I am not happy about this, Krunzle said.

Join the legion. And that was the last he heard from
Chirk for a while.

Krunzle had been climbing for quite some time with his
head down, seeing only the heels of the dwarf's boots
in front of him. He became aware of a change in the
quality of the light and looked up, over Glyff's head, to
see an oblong of daylight not too far ahead. The light
grew brighter as they ascended, and now came sounds
other than the monotony of their own steps: voices, male
and female; a clanging as of blacksmithery; a creaking
that the thief ascribed to pulleys and lifting tackle; the
rattle of iron-shod hooves and cartwheels over cobbles.

The sounds and the light grew in intensity until
suddenly their party emerged from the tunnel into full
daylight. Krunzle's first impression was that he had
never seen so many dwarves. There must have been at
least a thousand, of both sexes—he was certain he had
never seen a dwarven woman before—and of all ages.
And every one of them was busy.

The tunnel had fed them into a huge circular
space cut out of the same black rock the tunnel had
traversed. It might have been called an amphitheater,
except that its sides were sheer all around, not sloped,
and the walls were pierced everywhere with windows

and doorways. The impression was of a vast apartment building built around a huge central courtyard.

But this was more than just a dwelling space; it was at least a village, perhaps even a small town, compacted and closed in. Along the bottom of the curved wall, archways bigger than the tunnel's exit had been carved out. Inside were sizable rooms dedicated to a range of essential activities. In one, Krunzle saw flour-smeared dwarves kneading lumps of dough and loading them into iron-doored ovens set into the back wall; next door, a heavily muscled fellow with soot on his face was hammering glowing iron on an anvil—he looked to be making hinges; beyond the smithy, a dwarf with a pencil behind his ear was carefully chiseling a complex, interwoven design into a long, wide slab of dark hardwood.

Across the courtyard, behind closed doors but audible through the open windows, dwarf children were chanting a multiplication table. Dwarf women, presumably their mothers, were washing clothing in a multispouted fountain; others were hanging clean linen to dry on a rotating frame made of wood and rope. They were laughing about something, then one of them made a gesture with two hands that redoubled the mirth. Other dwarf women, leaning out of windows and balconies two and three stories above the laundry, joined in the banter as they worked ropes and pulleys to haul up baskets full of clothes.

When Krunzle looked up, he saw four tiers of windows and doorways cut into the cliffs all around, and glimpsed movement within many of them. Above those, dwarves with hammers and chisels, standing on platforms suspended from the cliff top, were carving out new accommodations.

Glyff and their escorts marched the three travelers straight across this hive of activity, dodging a train of dog-pulled carts carrying mounds of vegetables and hanging sides of beef and mutton to a multi-arched refectory next to the schoolrooms. Then they had to stop as a platoon of at least forty armed and armored dwarves marched across their path, reversed and marched back the other way, all of them chanting an alliterative verse about a young female dwarf named Agna who seemed to be renowned for her stamina and liberal nature.

So many were the sights and sounds around them that it took a few moments for the most remarkable aspect of the scene to register with Krunzle: not only had he never seen so many dwarves in one place— or cumulatively throughout his entire life, for that matter—but he had never seen them so happy.

Normally, the sweetest mood he would have expected to find in any member of their race would have been mild grumpiness. When a dwarf said things were "not bad," it was the equivalent of a human bounding about, wreathed in smiles and shouting, "Great day in the morning!" He would no more expect to find a smile on a dwarf's face than hair on an egg.

Yet here were cheerful, smiling, joke-telling dwarves. It was disconcerting. When the thief looked to see how Raimeau was taking it, he saw that the gray-haired man's eyes were wide and constantly moving; his legs shook like those of a man who has to pick his way across a shelf of stone on which a hundred rattlesnakes have coiled themselves to sleep in the sun. Krunzle doubted the trembling was solely a result of the long stair climb.

Past the platoon of marching dwarves, they encountered a squad practicing close-arm drills with spear and shield, then another seated cross-legged in a semicircle while a junior officer—to judge by the small brass crown on the front of his helmet—directed their attention to an easel that supported a blackboard on which squares and circles were drawn in chalk, with curving arrows connecting them. The officer paused at the sight of Glyff's party and gave the three travelers an unwelcoming gaze as he smartly returned the escort's salute.

And then they had crossed the great courtyard and were being marched through a wide archway flanked by two spear-dwarves in armor. Beyond was a long corridor, lit by more luminescent globes—though these were brighter—and with more arches on either side, all filled with closed wooden doors on which numbers and letters were neatly painted. Glyff took them to one that bore the legend *Torphyr, Senior Crown.* The red-bearded dwarf knocked, and when he heard an answer, told the three travelers to stay where they were while he went in. The order was accompanied by a meaningful glance at the armed dwarves who had come with them.

Glyff closed the door behind him. Krunzle could hear voices within, although not clearly enough to make out words. But, moments later, he did hear the scrape of chair legs across a stone floor—the sound of someone getting to his feet in a hurry. The door opened, and he found himself looking down at another grizzle-bearded dwarf in a mail shirt whose links had been gilded and which bore several impressive decorations. The officer ran his eyes over the three humans, and it was clear that the sight of them did not elevate his mood. He had been carrying a helmet and now put it on—the headgear, the thief noted, bore a larger crown than that of the junior officer outside, and it was gold, not brass.

Torphyr spoke to Glyff: "Go to Operations and report your news to Squadron Commander Glamwyn. Tell him I'll join him when I can. Meanwhile, I'll take these to the Head." He turned to the travelers and made a come-along gesture. "You three, with me."

Without waiting for an answer, he turned on his heel and strode down the corridor, his steel-cleated bootheels beating out a rapid tattoo. Their escorts, who had stood to attention while the crown had been speaking, made it clear that they had no option about obeying. Krunzle shrugged and complied.

They went deeper into the dwarven complex, turned a corner at an intersecting corridor, and came to a pair of wide wooden doors. The crown pulled a rope that came out of a hole in the wall and ended in a wooden handle. At once, one of the doors slid open, revealing a small wooden room. The officer stepped in and the dwarves behind the travelers made sure their three charges did likewise.

When they were all crammed into the small space—Raimeau had to stoop—one of the dwarves slid the door closed and pulled on another rope that came out of the ceiling. A moment later, the floor pushed against their feet.

"We're going up," Krunzle said.

Torphyr rolled his eyes. "Primitives," he said.

"Not all of us," said Gyllana. "We have ascenders in Kerse." She looked around at the walls and ceiling. "Though I must say I'm surprised to see one here in the upriver wilds. Who built it for you?"

The dwarven officer seemed to swell. Krunzle thought it must be through a combination of pride and indignation. "We built it!" he said. "Under the inspired leadership of the great Brond, we are restoring the glory of the Five Kingdoms. And, you of Kerse may take note, we are reclaiming dwarven lands that have been . . ."—here he seemed to search a moment for just the right term—"irregularly alienated from our rightful sovereignty."

The Kalistocrat's daughter afforded him a look that could have chilled boiling cabbage. "I trust you do not refer to the territory of the Kalistocracy. The land was fairly and justly ceded, after free and open bargaining."

The senior crown muttered something. The words "sharp practice" may have put in a brief appearance.

"I beg your pardon," said Gyllana. "I would not have expected that the Kalistocracy would have to remind a dwarf of the Five Kingdoms that without our mediation you would still be savaging each other in your pointless civil war."

"Just as I would not have expected," said Torphyr, "that a Kalistocrat would ever pass up a chance to remind us of it."

The woman drew in a long breath through her nose and was about to deliver an eviscerating reply when the ascender's upward progress came smoothly to a halt. A chime sounded from somewhere and the door slid open. The party exited into another hallway, this one wider and walled in glossy black stone, with a floor of gray granite that was polished to an equivalent sheen. The travelers followed the crown a distance along the passageway, which was decorated at intervals with large paintings featuring famous events from the history of dwarfdom—though Krunzle saw no representations of incidents, such as the fall of Koldukar, that had won dwarves no compliments for their valor. Between the paintings were niches that held statues of dwarves in heroic poses.

They came to a pair of tall doors of the same dark, polished wood the dwarf cabinetmaker had been working on in his shop off the courtyard. Each of the portals bore a circular cartouche in which something was written in an ornate form of the dwarven script that was too complex for Krunzle to read—at least in the short time he had to examine it. The time was short because, as they arrived, the doors opened inward—silently, and without any apparent agency—and the crown led them through and into an enormous room.

Like the corridor, it was walled and floored in black and gray rock burnished to a high gleam, except where vast carpets of black wool covered portions of what seemed to the thief to be a good half-acre of space. From the ceiling, which was far higher than any dwarf would ever need, depended ten great chandeliers of black iron and faceted crystal. The wall that faced the courtyard was pierced by a row of windows, each as wide as Krunzle could have reached with arms outspread, that started at that ceiling and, glazed in flawlessly transparent panes, went all the way down to the floor. Through these, the sun threw a series of parallel bars of light from one end of the huge chamber to the other.

At that distant other end, three broad steps led up to a wide dais. On this platform, a desk fashioned from more of the dark wood stood on legs made of fluted columns of the black stone, both substances gleamingly polished. The desk's working surface was so large that Skanderbrog would have seemed too small for its dimensions, if ever a troll could have been induced to sit behind a piece of furniture. On the wall behind the dais hung a grand tapestry of closely woven wool that featured a design formed from crossed pairs of edged and pointed weapons surrounding a central cartouche like the pair on the doors.

Krunzle now had time to work out the extravagantly curled and entwined script because it took almost a hundred paces to travel from the doors to the steps of the dais—and the dwarf officer who led them made it clear that they were to cross the distance at a ceremonial pace: slow and stately, with a pause between the placing of one foot and the lifting of the other.

The logo turned out to be a dwarven name: Brond. But most of the lettering formed a rendering of two dwarven words: "noble" and "head." Krunzle found himself puzzling at the meaning of the words—he could recall nothing from his smattering of dwarven lore to account for it. He would have liked to have asked Raimeau, but he had a strong sense that aimless chatter would not go well with the formality that the crown had imposed on the occasion. There were still two dwarves behind them with spears and axes, and the officer was probably still fuming from his passage of verbal arms with Gyllana. In such circumstances, Krunzle could easily imagine an innocent error in manners earning someone a beating. He would rather that someone not be him.

They had crossed, at a measured pace, some three-quarters of the distance. The thief could see motion behind the desk, but the height of the dais and the small size of the moving object made it impossible to get a clear view. His impression was that something pale, smooth, and rounded was moving back there, something that gleamed in the bar of light that the rearmost window threw across the desk, but what he was seeing was too small a fragment for him to deduce the whole.

They reached the foot of the steps. Torphyr held up a hand in the universal signal and they halted. Then the crown ascended the three risers, again at the same ceremonial pace. At the top, his eyes just level with the polished surface of the great desk, he stopped, snapped his heels together, struck his beard-hidden chest with his right fist, and said, in parade-ground tones, "Request permission to report!"

The voice that answered him from beyond the desk did so in a more conversational tone. "Do so."

In a series of staccato bursts of speech, Torphyr related the news of the collapse of Ulm's Delve, the deaths of Ulm and Mordach, Squad Leader Drosket's initiative in leading his patrol to secure the gold mine, and the arrival under escort of the three human outlanders who had brought the news.

There was only the briefest pause while the unseen recipient of these tidings absorbed them. Then the voice said, calmly, "Send reinforcements and supplies, including a company of engineers with tools and materials to build a strongpoint. Inform Drosket, son of Drosket, that he is promoted to junior crown and awarded command of the installation. Then prepare a briefing for the high command, and tell them to organize a wagon train and a full battalion for escort. Dismissed."

The crown struck his beard again, about-faced, and was about to march down the steps. Then he stopped, turned again and said, "Noble Head? The outlanders?"

"I will deal with them," said the voice. "Dismissed."

The officer repeated his salute and turn, then descended the steps. As he passed the three travelers, he gave Gyllana an upward and sidewise glance that invited her, with silent eloquence, to try her

Kalistocratic arrogance on the one who was about to "deal" with her and see what it would get her. The woman's reply—the merest flick of an eyebrow—was equally expressive.

But the three outlanders' attention was now drawn back to the dais. The thief heard the scrape of a chair being moved against a stone floor, then the footsteps of hard-soled boots approaching down one side of the huge desk. A moment later, a figure rounded the corner of the immense object and Krunzle found himself looking up into a pair of the stone-gray eyes that were common among dwarves. They were intelligent eyes, eyes that were accustomed to weighing and assessing the worth of persons upon whom their gaze might fall.

But as that gaze moved over the three travelers, the thief saw the coolness replaced by what could only be alarm. First the eyes widened, then they narrowed, and a pair of thick dwarven brows would surely have drawn in and down—except that there were no brows. Nor a pair of sweeping moustaches, nor an avalanche of beard from the cheeks and lower lip descending uncut to as long as it cared to grow. Lips, cheeks, chin, brow—all were bare, clad in nothing but smooth, pale flesh. There was not even a hair on the high-crowned and rounded head that gleamed palely in the shaft of sunlight from the window.

A bald dwarf, Krunzle was thinking. Whoever heard of a bald dwarf? And not just partially bald, but as hairless as a fish's backside. Like a great baby. It was a disconcerting sight, the thief decided. A dwarf without hair, without braids or shaggy locks, was a deeply unnatural occurrence. He glanced sideways at Raimeau and the woman, and saw that their reactions were much the same as his. The gray-haired man had even taken an involuntary step backward and the corners of Gyllana's mouth had turned down even farther than usual.

"Is one of you," said the unhirsute apparition—and the thief heard a tremor in the voice. The speaker was making an attempt to suppress the quaver, but with only partial success. "Is one of you . . . a thief?"

Krunzle adopted his blandest aspect, and looked appraisingly at each of his companions, as if one of them might step forward and admit to larcenous tendencies. He found Gyllana's finger pointing at him.

"I'd lay money that he is," she said.

Her statement drew the attention of the hairless creature atop the dais, "And you," he said, "are you a . . . woman who has been ill done by?"

"What woman," said the Kalistocrat's daughter, "has not?"

The gray eyes turned toward Raimeau. "Have you . . . a scarred back?"

Raimeau said, "What slave of the iron mines of the Fog Peaks has not?"

The bald dwarf's legs seemed to have lost their strength. He shuffled forward and sat upon the top step of the dais. The two dwarves who had been standing at rigid attention rushed forward to assist him, but he waved them off with a pale hand that, Krunzle noted, had no hairs on its back. Then the hand passed over the whiskerless face, and came away damp with sweat, so that its owner had to wipe away the moisture on the front of the black tunic he wore over gray trousers and black half-boots.

"Sir," said one of the spear-dwarves, "shall I call for—"

"Out," was the answer. "You and your comrade."

"Sir? Noble Head? Are you well?"

"Out!" The voice had recovered some of its authority. "I will question these three alone. Wait outside the doors until I call you."

"But they are armed," said the escort.

The opposition, even so hesitant, seemed to revive the bald one. He stood up, and now Krunzle saw no suggestion of babyhood. "They will do me no harm," said the dwarf. As if to himself, he muttered, "At least not here." Then he pointed at the faraway doors, and his posture defied all argument. In unison, the two escorts clacked their heels together, then turned on them and marched away.

The hairless dwarf brought his gaze back to the three travelers at the foot of the steps. He seemed calmer now, almost resigned. "So," he said, "you're real. And here you are."

Krunzle had been probing at the place in the back of his mind where the snake was usually felt. *Chirk?* he said, inwardly. *Are you aware of this?*

Busy, came the answer.

I think we're about to hear from another dreamer.

The snake said, *I wouldn't be surprised. Now, leave me in peace.*

Meanwhile, the hairless dwarf had pulled himself together and was studying each of them. Now he smoothed the front of his tunic, resettled around his waist the plain black leather belt that confined the cloth, and said, "Do you know who I am?"

Krunzle said, "You were addressed as the 'Noble Head.'" He looked at the cartouche woven into the tapestry behind the desk. "Would your name be Brond?"

The bald head nodded in confirmation. "You have not heard of me?"

"My mind has been concentrated on other matters," the thief said. He had a curious sense that, although this anomalous creature was plainly the power in these parts, Brond was somehow dependent on the three travelers—wanted something from them. *No, not want,* he thought. *The word is "need."* And in that realization, Krunzle scented opportunity.

The dwarf was gesturing in a way that said it was not important that the three had not heard of him. "We make an effort to keep ourselves to ourselves," he said. "For the time being, at least." He stroked his smooth chin and said, "The man who came through here yesterday, the mercenary, was he something to do with you?"

Gyllana would have spoken, but Krunzle was there first. "I am an emissary of Ippolite Eponion, Second Secretary to the First Commissariote of the Kalistocracy at Kerse. The man Berbackian has stolen an item of value from my employer, and I am charged with recovering the purloined property and restoring it to its owner."

"What is this stolen property?" the dwarf asked.

"I am not at liberty to say," Krunzle said, "but I am sure that the First Secretary—"

"I thought you said your employer was the Second Secretary," said Brond.

"Did I?" Krunzle made the same dismissive gesture the dwarf had made earlier. "No matter. But I was about to say that the Kalistocracy would be grateful for any assistance you could render in furthering the apprehension of the dastard, Berbackian."

"What sort of assistance?"

"It's a small thing, but my traveling funds were stolen from me by a parcel of rogues in the gold camp. If you were able to advance me a few gold pieces—say ten; no, to be safe, let's say twenty—I would be pleased to give you a promissory note on behalf of the Second Secretary."

"Don't listen to him!" said the woman. "Ippolite Eponion is my father, and Berbackian, until I discovered his true nature, was my intended. This rogue who is trying to separate you from your gold is merely a thief that my father has put on Berbackian's trail." She cast a scornful look in Krunzle's direction. "Apparently, my father thought the best way to catch a miscreant is to send one of his own ilk after him."

Brond turned this over in his mind, then turned to Raimeau. "And you?" he said.

The gray-haired man returned the dwarf's gaze. "I am an ordinary man," he said, "in pursuit of a dream."

"How long were you in the mines?"

"Ten years."

The dwarf's bald brows wrinkled in surprise. "Then you are no ordinary man. Tell me, what is your dream?"

Raimeau's face fell. "I only know that I am fated to perform a brave and significant deed. But what that deed may be . . ." He drew up his shoulders and let them slump.

At that news, Brond swore softly. "I had been hoping," he said, "that when you finally arrived, there would be more to you than . . ."—he made a rolling motion with both hairless hands—"than this."

"You were expecting us?" Gyllana said.

"All of my life."

Krunzle could not resist the obvious question. "Why?"

"I was hoping," said Brond, the Noble Head and founder of the Regulate, "that you would tell me."

Chapter Nine
"There Will Be a Reckoning"

Between two of the tall windows was a group of overstuffed armchairs arranged for conversation. Brond led them there and bade them sit. Since the furniture was scaled to dwarven dimensions, Krunzle and Gyllana were more comfortable sitting on the plush arms of their chairs, while Raimeau eventually settled for turning his completely around and placing his thin rump where a dwarf's head would rest, his long legs extended before him.

Then the hairless one told his tale. He had been born an ordinary dwarven baby to an ordinary dwarven couple in the ordinary dwarven township of Skagnoth. His father had been a porter in the cheese market and his mother a weaver of shawls. Until the age of twelve, Brond, son of Tottreuch, had shown no remarkable qualities at all.

"Then, on my twelfth naming day," he said, "I was struck down by a sudden fever. It came on quickly, and within hours I was tossing on my bed in delirium. My parents sent for the quacksalver, but none of his potions had any effect. For two days, I lay upon death's doorstep. My mother said my forehead was too hot to touch.

"Then, on the third day, the fever broke. Sweat poured from my every pore, and when my mother went to wipe my dripping brow, she found that the cloth had taken away my eyebrows. When I sat up, my hair remained on the pillow. From that moment on, I was completely bald, and nary a hair has grown on my body since."

But that was not the strangest part of the experience. In the deepest moments of his delirium, when he babbled and tossed and apparitions hovered over his bed, a part of him had remained cool and calm. A voice had spoken from within him, telling him not to worry, that not only would he come through but that he would go on to greatness.

The voice had spoken with such assurance, and carried with it such a profound presence, that young Brond had never doubted the truth of its message. And when he rose from his sickbed, pale and smooth, he no longer spoke or acted as a child. This, along with a lack of hair that made him unique among dwarfdom, made him a target of jibes and mockery from his age-mates— one of them dubbed him "the noble head"—but the bald dwarf youth was so oblivious to their ridicule that in no great time the chaffing simply ceased.

He had become a grave and thoughtful young dwarf. His manner gave rise to suspicion among some that he thought himself better than his equals—a guarantee of unpopularity—but his lack of boastfulness and constant, quiet humility won him praise. It was then that his insight and intelligence were finally noticed. Other dwarves, even his elders, began to ask his advice, and found his simple but clear-sighted responses to be charged with a wisdom that belied his years.

"By the time I achieved adulthood," he told the three travelers, "dwarves were coming from as far away as Highhelm to consult me. Thanes and potentiaries, as well as common folk of all classes. A number of them stayed on." He opened his hands to express mild wonder. "I found I had *disciples*. I decided that I had better think of something useful that I could do with all this . . . whatever it was."

He retired to a cave up in the hills above Skagnoth and spent some time meditating and walking in the quiet of the morning. Nothing came of it. He began to feel somewhat foolish. "I told myself I'd go back down the next day, made myself a supper of roots and vetch, and went to sleep by the fire. And I dreamed that the voice I'd heard in my illness—the voice I had never heard since—spoke to me once more.

"It told me to bring together as many dwarves as I could convince to follow me. It told me to build an organization—it was to be called the Regulate—that would be dedicated to a revival of our ancient skills and arts. It told me to create a community and an army and a workforce of dedicated artisans.

"I came down from the hills and went to work. I sent my disciples to scour bookeries in every corner of the Five Kingdoms, looking for practical texts on engineering, arts, crafts, architecture, metallurgy, hydraulics, geothermics. They brought back cartloads of scrolls and tomes. I studied as much of it as I could absorb, and that turned out to be quite a lot. I also encouraged others to read the old books and experiment with the techniques in them."

Over the centuries, dwarves had come to prefer hands-on apprenticeship over book-learning, but Brond's scholars reversed the dynamic. Others came to join in the renaissance. From a handful, they became scores; then the scores became hundreds. Whenever a student mastered an ancient discipline, he or she was promoted to the rank of instructor. The Regulate's knowledge and capabilities began to expand exponentially.

"Everything I had been told came to pass. It was as if dwarvenkind had been waiting for someone to say, 'Come on, this way, follow me.' I called, and they came. I led, and they followed. And now we have built all this. And it is wonderful."

But the voice had told him one more thing: that a day would come when three travelers would find their way to him, out of the world of men. One would be a thief. One would be a woman who had been wronged. One would be a man with scars on his back.

"When that happened, when the three came, then my destiny would reveal itself. And now,"—he looked at each one of them in turn and his mouth twitched at both corners, left, then right, then left again—"here you are. So, what can you tell me?"

Krunzle was determined this time to get in before Gyllana could forestall him. Rogues and swindlers lived for opportunities like this, and he was thinking that he'd be damned in four directions if he let this one pass him by. He had already contrived a sagacious expression for his face, and the architecture of a truly monumental piece of mountebankery was erecting itself in his mind.

But it was not the woman who tripped him up. As he opened his mouth, he felt a familiar tightening around his neck. *Now?* he shouted within the confines of his cerebrum, *Now you wake up and decide to interfere?*

The Noble Head was watching him expectantly, waiting for some revelation to deliver itself from the thief's still-open mouth. Krunzle shut the temporarily useless organ. He looked to Gyllana and saw what he expected to see: the product of generations of merchant breeding examining the hairless dwarf and no doubt thinking about ways in which the Regulate and the house of Eponion could do business—mutually profitable to be sure, though the mutuality did not imply that one side would not gain more than the other.

So, with one of the three paralyzed and the other weighing her options, it was the former mine slave who spoke for them all. "I think," Raimeau said, "that we are all paddling the same coracle. As I said before, I am here because—like you—I follow a dream.

"My friend Krunzle, who is a man of deeds and attainments, for all he thinks of himself as a fast-mover, has been drawn to this land by some impulse deep within him that he cannot account for."

"He is not your friend," said Gyllana.

Raimeau ignored the interjection. "And the lady Gyllana? Why, she is here because she fell in love with a man, and what is love but a kind of dream? Though it is one that, when we try to live it in the world of phenomenality, can often lead to a rude awakening."

This last thought won the gray-haired man a sharp look from the Kalistocrat's daughter, to which Raimeau returned a gesture of apology. Krunzle would have liked to have brought him up even sharper—who was a former mine slave to comment upon the motives of a rogue of his stature, after all?—but his vocal apparatus was still held hostage by the snake.

Besides, Chirk was speaking within his mind. *Ask him*, the snake said, *if all of this reviving of dwarven arts and skills has been for its own sake, or has it been directed toward a particular goal?*

I would rather ask him, the thief said, *where they keep their gold and whether they would appreciate having a qualified locksmith appraise their security.*

Do as I say, came the inner voice, accompanied by a warning twinge from his sacroiliac joints.

Krunzle said he would, but only under pressure. *But you and I need to have a conversation about this partnership of ours, a free and frank exchange of views. And soon.*

Partnership? said Chirk. *I was not aware we were in any such relationship. My impression was . . .* An image formed in the thief's mind, of a man seated on a horse, with reins in one hand, a whip in the other, and spurs on the heels of his boots.

I remind you, said Krunzle, *that when Skanderbrog had to be dealt with, it was my strategy that won him over.*

He expected a disparaging critique of his point, and was surprised when Chirk said, *That is true.* There was a pause, then the snake said, *At the time, however, your actions served your own interests. The question is: in less perilous circumstances, can you be trusted?*

I should have thought, Krunzle replied, *that the question is: how can we arrange matters so that my interests receive some decent level of consideration? Because, when they are, then I have shown myself to be a ready and willing actor.*

Another pause, then: *You are right. At least to this extent: we ought to have this conversation. But not now. Ask him the question I posed.*

Krunzle said, *Give me a commitment to discuss my concerns. And a time.*

Very well, said Chirk. *Before you sleep tonight.*

During this passage, Brond and Raimeau had been speaking about their dreams, and finding little in common other than the fact that they had both been motivated from within. The thin man had revealed, however, what Gyllana had admitted the night before by the light of their campfire.

The leader of the Regulate was now more than a little interested in Berbackian, the errant Blackjacket. "He also was drawn by a dream?" he asked the woman. "What dream? And what did it command him to do?"

Gyllana was reluctant to discuss it. "He may have been lying," she said. "It turns out he often did that, at least in my company."

"I wish we had kept him longer, then," said Brond. "But he claimed to be carrying dispatches from the First Commissariote of Kerse to representatives of the Lumber Consortium in Falcon's Hollow. The Regulate wishes to retain good relations with all of our neighbors."

"Though not Ulm's Delve," she said.

"They are not friends to dwarves. Or I should say 'were not,' now that you tell me the place has burned and its rabble are fled."

"That was Krunzle's doing," said Raimeau.

The bald head turned toward the thief. "Really? The Regulate owes you its thanks. They were a troublesome crew, and the gold should have been ours."

Here was Krunzle's opportunity. But even as he formed in his mind a suggestion that the Regulate's thanks be expressed in a tangible form—preferably a round, shining, yellow form—Chirk nudged him. *You will get more by asking for less,* the snake said. *Be modest, and ask about his aims for his movement.* The advice was accompanied by the tiniest, briefest pressure around the man's throat.

"It was nothing," Krunzle told the Noble Head. "Anyone would have done the same." He saw a momentary astonishment register on Gyllana's face, but pressed on regardless. "But, tell me, this movement you lead: where do you lead it to?"

The bald head held itself erect and the whiskerless chin jutted out. "To the reestablishment of dwarven civilization, here in the Five Kingdoms. And, if I live to see all my plans bear their final fruit, the five will be united into one great republic. And every race on Golarion will turn their gaze to these mountains and say, 'Behold, the dwarves are back.'"

Prompted by Chirk, the thief said, "That is a noble goal, but it will take more than a few thousand dwarves, however dedicated, to achieve it. How will you go forward?"

The gray eyes were thoughtful, then Krunzle saw the bald one come to a decision. "This is not something I would tell every passerby," Brond said, "but, obviously, we are not casually met. All of this,"—he gestured to include the hive of industry outside the windows—"is but the staging area for our true project."

He paused, theatrically, then went on. "Not far south of here lies Mount Sinatuk. It is a fire mountain, though it has not spewed brimstone and lava in living memory. Indeed, our oldest texts on geology make no mention of an eruption."

It was, however, a well-watered mountain. The abundant rainfall on the upper slopes sank deep into its substrata, where the moisture met heat and became steam. Brond's engineers had burrowed into the mountain to tap its energy, so as to convert it into heating and light and power for the Regulate. Grimsburrow was rapidly becoming the most livable dwarven settlement constructed since ancient times.

"How admirable," said the Kalistocrat's daughter.

"But there's more," said the Noble Head. "When they got deep into Mount Sinatuk's bowels, as with any volcano, they found lava tubes. And in some of those tubes they found diamonds."

"Diamonds?" said Gyllana, and Krunzle saw in her eye the Kersite merchant's unmistakable glint. "Mineable diamonds?"

"Just so," said the dwarf.

The woman leaned forward. "How well are you capitalized? Mining is a costly affair."

Brond fluttered a hand. "We are managing. Though, if Drosket brings back a wagonload of abandoned gold, it will certainly help."

Gyllana's gaze never left the hairless face. "And have you lined up customers for the mine's output? Or, better yet, an experienced merchandiser who could find you customers all around the Inner Sea?"

The dwarf gave her a bemused smile. "It is early days, yet," he said. "At this point, we have no more than a few samples. But our geologists are confident that, as we progress deeper into the mountain, the finds will become richer. And, individually, larger."

The woman was sitting forward now, her hands clasped over her knees. She had the look of a bird that had just spotted a particularly juicy caterpillar crawling amiably along the branch on which it was perched.

Krunzle, however, was following Chirk's lead, though where the snake's inquiries were heading remained a mystery. "Progress?" he said. "So your main shaft is not completed?"

"It is not," said the dwarf. "It is a difficult business, made all the more so by the fact that we are having to learn as we do. The techniques of mining into volcanoes are abstruse and complicated. Even our best are not yet up to the challenge." He paused and nodded, as if to confirm an unvoiced thought, then said, as much to himself as to his three listeners, "But we will be. We are learning as we go."

"I do not doubt it," said Gyllana. "Perhaps we could establish a preliminary arrangement for when you achieve your breakthrough? I would be delighted to see your samples and—"

Krunzle cut her off. "How far have you got?"

"As of yesterday's report," said Brond, "the tunnel is a little over six standard miles."

"And how large is the mountain?"

"Two miles high—but, of course, we are drilling down and at an angle to intersect the lava tubes above the main magma chamber. That is where the prize blues are to be found."

Gyllana's face now became very still. "Blues?" she said.

"Oh, yes," said the dwarf. "We have found some clears and some yellows, even a few pinks. But the majority are gems of the truest blue. If our geologists have accurately determined the trends, we will ultimately come upon blue diamonds of exceptional quality, and exceptional size."

"How exceptional?" the Kalistocrat's daughter said.

In answer, Brond held up one fist. Like any dwarf's fist, even a hairless one, it was of a substantial size. Then he moved the cupped palm of his other hand over it, perhaps a finger's width above the pale knuckles.

Gyllana took in an involuntary breath. "Exceptional size, indeed," she said. Her eyes glittered.

Krunzle knew that blue diamonds were of interest to wizards—something to do with focusing or concentrating arcane powers. *Is that it?* he asked Chirk. *Is that what we're after?*

The snake's answer was ambiguous. *I need to see the mine.*

Through my eyes?

Those are the only eyes I have, said the snake, then added, *at the moment.*

Why do you need to see it?

I'll know that when I do.

"May we visit the mine works?" the thief asked Brond.

Gyllana stepped in, suspicion molding her face as she said, "I don't think that would be a good idea."

"You think he will steal our diamonds," said the dwarf, waving Krunzle's protests to silence with a pale hand and a small smile.

"I think he would steal the mountain if he could find a buyer," said the woman.

"You might be right," said Brond, "under normal circumstances. But these are not normal circumstances. We are all part of a mystery, and I have a feeling—a strong feeling—that Mount Sinatuk is also a player in the enigma."

"Mysteries are well enough, in their place," said Gyllana, "which is in the library of an evening, with the brandy decanter ready to hand. But this is a matter of money." She quoted the old Kersite proverb about the man who let a thief inspect his trouser buttons.

"I am not worried about stumbling around with my trews about my ankles," said Brond. He spread his hands. "I have come a long way by heeding my presentiments; I will not stop now."

He raised his head and his voice. "Guards!" The two escorts and his own two sentries came through the doors as if they had been loaded onto spring guns, spears leveled and on the run toward the group. "There is no problem," Brond told them. "Stand down."

He began to issue orders: senior staff were to be advised that the Noble Head would make an immediate visit to the mining zone; two full companies of spear-dwarves and a company of axe-dwarves would provide escort.

While he was speaking, Senior Crown Torphyr entered the room: "Noble Head," he said, "you're not intending to take these . . ."—he appeared to discard the word he first thought of and substitute another—"these persons into the security zone?"

Brond looked at the officer as if he were a precocious child whose outbursts had to be tolerated. "I am, Crown," he said, "but if you are concerned, you may command the escort."

Another protest was on the officer's lips, Krunzle thought, but it was apparently trampled to death by Torphyr's acceptance of an assignment that would put him in close contact with the Regulate's ultimate source of medals, promotion, and prestige. The crown snapped his heels together, smacked his fist into his beard again, and rushed off to do whatever was required.

"In the meantime," Brond said when they were just the four of them again, "what about lunch?"

Krunzle had to admire the efficiency. By the time they had eaten a well prepared meal—the nut-brown ale was as good as any he'd ever tasted—a column had been assembled in the great courtyard. A half-platoon of spear-dwarves formed the vanguard and another defended the rear. A string of ox-drawn carts carrying rations and other military impedimenta occupied the middle of the column, with a half-platoon of axe-dwarves on either flank.

Krunzle was surprised to see these last troops; again, they were like something from a bygone age. Some of the dwarven armies of old that had fought against orcs and men—and anyone else who got in their way—had contained specialized units that used the long-hafted, single-edged axe, with a hook on the back of its head that could pull a horseman from the saddle. The axe-dwarves had been trained to fight in formation, twirling their weapons in a two-handed grip and in choreographed unison, so that an enemy facing them needed to be both resolute and handy with their own equipment. A platoon of axe-dwarves came on like a rolling mower of forty synchronized, razor-sharp blades, and very little had ever stood before such a force, never mind stopped it.

The three travelers' horses, fed, watered, and rested, were brought to them. They were to ride ahead of the wagons, with the Noble Head and his bodyguard of ten elite dwarven warriors; unlike the spear- and axe-dwarves, these were clad in articulated plate armor and carried body-length shields and two-handed swords longer than their wielders were tall. The shields were to protect the leader from missiles, but if any enemy came within spear-thrust range, out would come the greatswords.

"Impressive," Raimeau said to the thief as they sat on their horses waiting for the Noble Head of the Regulate to come out of his quarters.

"Worrisome, I would have said," said Krunzle. "This doesn't look like a ceremonial procession. They look like they wouldn't be surprised to find themselves in a fight."

The thin man's face rearranged itself as he considered the argument, then he shrugged. "I'm still dealing with the notion of being surrounded by dwarves and not having to be terrified of them."

Gyllana had also been assessing the force assembled around them. Her expression was thoughtful. "Orcs, Brond said. When was the last time orcs came into Druma in numbers that warranted ninety dwarves armed to their gritted teeth?"

"A hundred," said Raimeau. "You've left out the cart drivers."

"Perhaps your father should get into the arms trade," Krunzle said. "A new market opens."

"They're making their own," the woman said. She cast an eye over the armor of the bodyguard. "And it looks to be of more than just good quality."

"Then buy from the Regulate and sell it to other dwarves."

"That's all we need," said Raimeau, "a world full of better-armed runts." One of the elite sword-dwarves turned to look up at him, and the thin man said, "Sorry."

A trumpet blew and the entire column snapped to attention as Brond came out of the archway below the great chamber. Like his bodyguard, he wore gleaming plate, but carried a mace with a black iron head from which protruded short spikes of polished steel. He moved easily in the armor, and needed no help to mount the stocky, long-maned horse that one of his guards held for him.

He smiled briefly at the three humans and said, in a conversational tone, "Well, then. I suppose destiny awaits."

Senior Crown Torphyr, mounted on a horse of his own, rode back from the head of the column, saluted with fist to chest, and said, "Whenever you are ready, Noble Head."

The leader of the Regulate returned the salute and said, "At your convenience, Crown."

The trumpet blew once more, whistles sounded, and ninety dwarven left feet stepped forward. The cart drivers applied their whips and shouted encouragement to the oxen. Dwarves all around the courtyard ceased their labors and stood to watch the column depart through the great gates.

"We are all, of course," Brond was saying to Gyllana, "creatures of destiny. Each of us plays a part in the great performance. One's part may be a leading role or it may turn out that you are just the fellow who trims the lamp-wicks before the curtain rises — either way, the proper thing to do is embrace one's lot with courage and good cheer."

"But how do you know what your proper place is?" said the woman. "Our prophets, may their bounty ever increase, revealed to us the great truth that to strive for more is to put oneself into the eternal flow. For the struggle to dominate one's environment is surely the grand commandment graven into the heart of the world."

The hairless dwarf made a dismissive gesture. "Spoken as a true Kalistocrat," he said. "But piling up pelf is not a blessed cause; it is but a succumbing to the lure of greed. The truly superior being craves nothing more than glory."

"But to be rich is glorious," said Gyllana.

"To be rich," said Brond, "is merely to be rich. How can there be glory in grubbing for groats?"

"That 'grubbing' provides the fundamental energy that builds a civilization."

"Not so. My followers do not work to fill their purses. Pride, not greed, drives the work forward."

Krunzle was paying only partial heed to this debate. When the two disputants fell to citing examples from the animal kingdom—eagles versus ants was one of them—he turned his mind inward and spoke to Chirk. *There seems to be a good deal of talk about fate swirling around us. Most of us go through our lives without the need to be called to some grand quest. It is more than odd to me that each of us here—even I to some extent—has been summoned by dreams or visions. It worries me.*

The snake's response was a while in coming. Krunzle thought his remark had been ignored, or had at least gone unheard, and was about to repeat himself when he heard the quiet voice speaking from the back pastures of his head. *It worries me, too. I would be less concerned if I did not feel like a dreamer who stumbles about in a half-daze, never sure whether he is treading the labyrinth he sees around him or is still lying abed, his limbs twitching and his eyes trembling beneath closed lids.*

Krunzle said, '*Stumbling, treading, limb-twitching*'; *are those not unusual choices of imagery for a snake?*

They are, said Chirk, *and that worries me also. I have a sense that when I finally and fully awaken from this dream, I will be startled. And perhaps not happy.* There was a pause, then, *On the other hand, I may find that you and your companions are only parts of my dream. If so, you will all summarily evaporate and trouble me no more.*

I am no figment, said Krunzle.

Yet is that not exactly what any self-respecting figment would say? said the snake.

The thief withdrew his attention from his inner world. Gyllana and Brond were still nattering to each other about the supremacy of greed over pride—or vice versa—as an organizing principle for the fulfilling life. Raimeau was sunk in an apparently unhappy contemplation of being surrounded by dwarves, and did not respond to Krunzle's overtures. He allowed his head to nod and let the rhythm of the horse's gait lull him into a dream of his own.

When he awakened, he found the column halted. They had been climbing a sunlit slope when he had nodded off. Now they were following the course of a stream along the bottom of a narrow valley, closed in on both sides by dark, thickly packed evergreens. Not far forward, the watercourse curved away out of sight. A cold wind, blowing from the heights above, carried a sweet-sour smell.

The dwarves had not only halted but, as Krunzle came back to the waking world, were executing maneuvers. Those along the flanks of the column turned to face outward. The vanguard and rear guard companies reformed themselves into crescents whose points curved back to partially cover the baggage train and command party. Shields that had been slung from backs were repositioned to make a wall, and spears and long-axes were readied for action. The plate-armored bodyguard formed into two ranks on each side of their leader and unsheathed their two-handed swords.

Krunzle thought it a bad place for a fight. The stream took up most of the valley floor and the trees came almost down to the water. If anything came out of the forest, it would be on them in no more than three strides—two, if it was bigger than a man.

"What's going on?" he asked the world in general. Brond was engaged in a low-voiced consultation with Torphyr, and Gyllana was listening in, so it was Raimeau who answered him.

"Orcs."

The thief sniffed the air. "Dead orcs?"

"They've sent scouts up the creek to see."

The senior crown saluted his leader and went forward to where the spears of the leading half-platoon bristled. The dwarves stood silent, the only sounds the occasional creak of leather harness as someone shifted his equipment to settle it, and the shuffle of the cold wind through the tops of the evergreens.

There came the sound from up ahead of approaching footsteps. The shield wall tightened in a series of *clacks!* Then two spear-dwarves came trotting around the bend of the stream and halted before Torphyr to report. A moment later, the senior crown was bringing the news to Brond: The party that the leader had sent after Wolsh Berbackian had been ambushed in a clearing not far ahead. They were all dead.

The bald dwarf was not one to linger over a decision. The column would advance to the site of the ambuscade in battle order, and at the double. Krunzle wanted to suggest that they all head back the way they had come, preferably at a gallop, but even as the words were forming on his lips the column surged forward. One of the bodyguards seized the reins of his horse and he was left clinging to the saddle's belly-protector.

The ambush had been sprung at a place where the stream, filled with spring snow-melt, had long ago undercut a high bank. Year by year, the spring freshets had cut away and carried off more of the earth, leaving only a wide and curving field of stones. It would have been as good a place as any the narrow valley offered to stop and rest, refill water bottles, or kindle a fire for a meal.

By the evidence, the six dwarves sent after Berbackian had been engaged in all of those activities when a large party of orcs had sprung upon them from the trees. The six corpses were scattered between the trail and the water, all of them hacked and gutted—orcs were known to be fond of dwarf liver—and with their weapons missing. Amazingly, there were no orc dead.

"They may have carried them off," said Torphyr, when Brond commented upon the absence of enemy dead. But a closer inspection of the ground showed no splashes of blood or pieces of severed flesh that were not dwarven. The senior crown pushed back his helmet and scratched at the hair above his forehead and said, "I can't account for it, Noble Head. To take six of our lads by complete surprise? Orcs can't be quiet enough, long enough, to pull off an ambush. Unless . . ."

"Unless what?" said the bald one.

"Unless they're led by someone who terrifies them into silence and stillness."

"I think," said Krunzle, "that we should withdraw to Grimsburrow and consider our options." He half expected to be choked off by the snake in the middle of the sentence, but Chirk did not interfere.

Possibly, because it didn't have to. The hairless dwarf turned his pale eyes to the thief and said, "Spoken like a true rogue. Now hear a true dwarf speak." He raised his voice to be audible to all of the dwarves, arranged in a hollow square whose outer layer bristled with the weapons of spear-dwarves. Behind them stood ranks of axe-dwarves, while the center held the wagons and horses and the Noble Head himself, ringed by his bodyguard. "Enemies have come into our land," he called, "foul enemies who have struck down our comrades and feasted on their flesh! What will we do with these fiends?"

The answer was immediate, and issued from a hundred dwarven throats: "Kill them!"

The leader looked back to Krunzle. "Would you like to try to change their minds?"

A dwarf in plate armor was glaring at the traveler. "I think not," said Krunzle.

They wrapped the six bodies in tent canvas and put them in one of the wagons. The column reformed again, this time with its flanks strengthened by spear-dwarves from the forward and rear guards. A squad of the fleetest-footed young dwarves, sent ahead to scout, returned to report to the senior crown that the orcs had gone upstream. The officer relayed the information to Brond and added, "Something strange, Noble Head: a set of hoofprints in the wet ground beside the stream. One of them overlaps an orc print."

"Meaning?" said the bald one.

"Meaning that some orcs were waiting upstream while others got into position for the ambush. The human passed right through them. Indeed, my best tracker says they seem to have made way for him."

A cold shiver passed down Krunzle's spine. *Chirk?* he said, inwardly. *What is going on?*

The snake did not answer.

Brond was saying, "Are you telling me that the orcs ambushed our lads but let the Blackjacket pass?"

Torphyr nodded. "Almost as if they wanted him to get through and didn't want us to catch him."

"We need to think about this," Krunzle said. "I can feel it. Something is going on that is bigger than we are. Let us go back and—"

The bald dwarf stuck out his chin. "The only thing bigger than us is our destiny," he said. "I want this Berbackian. I want to know what a human is doing working hand-in-paw with orcs—orcs who are killing dwarves." He spoke to the senior crown. "We will go forward. There will be a reckoning."

Torphyr strode to the head of the column, ordered the scouts forward again, then in a parade-ground bellow, "Column will advance! At the quickstep!" His arm came down, and at the head of the vanguard an older dwarf with three arm-rings and a voice that could have battered down stone walls began to count off the paces.

Chapter Ten
The Battle at the River

The valley imperceptibly widened as they went on following the stream south, the slopes falling steadily back until they left a wide bottom for the stream to wander in. The column kept moving until, with the afternoon shading toward evening, their valley met an even wider one, almost at right angles. Here, the watercourse had to be called a river, though it now became a wide and shallow one.

Its banks were stony, spring floods having washed away the covering soil. The ground on the far side was gently sloped and thinly treed—at some time in the not-too-distant past a forest fire had taken all the timber on that side, leaving only blackened stumps. An expanse of long yellow grass had sprung up, broken by clumps of purple-flowered fireweed.

But it was not the river, nor the stumps, nor the grass and flowers that drew the attention of Krunzle and his companions as the dwarven column emerged from the valley of the ambush. It was the dark, shifting mass that stretched across the high ground beyond the river. The wind had died down, but now it brisked up again, bringing the same sweet-sour smell the thief had noticed downstream.

But now it was not a slight odor on the breeze; now it was a full-strength continuous stench, the reek of never-washed carrion-eaters who combed their shaggy manes with grease-smeared fingers and carried their next meal rotting in skin pouches hung about their waists. He recoiled, and as he did so the orc host sent up a bestial howl and clashed their roughly forged swords and axes together.

"There must be three hundred of them," said Gyllana.

"More like five," said Raimeau. "Look there, and there."

Krunzle followed the motions of the thin man's outstretched arm, and saw, to either side of the body of the orc force, dark shapes among the stalks of long grass. "They're lying down. They don't want us to see them." And then the realization struck. "They're showing Brond enough orcs to bring him on the attack. When he comes up to their center, the hidden ones will jump up and hit his flanks."

Gyllana was already saying to the bald dwarf, "Noble Head, this has the smell of a trap."

"I see the ploy," said Brond. "Surprising for orcs. They normally rush at you, all in a body. This looks almost like tactics."

"It also looks as if you're outnumbered five to one," Krunzle said. "With them holding the high ground."

The Noble Head gave the three travelers a bland look. "They're only orcs," he said. "Even if one of them has managed to formulate a battle plan and coerce the others into it, they will all lose their heads the moment we get things started. Then they will rush down at us in the same old way, and we will cut them down in the same old way."

"I know that quote," said Raimeau. "Taargick used to say that to describe his battles against orcs."

"You are well read," said Brond.

Raimeau waved away the compliment. "But dwarves have not always beaten orcs. Remember Koldukar, whose streets were littered with the bones of your unburied dead."

Brond's bald skull seemed to swell with suppressed outrage, but Krunzle knew the impression was just caused by the bulging of his eyes. "We are heavily outnumbered," the thief said. "We should withdraw."

"Six of my lads are in the wagons," said Brond. "What's left of them. Some of their flesh is over there in the bellies of those filthy gribbishers. We're not going anywhere except to walk over the stinking carcasses of dead orcs."

Gyllana would have joined in the argument, but the Noble Head was turning away. He kneed his horse forward and his bodyguard closed around him, putting themselves between him and the travelers.

"The conversation seems to be over," said the Kalistocrat's daughter. She looked at the two men. "What do we do?"

"Go back," said Krunzle.

"No," said Raimeau. "If these orcs are smart enough to stage a trap, they're smart enough to leave a force downstream to catch any stragglers."

He is right, said the quiet voice in Krunzle's head.

So? the thief replied. *What then?*

The snake answered and Krunzle repeated its words to the others: "We stay in the fort. It will be the safest place on the battlefield." Then he added his own counsel. "But be ready to run."

"What fort?" said Gyllana. Krunzle directed her gaze toward the wagons.

The dwarves had not been idle. Torphyr was giving orders and they were being efficiently carried out. The wagons had already been formed into a hollow square, with a gap at the rear. The oxen had been led a distance away and hobbled to keep them placid.

The three travelers entered the makeshift fortification from the rear, tied their mounts' reins to brackets on the inner sides of the wagons. All around them was a bustle of activity. Krunzle saw the dwarves who had been driving the wagons now pulling back the canvas load-cover of one of the carts, revealing lengths of iron-bracketed, squared timbers that they passed down to others who carried them off to the front side of the impromptu fort, facing the enemy. The wagons on this side were now topped by planks to make a fighting platform, and here the dwarves were assembling their burdens of wood and iron and twisted, corded rope into—

"Bolt-throwers!" Raimeau said. "I saw a picture of them in Uthorpe's *History*." He watched the dwarves working with methodical speed. "This will be something to see. Brond may well be right."

The dwarves at the riverbank were forming up in three ranks on their side of the water, arranged in five half-platoons: three units of spear-dwarves, separated by two of axe-dwarves. The remaining half-platoon of spears marched around to the other side of the wagon-fort, to form a rear guard or, if necessary, a reserve.

Brond and his bodyguard had gone forward and positioned themselves behind the center half-platoon of spear-dwarves. His seat atop his horse gave him a good view over his force's heads to where the enemy still stood along the high ground across the river. He raised his voice. "Company, about face!"

As one dwarf, the three ranks turned their backs to the foe and fixed their eyes on their leader. Spears and axes clashed against shields in salute.

Brond sat his horse and let his gaze roam over his small army. Then he began to speak in a conversational tone. "Dwarves of the Regulate," he said, "invaders have come into our land. They have killed our comrades in a cowardly ambush." A growl answered him from the ranks, loud enough for the orcs to hear; they set up a countervailing howl. The leader of the dwarves let the keening sound wash over them and die away before he spoke again.

"Now they dare us to punish them." He spoke loudly, letting anger seep into his voice. "They stand there with our comrades' hearts in their pouches, our friends' livers in their bellies!" Another growl, answered by another howling from the slope, followed by another wait for quiet. "What do you say, dwarves of the Regulate?"

The shout went up from every dwarven throat. "Kill them!"

Brond dropped his tone back to a businesslike calm. "Then let us begin," he said. "Each of you knows his duty. You've done this a hundred times in drill. Now we do it for real." He paused as another howl and clash of metal rose from the orcs. "Listen for the command whistles, obey your officers and sergeants, above all, hold your place in the line, and all will be well." He looked at them again, left, right, and center. "Are you ready?"

A hundred dwarven voices shouted, "Ready, aye, ready!"

"Then fight for revenge, and fight for the rebirth of dwarven glory!" Brond cried. "Company, about face!"

The three ranks turned again as one. Shields made a wall, and spears were charged, the second and third ranks aiming their points over the shoulders of their comrades in front. The axe-dwarves raised their long-hafted weapons, twirled them so that the fading light glittered on their polished blades.

And now, with perfect timing, the five bolt-throwers that the dwarven weaponeers had erected and loaded on the wagon-fort crashed in unison, each hurling ten iron-tipped, wooden-shafted missiles over the heads of their comrades. The fifty bolts rose in an arc, each one spinning as its four tail-vanes caught the air, setting up a whirring sound like nothing Krunzle had ever heard.

Then they plunged down and struck the orc host in a rain of death.

The orcs had no shields, no armor except here and there a rusted helmet or a slab of iron slung from a neck strap to lie across the chest. The fifty projectiles, each as long as a man's forearm, should have wreaked havoc among the densely packed mass. But as the bolts left the throwers, a single hoarse voice, somewhere on the grassy slope, shouted a command. Immediately, the orcs at the back of their mob stepped backward several paces; those at the front stepped forward; those left in the middle spread out. And all of them squatted down, placing their crudely made swords and axes between their heads and the death whirring down from above.

"That shouldn't happen," said Raimeau, as the missiles came down. Some missed entirely; a few bounced off orc weapons with a *clang!* Others struck home: Krunzle saw a big gray leap from his crouch, a dart stuck deep into the hunched muscle where shoulder met neck. With a roar of pain and rage, the orc seized the bolt's wooden shaft and yanked the iron point free. A gout of dark liquid fountained from the puncture, then another, and another, as the orc's heart pumped blood through a severed artery. Even as the orc flung the weapon toward the dwarven shield wall, his knees softened and he fell prostrate upon the grass.

Other orcs had taken wounds, but few of them were fatal. Some hurled the bolts back toward their senders, though even the farthest-thrown missile splashed harmlessly into the river. Now the mass stood up, clashed their weapons together, and laughed at the dwarves standing silent across the shallow stream. Krunzle had never heard an orc laugh before; it was a sound to chill the bowels.

Meanwhile, the dwarven weaponeers had recharged their bolt-throwers. They looked to their unit commander, a red-beard whose long hair was tied in two waist-length braids. He glared at the enemy, then shouted, "All sections, prepare to shoot! Section One, shoot!"

The captains of the named team struck with their mallets; the bow-staves of the thrower, thrust into tightly twisted skeins of rope, sprang outward; ten darts flew up and out toward the orcs. The commander watched them rise, then as they reached their apogee, and as the orcs crouched and covered their heads, he said, just loudly enough to be heard, "Section Two, shoot!"

A second swarm of razor-edged bolts followed the first. Section One's barrage fell among the enemy, and again the effects were minimal. But, again, the orcs stood up and, laughing, reached for missiles that had dug themselves fletching-deep into the ground, intending to hurl them back at the dwarves. And it was then that the second whirring hail of death came down upon them.

"Sections Three, Four, and Five, shoot!"

Thirty more missiles arced up and over the river. This time, Krunzle saw at least a dozen of the enemy drop lifeless, the iron tips lodged in their skulls or driven right through the torsos of those that had been stooped over to pluck up a spent missile. He heard others howl in anger and agony as the darts skewered legs and arms. He saw one thin-shanked orc bent over, trying to pull free the bolt that had nailed its foot to the ground, another staggering from their dark mass, reaching futilely backward with both hands to try to pull out a dart that had driven into the base of his spine. He fell to his knees, then sprawled face down, twitched a couple of times, and lay still.

The orcs howled their rage at being tricked, and one or two along the front line raced forward, brandishing their crude weapons at the motionless lines of dwarves across the river. But, again, the orc force remained where it was; not even one of the dark shapes lying half-concealed in the long grass to either side of the main body stirred and rose into proper view.

"This is not any kind of orc behavior I've ever read about," said Raimeau.

"Perhaps," said the thief, "there's an orc version of the Noble Head, reviving ancient skills."

"They never had any to revive," said the thin man. "This is . . . strange." He studied the orcs, still standing in loose order, still mocking the dwarves. One of them rushed forward and turned to present his scabrous buttocks, slapping them loudly with both hands, while the orcs near him hooted and jeered.

The weaponeers had reloaded, but their commander was looking to where Brond leaned down from his horse to confer with Torphyr. The senior crown saluted his leader, then turned toward the fort and made a hand signal that must have meant *wait*, because the artillery commander told his dwarves to stand by.

Whistles were sounding. The dwarven line was changing its orientation, with the outer half-companies walking backward, while the central unit went forward, all at oblique angles. In less than a minute, the triple line of dwarves had reformed into a wedge shape, an arrowhead whose point was aimed directly at the center of the orc host. Each of its two sides was made of three ranks of spear-dwarves, with the axe-dwarves clustered in the middle.

"I've seen this in the old books," Raimeau said. "Brond means to drive into the middle of them, then when the orcs who think they're hidden in the grass attack the sides of the triangle, the axe-wielders will swarm out around the ends of the lines and cut them down."

The dwarves had completed their maneuver. There was a moment's silence, then Torphyr ordered the advance. The entire formation moved forward in step, and the first dwarves entered the river, spears rhythmically clashing on shields in time with a deep-throated chant of *Huh! Huh! Huh!* marking every second footfall.

The orcs reformed themselves into a dense mass, screaming and roaring their hatred against the oncoming foe. They showed no order now, but it seemed to Krunzle that they were working themselves up into a berserker rage, the ones at the front leaping into the air, white foam spewing as yellow fangs clashed.

Still the dwarves marched on. They had crossed the stony verge of the far bank and reached the foot of the slope. Now they began to climb toward the enemy, still in tight formation, still clashing their shields and shouting their guttural chant.

At twenty paces from the orcs' front, a whistle sounded. The dwarves' spears came down, the shields interlocked, each one angled up to meet the downward blows of a taller foe. And now the chant ceased and the roar that went up from the spear-dwarves caused the hair on the back of Krunzle's neck to stand erect.

"I would not like to be an orc on any day," he said, "but especially not today."

"I don't know," said Raimeau, watching another flight of fifty darts fly over the heads of the dwarven army. The five bolt-throwers had crashed again at the moment the whistle sounded, and the missiles were tearing into the middle of the orc host, just as the first spearpoints of the arrowhead struck the center of their front. This time, the death toll was heavy.

In the center of the orcs' line, those who felt the first thrust of the dwarven formation went down fighting, but most of the blows from their weapons bounced ringing off the angled wall of shields or, at best, struck the well-padded helmets of the first rank of spear-dwarves. The wedge of spears drove deep into the orc mass, the dwarves thrusting and stabbing, stepping over the dead and maimed, while the axe-dwarves behind the spears finished off any orcs who still writhed on the bloodstained grass.

"I don't know," Raimeau said again. "Look."

The thief looked. The dwarven weaponeers could shoot no more bolts now, lest they risk hitting their comrades. The orcs in the middle were being pushed back and slaughtered, the destruction increasing as more of the arrowhead pressed into their mass. The three hundred orcs that had waited for the dwarves now folded themselves around the wedge, hacking and chopping, even as they were efficiently skewered by the long spears.

But the dark shapes lying in the grass on either flank had still not moved. "It's past the time," said Raimeau, "when they should have risen up and struck the dwarves' flanks. A few more minutes, and it will be too late."

"Perhaps they have decided it's not a good idea," said the thief. "I see a lot of orcs dying, and not too many dwarves." Only three short, mail-clad bodies lay upon the slope behind the advancing spears, and even as Krunzle spoke, one of them sat up, shaking his head as if to throw off a dizzy spell.

"Something is wrong," Raimeau said. "Look at Brond and Torphyr."

The Noble Head and his bodyguard had not followed the main force across the river. Now Brond was standing in the stirrups, the better to see how the battle was going. Then he leaned down to speak with the senior crown, who had remained with him. They were arguing, though Krunzle could not hear what either said. A moment later, whatever they had been discussing became academic. The battle abruptly changed course.

The entire dwarven arrowhead had crossed the river and passed beyond the wide stretch of water-worn rocks that lined the bank on the far side. The spear-dwarves had done most of the fighting, leaving a carpet of dead orcs behind them for the axe-dwarves to step over. But the orcs, for all their fierce displays, had not pressed the dwarves hard. They kept falling back before the spears, moving up the slope; few of them showed the berserker madness that made them willing to be spitted if they could only get within striking distance of the enemy.

The battle had thus moved steadily uphill, even to a height where the sides of the arrowhead—beset by orcs, though not heavily—had passed the level at which the dark shapes lay in the grass. But, whatever was lying there, none of them had risen to join the attack, even though their apparent numbers would have meant the dwarves would be fighting against odds of five-to-one.

Raimeau squinted, shading his eyes from the sun. "I think," he said, "those are only piles of earth. Decoys. Who ever heard of orcs using decoys? And, if they're not in the grass, where are the rest of them?"

He was answered by a new sound, scarcely to be heard above the din of the battle: a rattle of smooth stones sliding over each other. On the far side of the river, the wide expanse of worn stones suddenly heaved and billowed. From concealed pits, covered by earth-colored sacking over which a layer of flat pebbles had been laid, rose up orcs by the dozen, then by the score—big orcs, many of them with battle scars, all of them armed with heavy battering weapons: stone clubs, leaden mauls, long-hafted maces, and morningstars on iron chains.

Silently, with none of the usual orc stamping and roaring, they rushed uphill and fell upon the axe-dwarves, whose backs were turned toward the unseen enemy. In moments, a dozen dwarves lay dead or dying.

A whistle sounded from within the arrowhead. The rest of the axe company about-faced and engaged the attack from the rear. But the dwarves who turned to meet the orcs swarming up from the rear were pressed into the inside angle of the wedge formation; almost elbow to elbow, they lacked room to wield their long-hafted weapons effectively, and they had no shields. It was a fight where sheer force could outweigh technique, and the orcs battered at them without pause or mercy.

The rear rank of spear-dwarves, acting on their sergeants' commands, raised their spears, about-faced, and lowered them against the orcs attacking from the rear. But between them and the enemy were the dwindling numbers of axe-dwarves. These were being pushed back against the spearpoints of their comrades, those at the rear unable to even bring their weapons into play. The fight was losing cohesion, in danger of becoming a melee, and if it came down to every dwarf—or every orc—for himself, the outnumbered dwarves could not stand.

Brond was issuing orders. Another whistle blew three short blasts and a long, and now the twenty spear-dwarves of the reserve came trotting from behind the wagons. They paused at the riverbank to form themselves into a double line; then, spears leveled and shields to their front, they double-timed into the river, onto the stones beyond, and up the hill to take the enemy ambushers in the rear.

It was a precise piece of military maneuvering, and Krunzle thought it should have turned the battle, pinning the bludgeon-swinging orcs against the remnant of the axe-dwarves, with one rank of spear-dwarves to back them up. But the enemy had one more trick to pull, for not only had the orcs dug pits on the far bank, and hid in them with unheard-of patience—they had dug more pits on this side. And as soon as the reserve was across the river, fifty more orc veterans, armed with clubs and bludgeons, sprang from concealment to left and right of Brond and his bodyguard. They threw themselves screaming at the Noble Head and the ten plate-armored sword-dwarves.

The twenty spear-dwarves who had just crossed paused. Their officer looked back at the scene on the far shore, then at the orcs up the slope. Krunzle could see him debate which way to go. He put his whistle to his lips and blew a series of long and short notes. The twenty about-faced and went back into the river.

But the officer's hesitation had been fatal. Some of the orcs attacking the leader and his bodyguard on the near shore turned and met the reserve spear-dwarves in the water. It was not a deep river, but it was deeper for dwarves than for full-sized orcs, whom Krunzle thought must have been chosen for their height and bulk. Each of them was more than half again the size of a dwarf.

The twenty spear-dwarves tried to make a shield wall, but the river bottom did not offer good footing. They were less than halfway across, their line ragged and their shields unlocked, when the orcs battered into them, clubs and maces striking shields and helmets with a sound like an avalanche of scrap metal. The spears did their work, but dwarves began to go down. More gaps appeared in the line. Suddenly it was a melee, then just as suddenly, it was over.

When the arrowhead formation had gone across the river, Brond's bodyguard had formed a line between the water and their leader, facing the battle. But now orcs had come charging at them from both ends of their line. It would have been a matter of moments for the elite troops to reform to meet the double onslaught, but the enemy had not given them those moments.

These orcs, too, were armed with bone-crushing weapons against which plate armor, even backed by padded hauberks and helmet liners, was no protection. The dwarves swung their two-handed swords with parade-ground precision—Krunzle saw an orc's head fly from his shoulders ahead of an arcing fountain of blood; another raised his stone club only to see it fall with the hand that still gripped it—but there were too many of them, and they were coming all at once.

The dwarves in shining armor began to fall. Brond's horse reared, screaming, as the bald dwarf sought to draw his sword. But Torphyr, his sword already in hand, seized the reins and turned the animal's head toward the fort. He slapped its rump with the flat of his blade and sent it and its rider out of the slaughter zone.

"We need to get out of here," Gyllana said. Krunzle was struck by her calmness. All around them, the dwarf weaponeers were abandoning their bolt-throwers, drawing short swords and hand-axes. But the fort was indefensible against the numbers of orcs they could already see—and who knew if there were not more of them lurking, ready to leap at their throats?

The three travelers jumped down from the platform atop a wagon and found their horses. The animals were skittish, their nostrils distended at the scent of blood and orc, their eyes white-rimmed at the sound of screams and weapons-clash.

Krunzle swung into the saddle and spent a moment getting the gelding under control. *Chirk,* he said, *any advice?*

Run.

Which way?

Worry about that later, said the snake. *For now, just put distance between you and the orcs.* Then it added, *I need time to think about this.*

Krunzle pointed his horse toward the gap in the rear of the wagon fort, then cast one look back on the far side of the river. The axe-dwarves were all down now. The spear-dwarves had formed into two remnants, and were being hard pressed by orcs. The dwarves were dying well, taking as many of the enemy with them as they could, but it was clear to the thief that there would be no survivors.

Torphyr, the senior crown, had seized the two-handed sword of one of the fallen bodyguards. He was standing atop a heap of orc dead, his mail-shirt torn and his helmet knocked away. His grizzled braids swung in counterpart to each swipe of the long sword, the shining blade scything the air, sending a head or an arm flying with each blow, and his face bore an expression of determined concentration. But now a giant orc stole up from behind, raised a rough-hewn club of gray stone, and brought it down directly onto the dwarf's head. Blood and brains and bone sprayed. And the fight was over.

"Out!" said Krunzle. "Now!" He kneed his horse's ribs hard and it surged toward the gap. Gyllana was already through and out in the open, slapping her mare's withers with the reins. She turned to follow the river's course upstream, and Krunzle went after her.

"They're coming after us!" Raimeau shouted from behind the thief.

Krunzle looked back again. Most of the orcs on the slope had turned away from the last stand of the spear-dwarves. They were running down to the river, a few of them already splashing through the water's edge where the bodies of orcs and spear-dwarves floated. The group that had ambushed the bodyguard were not stopping to loot but had turned toward the fort, where the weaponeers stood stoically, their inadequate weapons in hand, waiting to die.

But, no, Krunzle saw—Raimeau was right. A few of the orcs were heading for the wagons, but most were careering around the carts, following the three humans.

Or maybe not, he thought. Because there was another quarry: Brond's horse, terrified by the stink of blood and orc and the din of battle, had taken Torphyr's slap on the rump as encouragement to run as fast and far as its short legs would carry it. The Noble Head was ahead of them, fighting to get control of the panicked animal. He did so, just as Gyllana reached him and swept past without a glance.

A moment later came Krunzle, who took the time to say, "It's over! Come on!" as his gelding veered around the other horse and kept going. He looked back and saw Raimeau hauling on his mount's reins, the horse skidding to a stop beside the bald dwarf. The thin man reached down, seized the dwarven horse's reins, and yanked the beast's head around.

"No!" Brond cried. He had dropped his sword in the struggle to control his mount, but he struck at his rescuer with a gloved fist. "I want to fight!"

"There is no fight," said Raimeau. "Only slaughter."

"Then let me die with my dwarves!"

"And let the Regulate die with you?"

"You care?"

"Strangely," said the former mine-slave, "I do."

The orcs were coming, though only about a dozen. The rest had already overrun the weaponeers and were looting the wagons, while others had turned toward the hobbled oxen. Orcs liked beef, especially raw and still bleeding.

Brond's shoulders slumped. Raimeau tugged on the dwarven horse's reins while he kicked his own horse into motion. The animals needed no more incentive to put distance between themselves and the pursuing orcs.

Krunzle turned his horse and waited for the man and dwarf to catch up, then rode along with them. He looked back at the loping pursuers, drew his short sword and said, "If they get too close, I will hold them off."

Raimeau looked at him in surprise. Krunzle returned him a steady gaze, though he was thinking: *The orcs will not pursue us far, while there's loot and fresh meat to call them back. And though the Noble Head has lost his army, he still has his blue diamonds to reward those who serve him.* Though, if the orcs did get too close for comfort, he hoped to throw them both the thin man and the Kalistocrat's daughter before he risked his own skin.

Any objections? he asked Chirk.

Save Brond, was the answer. *We will need him.*

I agree, Krunzle thought back, *but what use are blue diamonds to a bronze snake?*

Not the diamonds. The place where they grow.

The thief asked the snake if it was remembering more. *Perhaps you would like to share the information with one whose life you have been risking?*

You will know, said Chirk, *what you need to know, when you need to know it.*

Is this that talk you promised? Krunzle said.

Events are moving faster, came the answer. *Your desire for baubles grows increasingly less important.*

The thief thought a couple of short words back at the snake, but the action described was physically impossible and the suggestion received no acknowledgment. He looked back once more at the pursuing orcs. They were still following the four fugitives along the river, running at a steady pace but gradually falling behind.

"Noble Head," said Raimeau, "do you know a place where we could lose the pursuit?"

Brond's eyes were on his hands, which gripped his saddle front. But after a moment, he looked up and said, "Not too far ahead, the river curves and a stream comes down from the hills below Mount Sinatuk. If we are out of sight of the orcs, we can walk our horses in the stream and make them lose our scent."

"All right, then," said the thin man. "We'll find somewhere to hole up. Then we'll decide what to do."

The bald dwarf looked at Raimeau, then at Krunzle, but his eyes seemed to be looking through them and out across some great distance. "What we will do," he said, "is find out who taught those orcs to fight the way they fought. Then we will cut off his balls and feed them to him."

He fell silent, though Krunzle could see the muscles bunching at the hinge of his jaw. They rode on, the orcs falling behind—though they still followed at a jog. The sun was nearing the hills on the western horizon, and a chill was taking possession of the air. As the golden disc's bottom flattened against the line of a dark, forested ridge, Brond said to Krunzle, "The fellow you are chasing, this Wolsh Berbackian. He has a military background."

It wasn't a question, but the thief answered it. "He was an undercaptain in the Mercenary League for a while."

"And before that?"

"I do not know."

The bald head nodded. "And he passed unharmed through the orcs at the first ambush site."

"That was what it looked like."

The gray eyes were like stones in the twilight. "I want to find this Blackjacket," he said. "And soon."

They rounded a curve in the river where a ridge came down from the hills. The stream Brond had spoken of was there, its bottom formed of flat stones, black and gray with flecks of white quartz. They turned the horses into its cold, splashing current and began to climb.

Chapter Eleven
Desnertinizing the Flobbule

They picked their way up the slope in the gathering darkness. Even when true night came, they could follow the stream by its sound and by the star-speckled sky above the gap it cut through the evergreens to either side. They traveled silently, Brond leading the way, each immersed in his or her own thoughts. From time to time, they paused to listen for pursuit, but heard nothing other than the stream and the sounds of the night forest.

An hour or so after the stars came out, Krunzle noticed that he could almost see his hands upon the reins before him. A few minutes later, he could see the horse's ears silhouetted against the water. "I think the moon is coming up," he said, and when he looked backward, he could see the point of a thick crescent rising above the bordering trees.

They stopped to rest their horses and sat on a muddle of boulders and logs on the stream's bank. The thief was hungry; lunch had been a long time ago. He still had in his saddlebags his share of the bread, cheese, and ale they had bargained for with Drosket. Raimeau also had his supply, but Gyllana had left hers behind when they had joined the expedition. Brond had nothing.

"We will share," said the thin man.

Krunzle was tempted to use his advantage to exact concessions, but a moment's thought told him that Gyllana was the kind who would rather go hungry than submit to an unwanted imposition, whereas Brond seemed the type to remember a disservice as well as a kindness. So he said, "Of course. We must depend upon each other."

The meal, like the journey, was accompanied by silence, except for the gurgle of the stream and the rustling of small creatures in the undergrowth. Krunzle used the time to reflect upon the events of the day. He was not an expert in orc behavior, but he knew enough about the monsters to know that they were creatures of instinct and impulse. Their low intelligence gave them enough cunning to lie in ambush or to seek the high ground before a fight; but once the enemy was in sight, an orc warrior's bloodlust rose. He might pause long enough to work himself into a frenzy, but it would not be long before the urge to charge, howling and snarling, would become irresistible.

Yet the orcs at the river had had the intelligence to create decoys and the patience to dig pits on both sides. They had concealed themselves under sacks and rocks, then they had lain still and silent while the dwarves' main force had crossed over and walked right past them. Even then, only the orcs on the far side had leapt up and attacked. Those on the near side of the river had waited until Brond committed his reserves before attacking.

The thief was no great tactician, but he knew that today he had seen the work of a competent planner and commander—good enough to overwhelm a hundred dwarven soldiers who had looked to be as able as any such force in Golarion. But few orc chieftains had ever been that competent, and even if one such orc genius led this band, how could he convince several hundred of his stunted-brained fellows to restrain themselves long enough to carry out the battle plan?

It makes no sense, he told himself. Although it fit in all too well with the way his situation had developed since his arrival in Kerse. Here he was, however unwilling, on a mission to recover some object—he did not even know what—that a smooth-talking Wolsh Berbackian had persuaded a Kalistocrat's daughter to bring with her on an elopement. Apparently, the Blackjacket had been motivated by a dream, as had Raimeau, as had the Noble Head, as had Krunzle himself, in a general way. And coiled tightly around his neck was some kind of magical entity that felt itself to be waking from a dream.

Chirk, he said inwardly, *what's going on? Who's pulling our strings?*

I do not know, said the snake in the thief's mind. *Not yet.*

Krunzle pressed the issue. *But someone is pulling strings? Sending us dreams and organizing orcs?*

So it would appear.

To what end?

There was no immediate answer. The thief sensed that Chirk was straining to frame a response. Then the quiet voice said, *It is no use. I sense that the memory is there, buried; but I cannot uncover it.*

I do not like to be a patsy, Krunzle said. *It offends against my dignity.* He was surprised when the snake took him seriously.

I think all of us, said Chirk, *even Wolsh Berbackian and Ippolite Eponion, have been offended against. And I believe that there is worse yet to come.*

The prediction sent a shiver through the thief's torso. *How worse?* he said.

But Chirk had wrapped itself in its snake thoughts and would say no more.

The moon was high above the gap in the trees by the time they finished their meal. The horses had found little to eat, but Brond said there were meadows higher up, and caves they could shelter in. In the morning, they could follow a trail that would lead them, at the end of a day's ride, to the diamond mine.

"I'll be glad to see that," Krunzle said, climbing into the saddle. The pause to rest had made his legs and back go stiff, and his thighs ached as he heeled the horse into motion.

"And I would have been glad to show it to you," the dwarf said. "But now I will be bringing hard tidings to the miners. Many of those who fell today had fathers and brothers at the diggings." The thief heard him suppress a sob, then the voice hardened. "But Berbackian was supposed to stop at the mine. May Torag arrange for him to be there when I arrive."

The dwarf's mood argued for silent travel, though Krunzle would have liked to have known Raimeau's thoughts about what had happened today. The gray-haired man had sensed, even at the site of the first ambush, that the orcs were behaving oddly: They had waited in the bushes until the dwarves were at their most vulnerable. And they had let the Blackjacket pass through their numbers unharmed.

Could Berbackian be the brains behind the orcs' tactical brilliance at the river? But how could that be? Orcs hated men, except as food or, occasionally, as slaves. He knew that orcs would tolerate, for a little time, the few degraded humans who sought them out to trade with them, but the tolerance was directly related to the value the orcs put on the goods, otherwise unobtainable, that the traders brought. Even so, he had heard that at the end of a trading meet, with the orcs getting drunk on bad liquor, the men were wise to pull up stakes and be on their way, before some big buck decided to spit and roast them for dinner.

Krunzle had heard tales, but Raimeau had read books. He might know things that would not be talked about in the places where rogues gathered to exchange gossip. Krunzle would take the thin man aside before they slept and ask for his views. Because chances were they were not yet finished with orcs on this journey; or, worse, the orcs were not finished with them.

Another two hours, with the fat sliver of moon riding high overhead, and they came to a place where the trees petered out and an alpine meadow began. They were not yet on the slopes of Mount Sinatuk itself, but on the wrinkled lands that led up to the volcano's base.

"This way," Brond said, leading them out of the stream and up a gentle slope to a tumble of rocks. They threaded through them, crested a ridge, and on its far side found a place where a wide crack had opened in the earth. A dark passageway angled down.

Krunzle sniffed the chill air that came out of the crevice: a faint odor of carrion and old dung overlaid by a lingering scent of greasy smoke. "Something lives in there," he said, "or has done, not long since."

"A bear's den," Brond said, "but no longer—the beast must have been smoked out by hunters."

"The horses will not fit through the gap."

Despite the loss of three companies and his bodyguard, the bald dwarf still saw himself as in command. "We will tether them and let them graze."

They brought into the cave their saddles and horse blankets to serve as bedding, then Raimeau went to gather wood from the forest's edge. When he looked around the cave for somewhere to lay the fire, he found a rude hearth in the middle of the wider space at the foot of the down-sloping passageway. Firewood was stacked against the back wall.

"No bear did that," Krunzle said.

The dwarf shrugged. "Then a troll," he said. "Either way, the place is untenanted."

They sat around the fire, staring into the flames, each thinking solitary thoughts. After a while, Brond rubbed a hand over his hairless pate and sighed. He looked to Gyllana. "This Berbackian," he said. "What do you know of him?"

"That he is a liar and a rogue," she said.

Krunzle heard anger underlaid by some softer emotion. He waited to see if she would say more, and when she did not, he said, "You do not seem the sort of woman who is easily led astray. He must have been more than usually persuasive."

She gave him a sour look, but said, "It has all become vague now. Then it was excitement, adventure, certainty of outcome, present happiness, and the promise of even greater joy to come."

"It sounds to me," said Raimeau, "like ensorcelment."

The woman nodded reflectively, her eyes on the fire. "So it may well have been." She sighed. "Oh, he was handsome enough, and knew what to do and where to do it. But . . ."

"But it takes more than this," Krunzle said, making a rude gesture with the fingers of both hands, "to win away a daughter of a high Kalistocrat."

"Indeed," she said, still gazing into the flames, "and to make me bring him the—" She interrupted herself.

"The what?" said the thief.

She shook her head. "None of your business."

Now Brond gave her a look that said he was definitely still the one in charge. "Perhaps not his," he said, "but certainly it is the Regulate's business. More than three hundred of our warriors paid with their lives; as far as I'm concerned, that purchases the right to know what this is all about."

"The information is proprietary," Gyllana said. "My father would have to give his permission—"

"He did not give his permission," Krunzle interrupted, "for you and your charming Blackjacket to misappropriate the item. He sent me to get it—and you—back. Logic argues that you assist in that effort by clearing up the mystery."

She folded her arms and said nothing, but the determination in her face struggled with some other sentiment.

"Could it be," said Raimeau, "that the seducer laid more than one spell on you? Perhaps you will not tell because he does not wish you to?"

Gyllana's eyebrows rose, and she blinked several times. Then she swore. "I think you are right," she told the thin man. "Very well, my father collects arcana and mystical objects, particularly from the far east. Recently, he came into possession of an old amulet or talisman whose origins were obscure. He showed it to one of the wizards employed by the Kalistocracy to protect the Bourse in Kerse against unlawful manipulation."

"And what did the wizard say?" the gray-haired man said.

"That it might be a flippety-pertickety tundle-shrep." She stopped, perplexed. "What did I just say?" she said.

Raimeau answered her. "Something about a 'flippety-pertickety tundle-shrep.'"

"But that is nonsense!"

The gray-haired man stroked his nose. "I'm no spell-slinger," he said, "but I have heard of an incantation known as Fezzariot's Locutionary Jumble. Those who have been afflicted by it are prevented from disclosing specified information by mouth or pen."

"That is a sophisticated spell," said Brond.

"Not the sort of thing," Krunzle said, "that one would expect of an undercaptain in the Mercenary League." He turned to Raimeau. "Is it an incantation that could be employed at a distance?"

"Again," said the other man, "I am no expert, but distance means little when the caster has access to items that the target has handled."

The image of Thang-Sha came into Krunzle's mind.

"Could I draw a picture?" Gyllana wondered. "I can see it clearly in my mind's eye."

Raimeau handed her a piece of kindling and smoothed a space in the dust of the cave floor. But when she tried to sketch whatever was in her inner view, the image that appeared in the dirt resembled a child's drawing of a flower in a pot. Gyllana threw down the stick and swore again.

"Try this," said the gray-haired man. "Instead of telling us what it is, describe what it does."

"All right," she said, "if it is what the wizard thought it might be, it desnertinizes the flobbule."

"Hmm," said Krunzle. "That doesn't help."

Brond made a gesture of termination and said, "Enough! We do not know what the rogue took, but the fact that he—or someone else—went to such measures to prevent anyone knowing argues that it is an object of power more than of mere value. It *does* something."

"You are right," said Raimeau. "He does not want us to know what the thing does, because that would tell us what he intends to do."

"Which might also tell us," Krunzle said, "where he intends to do it, allowing us to try to cut him off before he gets there."

Gyllana was nodding in agreement. "Exactly," she said. "Berbackian means to desnertinize the flobbule—no doubt about it. So the question is: where will he find the flobbule to desnertinize?"

"I couldn't have put it better myself," said the thief. "But here's the question I've been pondering: what kind of power allows a man to make hundreds of orcs betray their natures, suppress their ungovernable instincts, so that they can spring an ambush like the one we saw today?"

Both Brond and Raimeau shook their heads. The bald one said, "No spell that I've heard of. Orcs feed off each other's emotions. You'd only need one to become so excited that he'd begin to break through the restrictions, even if it was just to growl. Then the one beside him would hear the growl and twitch in response, and then the next would let out a yip and a howl, and before you know it they'd all be up and stamping and lathering and charging off in all directions."

Raimeau concurred. "It would take not only a mighty spell, but a mighty wielder. The will of the spellcaster would have to be immensely powerful."

"Powerful enough," Krunzle wondered aloud, "to send dreams that would draw people from all over the Inner Sea?"

The faces of the others in the firelight changed as each dealt with the implications of the thief's suggestion. After a moment, Brond stuck out his chin and said, "As for me—"

A frightened whinny from outside the cave reduced the four of them to silence. Something was spooking the horses.

The two men and the dwarf drew their weapons. The passageway between them and the night was wide enough for two full-sized orcs to squeeze through. But that would not give them room to use their weapons. So it would have to be just one at a time.

"If we kill the first one or two," Brond said, "their corpses will make a barrier."

"Unless these orcs are being directed by our mage of great will," Krunzle said. "In which case, they'll do what the hunters did with the bear."

They listened. The horses were all voicing their fear now. The travelers could hear other sounds, too: brutish voices, several of them, and the snap and rattle of dry wood.

Krunzle peered up the passageway. The moon must have gone behind Mount Sinatuk by now, but there was still light enough in the sky for him to see dark shapes moving across the cave's narrow mouth. And something building there.

"They're going to make a bonfire," he told the others.

Raimeau took a look and concurred. "Another case of orcs being depressingly unimpulsive."

Brond gave orders: "We'll extinguish our fire, so that it does not draw theirs. But first let us see if we can use the blankets to make a barrier."

They tried, poking sticks through the coarse wool to make a kind of frame, and stitching two blankets together to make a sheet tall enough to cover the entrance to the passageway. But the only way to keep the flimsy barrier in place was for two of them to hold it against the uneven rock, and even then there were gaps.

While Gyllana and Raimeau held the blankets against the opening, Krunzle smothered the fire with dirt from the floor of the cave. Behind the pile of firewood was a longish, flattish bone that made a decent shovel. They were plunged into darkness, but only briefly—as soon as their eyes adjusted, they saw a yellowy glare of firelight flickering on the blanket barrier. When Krunzle touched the fabric, it was warm and growing hot.

"Water," said Brond. He threw the contents of his bottle onto the wool, soaking it, then collected all the others' water and did the same. The fabric began to steam, and the smell of stale horse sweat filled the cavern.

"It's not going to work," said Gyllana. "It's already drying. Soon it will char. Then it will burn. What will we do then?"

"Go out and fight them," said Brond. "Kill or disable as many as we can in the first rush, then all scatter. One or two of us may get away."

"No," said Raimeau. "I will go first. I will leap the bonfire and attack whatever I see. They will all try for me—orcs have no sense of chivalry—and when they do, you three can come after and take them in the back."

"It is a good plan," said Krunzle. "I only wish I had thought of it first."

"Your chances of survival are slim," Gyllana told the gray-haired man.

Raimeau shrugged. "I have long believed I am fated to perform a brave deed. Perhaps this is it."

Krunzle communed with Chirk. *Will my sword and boots serve me as before?*

If you use them to defend the others, particularly Gyllana, the snake said. *Otherwise, they might actually work against you. On the other hand, I would have no objection to your making a brave show and earning Brond's gratitude—and a few blue diamonds. Once my work is done.*

Aloud, the thief said, "I will go first and make the leap. You will not know it, but I am a prodigious vaulter. Also, not insignificant as a swordsman."

"I wish to be the first," said Raimeau. "Though I am grateful for your help in rescuing me from the gold camp, I must claim the honor."

"No," said Krunzle.

"Stop it, both of you," said Brond. "I am the Noble Head of the Regulate. You stand on my land. I will decide."

"Then do so quickly," said the woman. "My fingers are starting to burn." A stink of scorched wool now joined the odor of horse.

"Here is my decision—"

But Raimeau said, "Listen! Something is going on out there!"

They put their ears close to the now-smoking cloth. Above the crackle of the fire, they could hear angry shouts, orc howls, and the clang of iron on iron.

"They are falling out amongst themselves!" Brond said. "At last, orcs you can depend on! With any luck, there'll be only one or two left standing. Get ready to rush them!"

The air was growing more than smelly in the cave. Despite the blankets across the entrance, the bonfire at the end of the short passageway was drawing oxygen through and around the barrier, while the heat it was radiating was enough to sap their strength.

"If we don't go soon," Raimeau said, "we won't be going at all."

"Right," said Krunzle. He mopped away a flood of sweat from his brows and drew the short sword. "Pull it aside."

"No," said the thin man, "I will go first."

Brond said nothing, but moved, shouldering aside Krunzle then pushing Raimeau away from the entrance. The latter kept his grip on the blanket frame, pulling it out of Gyllana's hands. A blast of overheated air flowed into the cavern. The thief felt the sweat on his face dry in an instant, and when he touched a fingertip to his cheek, the skin was like old parchment.

The dwarf said, as if to himself, "I'll go for their knees." Then he hefted his morningstar and stepped through the gap.

The fight outside seemed to have reached its most desperate pitch. But now the commotion beyond the cave mouth abruptly ceased. Krunzle heard a sound of iron scraping on rock. The light from the bonfire dimmed. Someone was raking the fire aside, and the thief could scarcely remember a more luxurious sensation than the cool night air that riffled down the passageway.

Brond had stepped back, and the four of them stood expectantly, though with weapons in hand. Dim light from the remnants of the bonfire faintly illuminated the passageway, then it dimmed further as someone entered and made his way down to the cave—someone who filled the passageway that was wide enough for two orcs; someone that had to twist his shoulders sideways to fit through the entrance into the cavern, and had to stoop a little to keep from banging his head on the stalactited ceiling. When he was in, he took up most of the small space. The dark shape of his huge head moved as he examined the three humans and a dwarf, who had backed against the far wall.

"This is my cave," said the troll. "I smoked out a she-bear to get it." Then he laughed a troll's laugh, which none but a troll finds pleasant to hear, and said, "But you're welcome to stay for supper."

Krunzle stepped forward. "It's very kind of you, Skanderbrog," he said, "but we've already eaten."

The young troll sniffed the air. "Oh, it's you," he said.

"And me," said Raimeau. "You remember me. We helped free you."

"And," said Krunzle, "told you how you could settle scores with those two troll neighbors . . . what were their names?"

"Grunchum," said Skanderbrog, "and Brugga."

"And how are they faring?" the thief said.

"They are no longer troubled by the weight of their heads on their shoulders," said the troll. "I have put them in niches above the door to my cave."

"Well, then," said Krunzle. "How nice."

The troll quirked a corner of his mouth around one of his lower canines. "I suppose I shouldn't eat you," he said. "Or you." This with a head flick toward Raimeau. "My mother always said that a favor deserves a favor in return."

"A wise she-troll," said Krunzle. "I would like to meet her." He indicated Gyllana and Brond. "These are friends of ours," he said. "I would take it as a great favor if you didn't eat them either."

The troll's expression warned him that he was pressing his luck. "I've come a long way and I'm hungry," said Skanderbrog. "You work up an appetite, killing orcs." He was looking around the cave, his eyes glinting in the dimness.

"Have you lost something?" Gyllana said.

"The last thing my mother gave me when I left home."

Krunzle remembered. He stooped and came up with the deer's shoulder bone that he had used to throw dirt on the fire. "Is this it?"

Skanderbrog took it tenderly—for a troll, that is—and there was emotion in his voice as he said, "I seem to keep owing you favors." He cocked his head toward the passageway. "I suppose I could eat one of those orcs. One of them was fairly young."

"I have some salt and seasoning in my wallet," said Krunzle.

"That would help," said Skanderbrog. "They're gamy, even the young ones." He turned and wriggled his way through the opening. The others followed.

Krunzle and Raimeau reassembled the scattered remains of the bonfire and built it up again, a little distance from the cave mouth. They dragged the orcs' corpses off a distance, except for the young one the troll had selected. Again, Skanderbrog used the long iron chisel as a spit. He had brought his hammer, too, and used it to drive a couple of branches into the earth, then positioned the chisel and its gore-dripping burden so that it would sear without charring. The aroma of roasting orc began to permeate the air. The four travelers sat upwind.

"This is the third batch of orcs I've killed in the past two days," said the troll, turning the orc's cold side toward the flames. "The mountain is thick with them. My mother said you have to kill orcs as soon as you find them, otherwise they'll breed you out of house and home."

"We met quite a few down the hill there," said Krunzle. "They were surprisingly well organized."

"The ones I met did seem to be in a hurry to get somewhere," Skanderbrog said.

"What direction were they going?"

The troll moved his head to indicate the slopes of the volcano. "Up there."

"Tell me, Skanderbrog," Raimeau said, "have you had any unusual dreams lately?"

"Trolls don't dream," Skanderbrog said. He turned the orc again. "I don't know why."

Krunzle said, "Did you see any trace of a man? He'd be wearing black."

"I did," said the troll. "He went the way the orcs were going, until I interrupted their journey. He left a lingering smell on the trail. I didn't like it."

"What kind of smell?" the thief said.

The troll's snout wrinkled and he spat. "I've smelled something like it before, but not up here, in the world. It smelled like snakes, but not exactly. It is like the faint odor that lingers in some of the deep places where my mother said that someone used to do magic, long, long ago. But this is stronger. Ranker."

Chirk, Krunzle said inwardly, *are you listening to this?*

Yes.

What do you make of it?

It stirs something. I think I may be getting close to where the memory is buried.

What is the magic that troll was talking about? the thief said.

Old magic, I think, ordered by the old gods—the really old, old gods.

You may have forgotten, Krunzle said, *that you're some kind of a snake, yourself.*

A temporary condition, I'm increasingly sure, Chirk said. *I don't think I've been in my present shape for more than a few centuries. Ten at the most.*

What were you before?

I am still working on that.
But you're old, said Krunzle. *Are you really old, old?*
I think I might be, said the snake.
Do you dream? the thief asked.
I thought I didn't. Now I suspect that I do nothing but.
You promised a talk before we slept.
I think, said the voice in Krunzle's mind, *that the time for talk has passed.*

The four travelers slept in the cave while Skanderbrog lay beside his fire. When, in the morning, they looked for the horses, they saw that the animals had broken their tethers and fled from the orcs. But when Brond put two fingers in his mouth and blew a piercing whistle, his long-maned horse came trotting up and out of a distant depression in the alpine meadow. Moments later, the three horses came after. The beasts wouldn't come near Skanderbrog, but when the travelers carried their saddles and blankets out to where the horses stood, stamping and whinnying, they were able to calm the creatures down. Once they were mounted, they found the animals would tolerate the troll, so long as he did not come too close.

"Would you care to come along with us?" Krunzle said. A troll could be useful in woods full of orcs.

"Where? Up there?" Skanderbrog looked up at where the black cone of the mountain sent up wisps of smoke against the pale blue sky. "My mother told me about volcanoes—rivers of burning rock, boulders that fall out of the sky."

Brond said, "My geothermic engineers say there's very little chance Mount Sinatuk will explode in our lifetimes."

"If it explodes," said Skanderbrog, "that will be the end of all our lifetimes."

"Point taken," said the dwarf, "but it almost certainly won't go off in the next few days."

The troll twisted up his face in indecision, and Krunzle said, "I'll be blunt. You're a very useful troll."

Brond made a half-suppressed noise and the thief turned toward him questioningly. Raimeau said, quietly, "Dwarves and trolls don't usually get along."

Krunzle addressed himself to the Noble Head. "Skanderbrog is an exceptional troll. As an exceptional dwarf, you should be able to overlook old prejudices."

"You are right," said Brond. To the troll he said, "You are a valuable member of this company. You have my respect."

"That is kindly said," said Skanderbrog, "but I cannot eat your respect. And while I don't mind killing orcs where I find them, my mother advised me never to go looking for trouble."

"Good sense," said the dwarf, "but let us consider what a little trouble might be worth to you." He thought for a moment, then said, "The hammer and chisel are all very well, but have you thought about what you could do with a really good sword?"

Skanderbrog held out a hand, fingers spread, wide as a bushel mouth. "Can't find one to fit," he said.

"My smiths could make you one to scale. And of the best steel, not iron."

The troll's snout wrinkled and one canine gleamed. "Steel? My mother said steel was dangerous."

Krunzle entered the conversation. "And so it is," he said, "though it makes a big difference which end of the sword you're looking at." The troll conceded the point with a grunt. "In the hands of an intelligent, ambitious young troll, a good steel sword might open up a whole new world of opportunities."

Skanderbrog looked at the thief sideways and chewed one corner of his mouth. "Such as?" he said.

Krunzle made an airy gesture. "I am a stranger in your land. So I couldn't say how long has it been since there has been a troll king in these parts."

The troll's brows drew down. "I don't know. Long time, would be my guess."

"I imagine, and I'm just saying, a troll who became king would make his mother awfully proud."

Skanderbrog turned to Brond. "You have smiths up there at the mine?"

"And steel," said the Noble Head.

The troll looked at the smoke wisps rising from the truncated peak. "And it won't go off?"

"I promise."

The troll collected his chisel and hammer. He wound the deer's shoulder bone into his hair. "I'll bring along a leg of orc to chew on," he said.

Chapter Twelve
The Tunnel

Through the morning, they crossed the alpine meadowlands, the fields scattered with outcrops of broken stone and occasional pools of clear water. Krunzle surveyed the land ahead and saw that they were ascending toward a ridge of bare rock. Brond said the far side plunged down into a wooded valley with a stream of black water that the dwarves called Odrigg. Over the river, they would be at the bottom of Mount Sinatuk itself.

"There is a bridge—we built it—some distance that way," the bald one said, gesturing to the east. "It meets the road that runs from Grimsburrow to the mine works, but I have a strong feeling that we might encounter orcs if we go that way."

"Someone wants to stop us—or at least some of us—from getting there," Raimeau said. "I would like to know why."

"I would like to know who," said Krunzle. He looked at Gyllana, who had been keeping her thoughts to herself. "Berbackian?" he said.

Her face said the question pained her. "To me, he was just a dashing Blackjacket officer with a romantic plan to . . ." She knitted her brows. "It all made perfect sense when he explained it; now I can't even remember what he said. It's like . . ."

"Like a dream," Raimeau finished for her. "Is it possible your spirited cavalier was a spell-spinning wizard who wove a net of fancies to snare you in?"

"It must be so," she said, "though I thought I would know a mage close up." She shook her head.

"Perhaps," said Krunzle, "he wields a species of magic that you're not familiar with. Or any of us, for that matter. Mordach said there was an odor to it that he could not recognize."

Skanderbrog was striding ahead of the horses, but a troll's hearing can be sharp. "Snake magic," he said.

"You said that before," said Raimeau. "Can you smell magic?"

"No," said the troll, throwing the words back over his shoulder. "But a troll never forgets an odor. When my mother was teaching me, she took me down into the deep underworld, along tunnels and down sheer cliffs where no light has been shed for thousands of years. There are places down below—halls and chambers, altars and thrones—where old magic was once done. A stink still lingers there." He looked back at the travelers. "That smell is the one I scented from the tracks of your man. I could not mistake it. Nor would you if you'd ever smelled it."

Skanderbrog's gaze settled thoughtfully on Krunzle. "At first I thought there was a whiff of it about you, too," he said, "but it's just that metal thing around your neck." He paused to remember, then added, "That man who had his arms burned off—it was strong on the stumps."

"I cannot vouch for the object around my neck," the thief said. "I did not come by it voluntarily." He looked to the gray-haired man. "Raimeau, you've read books. Know anything about snake magic?"

"If it's what I think it is," said the thin man, "it's not really snakes that our trollish friend is talking about. Something older than snakes, much older than men or dwarves or even orcs."

"Long dead, then," said Krunzle. "That's a relief."

"Well," said Raimeau, "there's dead, and then there's dead."

"It comes in different strengths?" said the thief.

Raimeau's expression would have fit a professor of philosophy at one of the universities in Almas. "In a manner of speaking. Before the gods created mankind and the other races with whom we share Golarion, there were . . . precursors. Children of other gods, or wanderers who came here from other planes. We do not even know what they called themselves.

"Some of them built civilizations, empires, that warred against each other. They are supposed to be gone now, but they may live on in the deepest caverns of the Darklands. The thing is, they were different from us, had different powers—powers that were as natural to them as your ability to reach out a hand and seize a piece of the world is to you, powers that we would call magic.

"And their gods, or whatever made them, gave them different qualities of . . . being."

"You sound as if you're not sure of what you're talking about," said Brond.

"I'm *not* sure," Raimeau said. "Krunzle asked me what I had read. All I can do is relate what was in Captain Hdolf's library. There was a legend of snakelike beings—oddly enough, they were described as having heads 'something like lilies', whatever that means—and their wizards wielded great powers. Powers that are now long forgotten."

"What has this got to do with the smell on our missing Blackjacket?" Krunzle said.

Raimeau shrugged. "Maybe nothing. But some of these creatures, these lily-heads or whatever they called themselves, may still be with us, buried in a kind of half-life deep within the lightless regions far below the earth we walk, yet still able to reach out and touch the minds of lesser creatures, bend them to their will."

The gray-haired man looked up at the slopes of Mount Sinatuk. "They liked to entomb themselves beneath mountains—volcanoes, too. If a lily-head was looking for a place to lie low for a few thousand years, this is just the kind of neighborhood it would choose. And, if it wanted to accomplish something in the world, they could reach out and send dreams that would turn around a Berbackian or a passel of orcs, as easily as you or I would lace up our boots."

Brond's face had grown paler. "I would not like to think," he said, "that my life's work has been merely to fluff the pillows of some ancient snake with an oddly shaped head."

"Nor would I," said Raimeau. "Yet here we are."

Krunzle said, "My dreams are of my own making. Snakes do not enter into them." But he felt Chirk stir in the back of his mind, though the snake said nothing.

The dwarves' bridge was east of where they met the river; Berbackian's horse's tracks went toward the crossing, but the three humans, the dwarf, and the troll turned west and soon found a place where they could ford the rushing cold water on some boulders that formed a natural weir. Skanderbrog led the way. Not much farther on was a deep-riven gully. "Beyond here, the horses will not serve you," the troll said. "We will have to climb." But he promised they would encounter no orcs.

They set the animals free. From here on they would carry only their weapons and basic provisions. Skanderbrog slung the charred orc's leg from a thong over his shoulder. They began to ascend the slope, which soon rose steeply, its sides closing in, like a long, thin scar in the mountain's flank. In places, they had to scramble over loose slopes of gray, gritty scree; in others, they scaled near-vertical walls, the rock so new to the air that it had not yet weathered and so offered them plenty of toe- and finger-holds.

It grew cold as they climbed higher, the sun doing little to cut the mountain chill. The same sour-smelling wind came whiffling down the gully, making their faces feel stiff. They did not talk. Krunzle kept his thoughts to himself. They centered on blue diamonds and the options that might come open to him once Wolsh Berbackian had been dealt with, the stolen item returned, and Chirk removed from his neck and his mind. He might return to the northern shore of the Inner Sea, find a congenial city, and set up a training academy. A wallet well filled with rare gems would buy him a senior position in a rogues' guild. His colleagues would clamor to have him educate their children in his imitable techniques, and the fees could be whatever he wanted them to be.

With these pleasant considerations to ward off the chill and take his mind off the disagreeable labor of climbing Mount Sinatuk, Krunzle followed Skanderbrog until the young troll led them up a last low cliff and delivered them onto a sloping trail carved into the volcano's side by dwarven steel.

"I know where we are," Brond said, looking about. "That way"—he pointed up the smooth-floored track— "is a thermal vent that jets steam at regular intervals. It is caught in a copper hood and piped down to the mine works"—now he pointed downslope to where the trail disappeared around a protuberance of porous gray tufa—"where it is fed through a network of tubes beneath the floor of the administration offices and the workers' baths and accommodations. The pipe runs beneath the track."

"Impressive engineering," said Raimeau.

"Let us follow the path down to the mine," said the Noble Head. "We need to warn my people there about the orc threat."

They followed the trail to a place where the slope steepened and the smooth rock floor became a series of descending steps, curving around the girth of the mountain, with the hot-water pipe running beside it. Now Brond led the way, and the nearer he came to the place where dwarven skill and energy had laid an economic base for the Regulate, the more upright his posture became. At the end, he was almost skipping down the steps with a lightfootedness as unusual in a dwarf as his hairless head.

There turned out to be no need to warn the miners and their guards about the orcs. They came upon the first bodies before they had even reached the bottom of the steps: a pair of engineers, their bodies hacked and eviscerated. A few dozen steps farther down—Brond was not skipping now—and they rounded a last curve and had a clear view of the mine adit. And of the death that had come to roost there.

Raimeau had read military history; he could tell what had happened from the arrangement of the bodies.

The mine guards had not been taken by surprise. The last stretch of road leading up to the mine head had to traverse a slope too steep for oxcarts, so the dwarven road builders had cut a series of switchbacks back and forth up the incline. The orcs had come up it in a stream, but not fast enough to take the mine guards by surprise.

Fifty spear-dwarves had formed a shield wall where the road reached the broad apron of flat stone carved out of the mountain in front of the main tunnel. They should have been enough to handle twenty times their number. But again, the orcs had not come on in the same old way, flinging themselves against the spearpoints, piling up a wall of their own dead from atop which the dwarves' long spears would continue to methodically skewer them.

Instead, the orcs had cut down a big pine, below the tree line, far, far down the mountain. They had trimmed it, leaving stubs of branches sticking out as handholds, sharpening the wider end to a crude point. Then they had carried the log all the way up the switchbacks, forming up as a column with its pointed end at their front.

"You can see, there," the gray-haired man said, "where they drove through the wall. The rear rank of the guards threw their spears over the heads of the other three ranks. They did fearsome damage, but it was not enough. Other orcs seized the handholds and bore the ram forward.

"The shield wall broke. The guards tried to reform into two platoons, with the orcs squeezed between them. But the orcs did not give them the opportunity. Before the two bodies could get their shields and spears in place, the enemy raced through the breach and attacked the ends of the broken lines. The dwarves fought well, but they were overwhelmed."

The orcs had killed them all, the guards and a few miners who had not made it into the tunnel before the great doors had closed. But it would not have made any difference if the stragglers had gotten inside—the invaders had immediately picked up their ram and thrown themselves against the portal, which had been designed to keep out weather, not blood-fired orcs. The doors hung askew from their torn-out hinges; behind them, the proofs of slaughter continued. The miners had fought with their iron tools and had even hurled chunks of shattered overburden. Pools of orc blood, shreds of orc flesh, fragments of orc bone, and even severed orc limbs lay among the scattered bodies of the dwarves.

"They took their dead away," Raimeau said, shaking his head as they stepped among the carnage. "When have orcs done that?"

Brond moved quietly among the fallen, his hairless face ashen. Here and there, he stopped and softly spoke a name, or bent and rearranged an ungainly sprawled limb or closed a pair of sightless eyes.

Skanderbrog had gone beyond the densest part of the killing zone, his nostrils distended to catch the scent that came from farther down the tunnel. Here the place was illuminated by sunlight; deeper into the downward-sloping shaft, globes of light should have lit the way. But the tunnel was steeped in darkness. A set of wooden rails, laid into the stone floor, disappeared into the gloom.

"They went down there," the troll said, gesturing with his chin at the closed-in blackness. He sniffed again. "But I don't think they carried them. I think they walked."

Krunzle could catch the sour odor—stronger now—and under it, it seemed, something else—something sharp and rank that went straight through his nose to the oldest part of his brain, to stir up nameless animal fears from the times before a human ever opened his eyes on a Golarion night. "Dead orcs don't walk," he said

"These did," Raimeau said. "Look at this track." He indicated a splotch of congealed blood on the tunnel floor. "The orc who made that was missing half his foot. Yet he was walking on the stump. And he wasn't the only one. Look there." Smears of blood could be seen on the stone floor and the rails, as well as on the walls.

The troll sniffed again. "There it is again," he said, "snake magic. Strong." He summoned up phlegm and spat, then looked back toward the shattered doors and the sunlight beyond. "I don't think I'll be getting a steel sword today."

Gyllana's face was as bloodless as Brond's. She said, "What about Berbackian? Can you smell him?"

The troll's educated nose drew in more air from the darkness. "He went down there," he said.

"And has he come out?"

"No."

"I have to find him," she said, looking at Krunzle, "and so do you."

There was no point asking Chirk. The thief could feel the snake stirring around in his mind. Somehow the sensation was sharper now, as if the strange being were finally coming into focus.

"I have to go, too," said Brond.

"And I will go," said Raimeau. "Whatever I am meant to do, I sense that I am meant to do it here."

They all turned to Skanderbrog. The troll shook his head. "I would still like the sword. I would fight orcs for it. But what is down there is more than orcs, worse than orcs. I will heed my mother's advice and let it lie."

Brond ran his hairless hand over his browless, whiskerless face. He had aged a great deal since the fight by the river. "We cannot fight the orcs alone," he said, "and I must go to see what has called them and made them . . . strange. I could not live, not knowing."

"You might die, finding out," said the troll.

Brond's mouth moved, almost like a tic. "Let me offer you this: come with us and fight the orcs and I will give you a finer set of steel weapons and armor than any troll has ever owned. But if we find something that your mother would not have approved of, you may leave us and I will still honor the agreement."

"How, if you are dead?" said Skanderbrog, then with a shudder, "Or worse?"

Brond went to the mine office, found pen and paper, and drew up an order to the chief of the Grimsburrow smithy. "Present this and it will be honored," he said.

The troll looked at the paper then showed it to Raimeau. "Does it say what it should?"

"It does," said the thin man.

The troll rolled up the document into a scroll and tied it into his hair. "I will come," he said.

The tunnel bent as it went down into the bowels of the mountain. The dwarven engineers had scried the locations of lava tubes in which the blue diamonds would be found, and had directed their tunneling appropriately. The curve meant that soon they had left behind the sunlit entrance, but Brond had found oil lamps hanging from chains in the mine offices, and they hung these from the ends of lathes of wood and lit them. Thus they proceeded constantly into a gold glow, leaving darkness behind them.

Along the floor of the tunnel were laid two parallel tracks of hard wood, their upper surfaces polished by the traffic of grooved wooden wheels. A little way into the darkness, they came upon a cart. Krunzle climbed onto its yoke and held his lamp to illuminate the interior. He was hoping for a glint of blue light, but the cart was empty. Still, they pushed it ahead of them, Brond having reasoned that it would serve as a defensive barrier should a rush of orcs suddenly come out of the dark.

The tunnel was more than tall enough for dwarves, just comfortable for a man as tall as Raimeau, and tricky for a troll—Skanderbrog had to crouch, his knees bent and his head constantly in danger of banging against the ceiling. After a timeless time, they reached the first lava tube. It was a wide vertical shaft, almost cylindrical, that had formerly been filled with porous tufa. The dwarves had hollowed it out, above and below, extracting the gems they found lodged in the soft volcanic rock. They had also erected a wooden trestle from one side of the excavated tube to the other to support the wooden rails that crossed it to where the tunnel recommenced on the other side. Beside the tracks ran a walkway, again wide enough for dwarves and men, but difficult footing for a troll. Skanderbrog solved the problem by straddling the tracks and walking with one foot on each side. At least here he could stand straight.

As they passed through the empty space, Krunzle again lifted his oil lamp, hoping for a glint of blue from the walls. But it seemed that the dwarves had taken every gem.

They passed through two more lava tubes, each as empty as the first, then came to a stretch of tunnel that angled steeply down. The walls were fitted with strong timbers and iron rings to which blocks and tackle could be attached, for here the grade was too sharp for an ore cart to be easily dwarf-handled upward.

The passageway was black as pitch. The glow from their oil lamps scarcely illuminated the track ahead of the cart. They had not had to push the vehicle since they had left the reach of sunlight; gravity had pulled it along before them, and now the job of keeping it from rolling away on the steeper incline was left to Skanderbrog, who held it back with one hand gripping its rear wall.

"That's an orc," Raimeau said, holding his lamp aloft and peering with the others at the object the front wheels of the cart had bumped against, stopping the vehicle.

"It only has one arm and one leg," said Krunzle.

"And yet," said Brond, "we're supposed to believe it crawled all the way from the entrance." He looked around, moving his lamp to illuminate the area. "At least, I don't see any severed limbs. That makes no sense."

Another few hundred paces into the mine, they found a second orc, as dead as the first. This one had all its limbs, but its belly had been slit open by a razor-edged dwarven spear and its ropy entrails straggled behind along the track. It had finally expired with one hand outstretched, as if struggling to move one more span toward whatever had kept it moving.

Raimeau felt its arm: the gray flesh was cold. "It didn't die here," he said. "It's been dead for hours. Yet, dead, it staggered here until finally it no longer had enough of whatever had been enlivening it and keeping it going."

Brond's face twisted in disbelief. "Wounded orcs drag themselves away from things that might finish them off; they don't drag themselves *toward* anything. An orc, wounded or not, is a simple collection of appetites: it hungers, it lusts, it hates, it covets. A dead orc doesn't do anything."

"Somewhere," the gray-haired man said, "I've come across a mention of this kind of thing."

"Undead orcs, marching to . . ." Apparently, Brond could not think of anything undead orcs might march to, and ended by waving away the notion with a brusque gesture.

"No," said Raimeau, his brow furrowed in an attempt to catch a wisp of memory. "Something that could reach into another being's mind and bend it to its will—and do so with such power that the master could keep the mindslave moving and doing despite injuries that ought to have been fatal."

"Perhaps your flower-headed snake?" said Krunzle. "The one that would choose the middle of a volcano as its preferred lurking spot?"

Raimeau frowned. "My memory is capricious," he said. "Too many nightmares, all those years in the iron mines. But it could have been a lily-head."

"Well," said the thief, "if we keep going down this tunnel, we're liable to find out, aren't we?" He sighed, hitched his sword belt so that the weapon's hilt was close to hand, lifted the lathe of wood from which his oil lamp hung, and set off. A few steps on he stumbled and cursed. "Another one," he called back over his shoulder.

Answer me one question, Chirk, he said in the quiet of his mind, *will this end happily for me?*

Define happiness, from your point of view, said the snake.

The thief's response was instant. *A trove of blue diamonds.*

Then, yes. Your happiness is assured. Think of the biggest blue diamond you could ever imagine.

Krunzle did so. *Mmm,* he said.

Then double it.

Mm-mm.

And even that's not big enough.

Krunzle smiled to himself. Then another question occurred. *And the opportunity to sell it for a fortune?* he said.

You asked me to answer one question. I did. Now keep moving.

Krunzle swore and stopped to let the others catch up.

They found more orcs as they went on; many of them had lethal wounds. "Your guards gave a good account of themselves," said Raimeau. "And your miners."

"Dwarves do not die easily," said Brond.

Krunzle put a question to the gray-haired man. "Why do we see dead orcs, but not dead dwarves?"

Raimeau did not know, but said if he had to guess it would be that orcs were simpler-minded. "The clockwork of their minds would be easier to disrupt."

"But Berbackian must have had a subtle mind," the thief said, "to have put one over on the daughter of the Second Secretary to the First Commissariote of Kerse."

"Indeed," said Raimeau, "but perhaps his intellect was debased by overindulgence in certain appetites."

Now it was Krunzle's turn say, "Indeed?" An idea formed in his mind and he turned to the woman. "Was he a flayleaf addict? A devotee of pesh? Or perhaps the drug called shiver?"

"None of your business," said Gyllana.

Brond spoke. "I must differ. We are here because of a train of events your lover set in motion, whatever their end might be. Any knowledge about him may be germane to our situation, and thus we have a right to know."

For a moment, she faced them down, standing on the eminence of her social rank. Then her face crumpled. "Flayleaf," she said. "He introduced me to it . . . but I take responsibility. I liked it. It made . . ."—she took a breath, looked away, and continued—"it made certain pleasures more pleasurable."

Krunzle saw the shape of things. "He plied you with it, and while you lay inert and replete from his attentions, he stole the talisman from your father's strongroom."

"It wasn't in the strongroom," she said, as if the thief had proposed an obscenity. "I am a Kalistocrat's daughter; I would never have admitted one who was not of our blood to the inner sanctum of our house. The object was on a tabletop on my father's study, part of a collection of curious oddments he had picked up at a house sale. A minor wizard had misjudged the strength of a spell and blasted himself into oblivion, and his effects were auctioned. I told you that my father collected mystic curiosities from the East. He had bought a box full of such bric-a-brac at the sale. Thang-Sha was known to be an expert on such things; my father had taken objects to him before for valuing. He did so again."

"What did Thang-Sha say?"

"That the thing was obscure, probably of little value. He asked my father if he could keep it while he consulted his reference books." She shrugged. "My father is a Kalistocrat. It is foreign to his nature to part with so much as a stepped-on bean, even on loan. But he did invite the wizard to take up residence in the old wing. He could strengthen the mansion's defenses—free of charge, of course—while he studied the object to his heart's content."

She thought back, and spoke as if remembering a dream. "Then Berbackian was in the house for one of our trysts. He saw the whatever-it-is and asked if he could take it. I said no, of course." She shook her head gently, amazed at her own folly. "He said it was a test of my love, and for some reason I cannot explain, I did not laugh in his face and explain what love meant to a Kalistocrat's daughter.

"I remember thinking, 'It's just an old thing from who knows where. No one knows what it's for.' It was like someone else's hand picked it up and handed it to him. Then came the morning after. Thang-Sha made a fuss. My father was outraged that one of his possessions had been taken." She made a sound that might have been laughter. "He wanted to send the Blackjackets after Wolsh."

"But he didn't," said Krunzle.

"No. Thang-Sha said we should avoid the scandal of anyone knowing that we had been robbed." She made a chagrined face. "It is a great shame to be taken."

"So they sent you," Krunzle said. "And you, once again, succumbed to Berbackian's manly charms."

Now she made a face that expressed no respect for the thief's opinion. Krunzle began to offer a detailed analysis of Gyllana Eponion, but Brond shut him off with a wave of his hand. "What happened?" the dwarf said.

She made a helpless gesture. "I went to Berbackian, asked for it back, this trifle, this nothing. He said he would give it to me—of course, he would give it to me; it was around there somewhere. But first, let us kindle the pipe one more time. We lay on his bed, smoking."

Krunzle could imagine the rest, and took pleasure in saying it. "When you awoke, you were on the barge upriver, then you hitched a ride to Ulm's Delve with a wagon string, and there he decided to sell you to Boss Ulm. You were lucky that I had already come by and dealt with the riverside welcoming committee, or your introduction to the Ulm's Delve way of life would have taken the form of three bandits and a half-orc."

She nodded, not looking at any of them. "Even by the time he carried me onto the barge, I had become completely inessential to his plans. But he did not want anyone to know where he was going. I would like to think that some vestige of affection kept him from just killing me, but probably it was sheer happenstance. We were never alone. His true nature became clear when we reached the gold camp. Ulm saw me and made an offer: me for Berbackian's freedom. It was accepted."

"That must have been hard," said Raimeau.

She sighed. "Until that moment, I had been able to tell myself that it was all a romantic adventure. The flayleaf helped in that regard. But then they took my clothes and locked me in Room Thirteen while Ulm worked out whether he would make more money ransoming me to my father or auctioning me in the camp. Some of those gold seekers had coffers full of nuggets buried under their cabin floors."

Krunzle said, "I weep great, salty tears for you. Let us get on and get this finished."

Raimeau said, "Do you not feel for her? She has been much wronged."

"Someday," said Krunzle, "when we're not deep inside a mountain, facing unknown but doubtless horrific perils, I will explain my point of view."

They went on, the troll still keeping the ore cart ahead of them. The next time they came to a played-out orc, and the one after that, Skanderbrog bumped the wheels over the corpse and kept rolling.

They crossed another hollowed-out lava tube. At either end of the trestle that supported the wooden rails, ladders had been nailed to the soft rock. These led to narrow platforms—only two planks wide—suspended from chains attached to iron spikes. Looking up, Krunzle saw glints of blue reflecting the lamplight. The dwarves had not yet cleaned out this lode. He would have liked to have climbed and inspected the size and qualities of the gems, but even as the idea formed in his mind, he heard a sardonic chuckle from the back of his mind.

You know what the talisman is, the thing that Berbackian stole, don't you? he thought back. *You've known all along.*

Yes, said Chirk, *and no.*

What is it, then?

The stuff of dreams, said the snake, and laughed and would say no more.

After the lava tube came yet more tunnel, but after a few hundred paces the rails ended. Raimeau held his lamp beyond the wooden bumper that had arrested the ore cart and said, "What now?"

Brond said, "This must be almost as far as the miners had dug. The last report I had said they were getting close to the main lava tube, the one that went up to the volcano's mouth far above as well as down to the magma chamber. The others were just cracks in the cone where lava had forced its way through. My geologists were confident that there would be some outstanding specimens there."

"By specimens," Krunzle said, "you mean gems, blue diamonds."

"Yes."

The mental image Chirk had shown him—his hands around an incomparable, giant gem—came back. "How far to the diamonds?" he said.

"The tunnel does not go that far. My miners had yet to dig it."

"I'll bet it does now," said the thief. "That's what the orcs were for." He drew his short sword and sent a question to Chirk.

Yes, came the answer, *it will still defend you.*

"Then let us go," said Krunzle.

A pattern was forming in the thief's mind. It all came back to the diamonds. Any diamond of good quality was valuable—even the lesser stones that were used as cutting instruments in artisans' workshops or set into clockwork by watchmakers—but blue diamonds commanded the highest prices of all in Druma's markets. The dwarves had built all of their works—the road, the bridge, the mine itself—to get their hands on blue diamonds, because the gems would pay for all of Brond's grand schemes to revive the Five Kingdoms as a true republic.

Gyllana wanted revenge, but she was here for the diamonds, too. No daughter of a Kersite Kalistocrat could ignore the opportunity. The Regulate would need an agent to sell the mine's output; Ippolite Eponion, Krunzle was sure, would turn out to be a dealer in such rarities. A commission of even ten percent on sales would amount to a fortune, and the thief had no doubt that the Kersite would haggle for twice that.

But it wasn't just money. He'd heard that blue diamonds were prized by wizards as crystals of great power. Krunzle had no command of the arcana of sorcery, but he knew that gems of exceptional quality could be used to focus the most powerful of esoteric powers.

Suppose the stolen talisman was a diviner's tool that, in the hands of one gifted in divination, could show the way to a blue diamond of unheard-of quality. Suppose Berbackian was one of those who possessed the rare and special gift of divination. He learned somehow of the existence of the talisman, traced its ownership to the house of Eponion in Kerse. He came, saw the opportunity of access through the daughter, and used his charms—and the power of the herb known as flayleaf—to make her pliable.

He gained what he desired. The moment he held the divining tool in his hands, it pointed him toward Mount Sinatuk. He set off immediately, disposing of the impediment of Gyllana Eponion as he passed through Ulm's Delve. A plausible rogue, he talked his way through the gold camp and through the Regulate. Somehow, he also talked his way past a grand war party of orcs—Krunzle was not sure how that had happened—but no doubt it would be revealed in time. Or made irrelevant, once the thief was on his way back to the shores of the Inner Sea, his wallet abulge with a huge blue diamond.

Thang-Sha must also be a diviner, must have been on the same search as Berbackian. But the rogue had beaten the mage to the prize. Or perhaps the Tian mage's wizardry had been able to discern the talisman as soon as it became active in the Blackjacket's hands. Then he had gotten close to Eponion, identified Krunzle as a useful operative, and sprung the trap that led to the thief being sent on his mission, with a bronze snake in charge of his windpipe.

It made a rough kind of sense. Although it didn't explain the orcs, especially the dead orcs that had still struggled down the tunnel. But now Krunzle wondered if Thang-Sha might have played a part in that, too. The wizard did not trust Krunzle to do his bidding—hence the imposition of Chirk as his taskmaster. But perhaps Thang-Sha did not entirely trust Chirk, and so had attached a second string to his zither: if Krunzle did not find Berbackian and recover the talisman in time, the ensorcelled orcs would overpower the Regulate's dwarves and seize the riches of Mount Sinatuk for their spell-slinging, string-pulling overlord.

So there it was. Down at the end of the tunnel, they would find Berbackian and the talisman, waiting as the last of the orcs cut through the remaining few yards of rock to the magma chamber where the great blue gems waited. Thang-Sha, keeping a watching brief by isinglass or mercury pool, might even be preparing to transport himself to the place and take charge. At that point, Krunzle's assignment would be at an end. Chirk would be removed from his neck. Once that happened, there ought to be an opportunity for an enterprising rogue to fill his wallet with gems.

He decided to ask the snake the crucial question. *Chirk,* he said inwardly, *Once we have recovered the talisman and dealt with Berbackian, Gyllana will want to go home to Kerse. She is very unlikely to want me as her escort. Brond will provide her with one, especially if he is going to do a deal with her father to market the gems. If so, will you need to manage me quite so closely?*

I am sure not, came the reply. The voice sounded strong and certain.

So I will be free?

Who of us is free? said the snake.

Under the circumstances, said Krunzle, *I would prefer a less philosophical answer.*

Your preference has been duly noted.

The snake would say no more, and when Krunzle grew insistent, Chirk sent him a warning tingle and a gentle squeeze about his neck.

Chapter Thirteen
Necessary Sacrifice

Listen," said Skanderbrog, stopping in the darkness. The troll's ears were better than Brond's or the humans', but when they went cautiously forward a few more steps, they heard a faint *chink, chink* from down the tunnel. Skanderbrog's nostrils distended as they took in a great breath, then he sneezed. "Orcs, all right," he said.

The distant sounds ceased. The troll handed his lamp to Gyllana. In a matter-of-fact tone, he said, "They're coming. Give me room." He stepped in front of the others and said, "If any of them get behind me, kill them fast. They like to go for the hamstrings."

There was none of the stamping and roaring of a normal orc attack. First a rustle of sound from the darkness, growing clearer as it grew nearer, to become the slap of flat-footed steps rushing toward them. Then the hoarse breathing, coming louder, and a few glints of reflected light from the oil lamps, glistening off black eyes and exposed tusks.

And then the orcs were on them, the tunnel only wide enough for three or four. Their mouths gaped rather than snarled, and the froth on their lips was more of exhaustion than frenzy. Still they swung their swords and lunged with their crude, jagged halberds, those that didn't brandish picks or hammers that were clearly dwarven-made.

Four of them came first, pressed shoulder to shoulder in the narrow space. Skanderbrog roared in their faces, a bellow that would have emptied Krunzle's bowels if he'd been on the receiving end of it. The orcs paused only a moment in their advance, but that was enough. With his left hand, the troll thrust the long black spike of his chisel through the chest of a big brindled buck, gouging the rock wall behind him and pinning his torso to that side of the tunnel. Meanwhile, the huge right hand swung the iron-headed hammer in a flat arc, crushing the heads of the three others—one, two, three—in a spray of blood, brains, and bone. As they dropped, the troll shook the first one loose from his chisel and laid the corpse crosswise across the other three.

"Make a barrier of their dead, she always said." He seemed to be speaking to himself, even as he repeated the exact same motions to kill four more orcs that leapt their dead hordemates to get at him. In a moment, the barrier was knee-high to the next attackers, who stumbled as they were forced forward by the pressure of those behind. Skanderbrog smashed and skewered them with deliberate care, and now the barrier was waist-high.

"He fights well," said Brond. "Brains as well as brawn. I think he is an exceptional troll."

The troll was reaching over the barricade now, thrusting with the hammer to hold off some attackers while he judiciously transfixed one after another with his chisel. These he pulled forward before yanking free the spike, the better to raise the wall of dead between him and the foe.

"Still, they make no noise," said Raimeau.

"Indeed," said the bald dwarf, "they are unusual orcs. Look at that one."

The warrior he had indicated was shuffling forward along the right side of the tunnel, a dwarven spear in his hands, trying to stab the troll under the arm that wielded the spike. But the orc was hampered by a grievous wound to his forehead—pink-gray brain matter was visible through shattered bone—and a flap of skin hung down over where his brow ridge should have been, obscuring his vision.

"That wound is hours old and should have been fatal," said Brond. "Yet he still fights."

"Not any more," said Krunzle, as Skanderbrog's hammer swung to finish the damage to the orc's cranium that a spear-dwarf's thrust must have done in the earlier fight. The orc fell across the barricade and lay still. "It looks as if crushing the brain puts an end to even the walking dead."

The barricade of slaughtered orcs now reached half the height of the tunnel. Krunzle estimated that Skanderbrog had killed more than twenty of them. The attack stopped, as abruptly as if someone had blown a whistle, and the orcs fell back. Krunzle could hear snuffles of breathing from the darkness and sounds of movement. "Are they regrouping for another attack?" he said.

Skanderbrog applied his sharper hearing. "Maybe," he said. "Maybe not."

They listened as the time stretched on. No new attack came. Then they heard, faintly, the *chink, chink* of metal tools on rock.

"They've gone back to work," Brond said.

"Not all of them," said the troll. "There's a bunch a little ways down the tunnel, just outside the lamplight. See the faint gleam of their eyes. It comes and goes as they blink."

The dwarf went to the barricade, climbed on a convenient knee, and peered down the tunnel. "They're to keep us away until they get at whatever it is they're after."

"Do you want to let them?" said the troll.

The dwarf turned to the others. "What do you think?"

Chirk? Krunzle passed along the question.

Get there first, said the snake. *Seize it.*

Raimeau was saying that the orcs seemed to have the benefit of an able strategist, judging by their success against well-trained dwarves. "If they're after something down there, it must offer them some advantage."

"I agree," said Krunzle. "We should get it first."

Gyllana shrugged. "'Deny the enemy what he seeks' is usually good strategy."

"Then let us be about it," said the dwarf. He issued orders, and moments later they pulled down the barricade and rushed the orc remnant that stood between them and the end of the tunnel. Skanderbrog led the charge and did most of the carnage, smashing through the plug of orcs that blocked the tunnel—many of them already dead but still capable of pointing a spear or slashing with an axe—while the dwarf and the humans followed on his heels, breaking the heads of any of the orc fallen that still showed motion.

The tunnel ended at a crack not much wider than a man. From within came the sounds of hammer and chisel—at least one orc was still trying to break through to the last lava tube.

"That snake magic smell is stronger now," the troll said. His snout wrinkled in disgust.

Raimeau thrust his lamp on its lathe into the space; it illuminated a second orc with a spear, who immediately knocked the lamp to the floor, spilling its oil, and lunged at the gray-haired man.

A giant hand on Raimeau's shoulder pulled him back, and Skanderbrog reached into the crevice with his chisel. When he withdrew the iron spike, an orc was struggling on it like a gaffed fish. The troll brought his catch out into the tunnel, where Brond's mace dispatched it with a brain-spilling crunch.

The sounds of metal on metal still came from the crack in the rock. Gyllana looked at Krunzle. "Your turn," she said.

The thief had his sword in hand, but it had seen little use except to fend off ineffectual blows from wounded, fallen orcs as Raimeau or Brond put them down for good. *Chirk,* he thought, *do I have to wait until the orc attacks before this will serve me?*

No. Now, get on with it.

Krunzle slipped into the crack in the rock, sword first, his lamp held above his head, his buskined soles crunching on fragments of rock that littered the floor. At the end of the crevice, a big orc warrior, dappled gray on gray, was frantically driving a dwarven hammer against the head of a black chisel. The man approached cautiously, but the orc paid him no heed, as if survival meant nothing, and the work alone was his reason to exist.

Rock fragments flew. The *chink, chink, chink* of iron on iron was almost continuous. A tiny mote of bright blue light appeared at the tip of the orc's chisel. Another blow, another fragment of rock flown away, and the mote was larger, brighter. It illuminated more of the crevice than the thief's guttering oil lamp could manage, showing him that something indistinct lay on the rock-strewn floor. Cautiously, the man knelt and touched: he felt cloth; and through the cloth, skin; and through the skin, bone.

The orc paid him no heed, only hammered at the black rock. Krunzle brought his lamp closer to the thing on the floor. *That's not an orc,* he thought.

Get it out of the way, said Chirk.

What is it?

What do you think? Berbackian, of course!

The thief dragged the body out of the crevice, back into the tunnel. It was curiously light, and he heard its bones rattle within the skin. "Gyllana," he said, "will you come and tell us if this is Berbackian?"

The woman's drawn face grew paler in the lamplight, but she moved toward the front of the cart. Krunzle heard her swear, too, then make a noise as if she was fighting nausea. The thief bent forward to take a better look, then said, "If that's Wolsh Berbackian, I honestly don't see what you saw in him."

"Shut up!" said the Kalistocrat's daughter. She looked down again at the thing on the floor and dry-retched once more.

The other travelers brought their lamps to bear. The combined glow caused shadows to move over shadows, so that the corpse's face seemed to be still possessed by a kind of life—until the thief looked closer.

He had heard tales of caravans crossing the wastes of northern Garund, where the wind piled the dunes high against the horizon. Sometimes, the *khamsin*—the hot desert wind—would spring up, blowing searing grit that could scour the flesh from the bones of man and beast, and the caravaneers would hunker down beside their camels to wait it out. But, occasionally, the wind blew longer and stronger than a man could endure, and the sand would pile up against the weather-side of the animal, deeper and deeper as the hours turned into days.

The sand heaps would become sand mountains, and then they would *move*. The fiery sand would first bury the wayfarers' limbs beneath too much weight, then fill their mouths and noses, smothering them and entombing them in one action. And there they would lie beneath the newly formed dune, their bodies flattened by its weight, the last drop of their moisture leached out by the shining grains to be spirited down into the subsoil to sustain the vermin that lived there.

And then, a decade, a century, a millennium later, the wind would tear down the dune and carry it off to some other place, and the buried, mummified dead would lie upon the face of the desert, to be found and wondered at by the next troupe of men and camels to come that way.

Krunzle had heard that these once-human relics appeared shrunken to dwarven size, their skin like seared paper, their eyes dried to the size of peas in their sockets. He had heard that to come across one unexpectedly in the sandy wastes could deliver a shock even to the hardiest desert tribesman.

How much worse, then, to come across such an object in the deepest, darkest bowels of a mountain? the thief thought, putting out a toe to lift and let fall one black-sleeved arm. He heard the rattle of bones within the fabric; they sounded barely connected. "It's definitely him?" he asked Gyllana.

In answer, she swore again, but not at him—more at the world in general.

"What has happened to him?" Krunzle said. He stooped and held his light nearer.

"Something," said Raimeau, "has sucked all the life out of him. Blood, juices, every drop."

"Orcs?" said Krunzle.

Brond answered. "Not orcs."

"A lily-head?"

The dwarf turned his bald head toward Raimeau. "I don't know," said the thin man.

Chirk? the thief asked, inwardly. But the snake did not speak in his mind, though Krunzle had a clear sense that the creature was fully alert, fully engaged in this moment. Aloud, Krunzle said, "Raimeau, take my lamp," and when the thin man took hold of the lathe from which it hung, the thief knelt and expertly ransacked the corpse's pockets and wallet. The motions of his hands several times caused the dry bones to rattle and rasp against the equally dry bag of skin to which Wolsh Berbackian had been reduced.

"Nothing," the thief said, when he had finished his search. He swore and rose, taking back his lamp from the gray-haired man. "For a moment, I hoped that my part in this adventure might have finally come to a conclusion."

Far from it, said the voice in his mind. It was louder and firmer than ever, and there was more than a hint of sardonic humor in the comment.

"If he did not have the talisman," said Gyllana, "where is it?"

Raimeau looked back along the blackness of the tunnel and at the crevice whose mouth was limned in blue light. "An orc must have taken it."

"Why?" said the woman. "What use is it to an orc?"

"What use was it to Berbackian?" said Krunzle. "Except to lead him to an unappetizing death?"

Brond took hold of the mummy's doublet and hauled the corpse off to the side, where lay the orc Skanderbrog had skewered. "The answer," he said, "is at the other end of this crevice. I'm going in there. I want to know what's going on in my mountain."

"Bad stuff," said the troll. He indicated the mummy with one claw-tipped finger. "That thing stinks of snake magic. And, if you want my opinion, I don't believe this mountain thinks of itself as belonging to you."

"I'm going in there," said the dwarf. "You don't have to come." He looked around at the three humans. "That includes you."

"Well, in that case—" Krunzle began, but found himself unable to complete the sentence.

No more jokes, said the voice in his mind as the snake loosened its strangler's grip on his throat.

"I need to know," said Gyllana. The thief watched her and thought, *And you need to see the diamonds.*

Raimeau only shrugged. "Somehow," he said, "this concerns my destiny."

"My mother always said, a promise is a promise," said Skanderbrog. "But I agreed to fight orcs for a steel sword. I've done that, except for one hammering at the rock in there. If you want me to, I'll kill him, too. But after that, it's a whole new game of scuffle."

"Scuffle?" said Raimeau.

"Young trolls play it," was the answer. "You start by tying your ankles to your opponent's with a couple of cords about this long. Then you each take up a short cudgel—"

"Enough said," said the gray-haired man. "I'll imagine the rest."

Chirk said, in Krunzle's mind, *You go back in. Kill the orc. Cut your way through the rock.* The snake's tone left no room for argument. The thief readied lamp and sword once more and, signaling to the others that they should wait, stepped back into the crevice.

The orc warrior was hammering, his huge back and shoulder muscles bunched with effort. He paid no heed to the man creeping up behind. Krunzle paused to watch, no more than an arm's length from the orc's back, wary of some trick; orcs, after all, rarely offered an enemy such an opportunity. But then, these were no ordinary orcs.

Get to it, said the voice in his head, *or else.* The nature of the unspecified threat was made clear by a brief contraction of the bronze ring around Krunzle's throat. He growled, left with no option, and moved forward, sword arm extended. With his full weight behind it, the weapon's point touched the back of the orc's neck while the creature was in mid-swing of the hammer, and passed clean through, half-severing the head from the body. Blood spurted rhythmically from a bisected artery.

The orc shivered but did not even pause in completing the strike of hammer against chisel head. It shook again, then drew back the instrument for another blow.

Finish it.

Krunzle obeyed the voice in his head. He sawed the sword blade sideways, the magically enhanced edge cutting through the other half of the orc's neck as if through water. The head toppled from the stump of neck with one last gout of arterial blood. The orc's legs folded and he fell to kneel against the end of the crack, his tools striking the ground with a last, single ring of metal on stone. His head lay beside him, eyes open and staring up at Krunzle with a resentment that, in a moment, faded into the glaze of death.

The man looked up from that meeting of gazes to where the orc had been hammering near the top of the crevice. The glint of blue that had been there before was now the size of a robin's egg. A sensation like a jolt of cold energy erupted from the back of his mind, but he was already moving to sheathe his sword and reach for the tools. A moment later, even as Chirk said, *Yes!* in Krunzle's head, the thief was straddling the dead orc, driving hammer against chisel. Both were slippery-sticky with orc blood, but he paid no heed as he hammered and levered, hammered and levered, his arms extended to their full length over his head, cracking off chunks of the friable volcanic rock, the detritus striking his chest and shoulders, then falling to pile up on the floor and the corpse.

The patch of blue grew to the size of a Kersite silver piece, then as the chips flew it quickly grew to the size of Krunzle's balled fist, then to that of a saucer. At first he'd thought he was uncovering a gem of great size, but it soon became clear that "great" would have to be replaced by "gargantuan and then some." The more he chiseled, the greater the expanse of blue diamond became.

The barrier of rock separating the end of the crevice from the gem was about two hand-widths thick. As he cut away rock, the narrow space filled with light. From the diamond poured a cold, blue radiance that lit up his hands and arms, and dazzled his dark-adjusted eyes.

He paused for a moment, the better to see what he was about, and instantly felt a constriction about his neck. *Work!* said the voice in his head.

"I will," he said aloud. "I stopped only to see how best to go about it." The snake subsided, but the man was aware of a stir of tension in the place within him where Chirk was to be felt. "The body is in the way."

Brond's voice spoke from behind him. "Raimeau and I will drag it clear."

So intent had he been on his hammering, Krunzle had not heard them come up behind him. He squeezed against the wall of the crevice while they seized the dappled orc's headless carcass and pulled it rustling across the stone-strewn floor. The gray-haired man came back for the head, which he nonchalantly threw out into the tunnel.

Krunzle readdressed himself to the hole, but his hands were unused to the labor and began to tire. "We could use Skanderbrog in here," he said, "to widen the fissure."

"He is gone," said Raimeau. "He reminded us that he was with us only until the last orc fell."

"Let me," said Brond, reaching for the tools. "It is the kind of work we dwarves do best, after all."

Chirk made no objection, so Krunzle handed over the hammer and chisel. The dwarf could not reach as high as where the blue smoothness began, but he set to work below the spot with a dwarf's metronomic stroke. And soon a second source of blue light shone into the crevice. Brond paused and put his eye to it.

"Can you see anything?" said Raimeau, hovering over the bald one's shoulder.

"Nothing," said Brond. "It's too bright. It's like staring into a star."

Krunzle stooped and looked. He, too, saw nothing but a prismatic dazzlement, with no way to guess the size of the crystal into which he gazed. *The gem might be the size of a room,* he thought, *wealth beyond even my dreams.*

Fool, said Chirk. *Keep at it. We will not have much time.*

They took turns, the two men and the dwarf. First the two exposed regions became the ends of a narrow band, which they then extended to the floor of the crevice.

Then the band was gradually widened, starting at the top. Krunzle was working the upper segment when the voice spoke in his head again: *Wait!*

What? he said.

Put your hand against the surface.

The man did so.

Now, run your finger down. What do you feel?

Nothing. No, wait, what was that? His finger had found, just where the left side of the strip of gemstone disappeared into the rock, the edge of an indentation.

Clear it! said Chirk. *Quickly!*

Krunzle applied his chisel to the spot and in moments had uncovered a circular depression in the blue hardness. It was a little larger than the tip of his finger. When the snake told him to put his finger in and push, he did.

Something clicked and the smooth surface receded, as if it were a door that had swung inward on a silent hinge. "It's a door," he said. And beyond it was a hollow space of unknown size from out of which the blue light shone with even greater brilliance.

The gap it left, between the two sides where the edges of the crevice ended, was just large enough for Krunzle to push his head through and look around.

"It's a cavern," he said, twisting his head up and to the sides. "But I can't see how big it is because it must be completely lined with blue gems. And there has to be some source of light, because it's reflected from all sides. I keep waiting for my eyes to get used to the glare, but they don't. I can't see anything but blue brilliance."

"Let me at it," said Brond. He took the hammer and chisel, and for a while there was the steady *chink, chink* of his labor, while the light spilling from the widening crack grew ever brighter.

When Brond tired, Raimeau did not offer to take a turn. Instead, the gray-haired man was seated on the floor of the crevice, a piece of wood in one hand and a small knife in the other. He had cut one of the lathes into portions the length of his hand and was whittling at one of them. Krunzle could not see the use of what he was doing, but Chirk did not give him time to dwell on it. *Cut!* said the voice in the thief's head, and he took up the tools and got busy widening the base of the opening.

The volcanic rock was easier to cut than granite or marble, but it was still a time-consuming and painstaking process. Gradually, the hole grew. The thief pulled back. "I might be able to wriggle through," he said.

"If you can't," said Raimeau, looking up from whatever he was doing with the knife and wood, "I may."

Let him try, said Chirk.

"Be my guest," said Krunzle.

The thin man swept away the rubble of rock fragments and lay on his back. He stretched his arms through the gap, tested his shoulders against its width, bent his knees, and pushed and wiggled his way into the blue radiance. A moment later, he said, "I'm through," then his legs and feet followed the rest of him out of sight.

"Can you see anything?" Brond said.

"Oh, yes," came the answer. "Take a look for yourself." Through the gap came Raimeau's hand, holding a piece of the lathe he'd been working on. Two narrow slits had been cut lengthwise into the flat surface. "Look through it," he said, then offering another to Krunzle as Brond took the first, "and here's one for you."

The thief looked high while the dwarf looked low. Peering through the slitted wood canceled most of the glare. Now when he looked through the gap he saw shapes: on the far side of the space, columns of blue crystal stretched up from a floor of the same stuff, a series of broad steps leading up to a dais, on which stood a carved . . . "It's a throne room," Krunzle said.

"No," said Brond, "it can't be, buried in a mountain. I say it's a tomb for a king." He put down the wooden slit-goggles and took up the hammer and chisel again. "We must get through."

"Give me tools," said Raimeau. "I can work from this side."

There were tools scattered about in the tunnel, dropped by dying—or in some cases, already dead— orcs. Krunzle went to get them, with Chirk encouraging him to hurry. At the mouth of the crevice he found Gyllana, arms folded across her chest, staring into the narrow passageway, one foot tapping with impatience.

"When?" was all she said.

"Soon," was all he answered.

Moments later, he was hammering above Brond's head while the dwarf enlarged the lower part of the gap, and Raimeau gouged and cut away rock from the other side. Now the hole widened quickly, and it seemed only moments before the bald dwarf could put down his tools, turn himself sideways and scrape through the opening. Krunzle came right on his heels, then Gyllana.

"You are right," said Raimeau, looking about through his slit-goggles. "It is a tomb."

"But not for a dwarf," said Brond.

"Nor for a man," said Gyllana.

Krunzle said nothing. He had made his way to the throne and was running a hand over its carved back and arms. Even with the vision-aid Raimeau had fashioned, it was difficult to make out the intertwined shapes of the carvings; they seemed to flow into and through each other like a nest of amorous snakes. And they were all cut from blue gemstone—indeed, from *one* great blue diamond, he realized—and the throne, the steps, and the pillars were themselves only smaller parts of a single, truly immense stone from which, and within which, the entire chamber had been fashioned.

With the goggles, it was possible to tell that the source of light was coming from above. There must be a shaft reaching from the gem to the light of day, perhaps a mile or more above them in the cone of the volcano. And the shaft itself, he theorized, must be lined with light-catching and reflecting diamonds, in order to bring the radiance this far underground.

"These are no ordinary gems," he said. He had spoken aloud, though to himself, but an answer came from within: a disdainful clucking of tongue against teeth that no snake could ever have made, but it was followed by Chirk's voice saying, *Of course not, fool! Now, look around and find the sarcophagus!*

You know what this place is? the thief said.

Do as I say! There is no more time left for chatter!

A jolt of white-hot pain shot up the man's spine and down both legs. He went rigid for an interminable, agonized moment, until the snake let loose of his nerves. "All right," he said. "Where do I look?"

"What is the matter?" Raimeau was beside him.

"This," Krunzle said, indicating the metal coiled about his neck. "It lacks patience."

Chirk said, *Do you need another?*

No. To the thin man, Krunzle said, "He says there is a sarcophagus here, and wants it found."

They both put their goggles to their eyes and looked about. The chamber was deceptively large—even with the vision-aids to reduce the glare, it was difficult to see where floor met wall or wall met ceiling; distances seemed to grow or shrink as they looked across them.

"There is more than light playing tricks here," Raimeau said. "But there is something large on the other side of the chamber."

Chapter Fourteen
"Call It My Fate"

Krunzle and Raimeau made their way from the dais and throne across the glistening floor. Brond joined them. "You're right," he told the thin man. "If Skanderbrog were here I think his snout would be wrinkled all the way up his forehead and he'd be complaining about a stink of snake magic coming from every quarter."

"This does not look like a sarcophagus to me," Krunzle said. They had reached the object where it stood against the far wall and, at closer range through the anti-glare goggles, could make out its shape and size: an oblong that was waist-high to Krunzle, twice his width, and as deep as his forearm from elbow to wrist. "A cabinet," he said, running his hands over its surface. It too was carved with interpenetrating serpentine shapes, all of the same blue gemstone, and it too was one with the floor from which it rose.

His exploring fingers found a groove in the front, leading to a hole, just like the one that had opened the door into the chamber. He slipped a finger into the space, pressed, and felt something give. With a tiny click, the front of the cabinet opened on hinges of carved diamond. Krunzle stooped and looked inside. "Well, now," he said.

Inside were objects made not of diamond, but of pure gold. He reached in and lifted one, saw that it was a vessel of some kind, but empty; another was a beaker with a spout for pouring; and there was an assortment of plates and other vessels.

Raimeau squatted beside him and examined the cabinet's contents. "Not a king, then," he said, "A wizard."

"And still not a man nor a dwarf," said Brond. "See, there is script of some kind on some of the items, but like none I have ever seen."

Gyllana said something, then, but Krunzle did not hear it because he was distracted by another searing burst of pain that shot from coccyx to pate, followed by a voice that grated in his head: *The sarcophagus! Find it!*

He had dropped the glare-goggles when the agony struck. Now, cursing, he bent and picked up the piece of wood, and as he did so, he noticed a discrepancy. "There is a smudge here," he said, pointing to the floor.

Raimeau joined him and peered through his own vision-aid. "No, not a smudge. There is something below the floor. You can just see it through the diamond."

There will be a lock, said Chirk. *Find it!*

Krunzle knelt, and felt with fingertips above the indistinct dark shape he could see through the gemstone floor. His spine still glowed with a residual ache from the pain Chirk had dealt him, and he thought about revenge, until another jolt made him yelp. After that, he concentrated his mind on the task at hand.

The others had joined him, quartering the floor on their hands and knees, and it was Gyllana who said, "Here! I have it!" Her finger touched a spot on the floor—a spot like any other to the thief's eyes, until he slid his finger next to hers and felt, not a depression, but a small piece of gem that slid aside when he pressed it in the right direction. Below was a hole.

Step back! the snake ordered. *Tell them!*

The man did as he was told. Then Chirk ordered him to inspect the hole, by eye and by touch, and he knew that the snake was experiencing the same sensations, transferred to it through his own sensorium. At last, he heard a grunt in his mind, and Chirk said, *Good, we are in time. It has not yet begun to stir.*

What hasn't? Krunzle asked inwardly. *What is it?* But he received no answer. After a moment, he said, *Now what do you want me to do?* Again, he heard no response, but he had by now enough experience hosting the creature in his mind that he could sense some of its moods. Chirk was waiting.

Gyllana had put her finger to the hidden hole. "I think I know what's in there," she said.

If she tries to open it, Chirk said to Krunzle, *kill her. The same goes for any of them.*

Krunzle relayed the information to the others. Gyllana and Brond reacted as their natures dictated, both of them showing more affront than fear. Chirk spoke in Krunzle's mind again, and again the man passed on the information received: "Chirk says that to interfere with the personage in the tomb would bring an instant and horrific death. Worse, it would unleash widespread destruction. We should look for the talisman."

Brond weighed this news and put a hand on Gyllana's arm when she expressed a disregard for the reliability of the messenger. "The snake knew about the lock. It may well know about what's under the floor."

Raimeau clucked his tongue against his teeth thoughtfully, then crawled closer to where the thief knelt above the hidden sarcophagus. Holding his slit-goggles to his eyes, the thin man bent his head to examine the bronze snake closely and from several angles. "Ah," he said, settling back on his heels.

"Ah?" said Krunzle. "What kind of 'ah' was that?"

"I have a hypothesis."

Gyllana had gone over to the cabinet of gold objects. She held up the golden beaker, examined it for a moment, then replaced it and looked at something she held concealed in her other hand. Then she held the hidden object out where they could all see it. "Does your scheme include this?"

In the glare it was difficult to see what dangled from her fingers, even with the anti-glare goggles. Brond spoke for them all: "What is that?"

"The item we were supposed to be looking for," she said, "before we were distracted by diamonds and . . ."—she fluttered her other hand—"snake magic."

Krunzle stood up and went to her, his anti-glare device before his eyes. Hanging from her fingertips on a thread of braided gold was what appeared to be a pendant of some dark metal, shaped like a flower rising from a coiled basket—a flower whose head was slit into several sharp petals. He found it hard to focus on the object because of the surrounding glare.

"It was under the orc's body," she said. "It must have been hung around his neck and you didn't notice when you cut off his head." She held it higher. "Look."

Krunzle peered closer. The thing swung in a circle at the end of its plaited thread, like a diviner's bead circling over a map. The longer she held it, the faster it spun. She reached with her other hand and stopped it. "Here," she said, pointing with one fingertip to a line of sinuous characters that ran in a raised relief along the back of the pendant. "What does that look like?"

Krunzle looked and saw, but it was Raimeau who answered. "That is the same script as is graven into the things in the cabinet."

"And the shape of the thing," the woman said, "is it one of those creatures you talked about, the ones with bodies like snakes and heads like lilies?"

"I think it must be," said the thin man.

"Indeed," said Brond. "So this is the object that led Wolsh Berbackian and the orcs—and after them, all of us—to this chamber." The bald dwarf looked around. "The question is: why?"

Chirk? Krunzle tried again, but no answer came from the snake in his mind. He was thrown back onto his own powers of deduction. "I have been thinking," he said, "that Thang-Sha, the wizard who put this snake around my neck, is behind all of this."

"That would make him an exceptionally powerful wizard," said Raimeau.

"What does your snake say?" said Gyllana.

"Nothing," said the thief. "Now that it is assured that the sarcophagus is untouched, it seems to have lost interest. I suspect that it is waiting for something to happen." Inwardly, he said, *Is that the way it is, Chirk?* but again he received no answer.

"I am concerned about something," said Raimeau. "What happened to Berbackian? Something sucked the life out of him. Was it the talisman?"

Gyllana looked sharply at the object in her hand and quickly placed it on top of the cabinet. "I want to leave this place," she said.

"In one way or another, we have all been led here by dreams and magic," said Raimeau. "In Berbackian's case, the lure was fatal. I would like to study the place, and especially the creature entombed below the floor, but I'm beginning to think that we should leave before what happened to Berbackian happens to the rest of us."

"Yes," said the dwarf. "I will send a guard and some of my best minds to investigate."

"I agree," said Krunzle, "though I think we should take the gold with us. For safekeeping," he added, when the suggestion brought him hard looks from the other three. Meanwhile, he asked the snake, *Chirk, may we leave now?*

"I don't think so," was the answer, but it came aloud and they all heard it. It was a new voice that spoke from the side of the chamber where stood the dais and the throne, a subtle voice that the thief had heard on one other occasion.

The four of them turned toward the sound and saw, seated upon the throne, a diminutive figure whose face was as wrinkled as a winter crabapple, and whose long, sparse whiskers touched a robe of silk figured in arcane designs and Tien characters.

"Because," Thang-Sha continued, "we've only just begun."

The wizard moved one hand in a sharp gesture then struck the heels of both palms together while uttering a single syllable. The door of the chamber swung silently shut and they all heard a discreet *click* as it locked.

"Now," said the wizard, "we may begin."

"*You* may begin," said Brond, striding to the base of the steps, his piece of slitted wood across his eyes, "by giving an account of yourself. You are within the territory of the Regulate of Grimsburrow, and I am—"

Thang-Sha made another complex gesture and muttered something. Brond's voice disappeared, and the dwarf choked and put a hand to his throat as he tried to speak again.

"The harder you try," said the wizard, "the more it will hurt."

"Leave him be!" said Gyllana, stepping forward. "My father will hear of this, and you can be assured—"

The wizard's hands made the same motions and the woman was silenced. "This will all go much more smoothly," he said, "if you keep quiet and do as you are told. Is that clear?"

Four heads nodded. The spellcaster made another gesture and said, "Your voices are restored. But only on sufferance." He pointed at Gyllana, then to the cabinet. "Bring me the finder."

She crossed the room and retrieved the talisman. Thang-Sha would not take it directly from her, but produced a glass rod from within his robe and bade her slip the talisman's thong over it. He brought it close to his face, studying the design on one side and the script on the other. A thin smile of satisfaction played around his lips, then he set both objects on the floor beside the throne. "And Berbackian?" he said.

Raimeau gestured with a thumb toward the door. "Dead and dried as last year's corn husk."

The wizard nodded as if this news confirmed his expectations. His eyes went to the floor. "Did he make it inside?"

"No," said the thin man.

That news caused Thang-Sha to stroke the half-dozen long whiskers that sprouted from his chin. His small, dark eyes went to the floor. "So he did not open the tomb?"

"None of us did."

"Good." The wizard said nothing more, but sat with his chin in his hand and regarded the dark shape beneath the floor of brilliant gemstone. After a while he said, "Good," again.

Chirk, Krunzle thought, *what is going on?*

The snake did not answer. Instead, the question drew Thang-Sha's gaze to the thief. "Struck up a relationship, have you?" the wizard said.

"I would not object to ending it," said Krunzle, "now that I have done what you wanted."

"Your mission," said the wizard, "was to recover that"—he indicated the talisman—"and return it and the daughter to Ippolite Eponion."

"That," said the thief, "was Eponion's understanding of the task. I don't think it was yours."

The wizened face rearranged its wrinkles into a smile that revealed small, yellow teeth. "You are more perceptive than I took you for," said Thang-Sha.

"So may I be relieved of the neckpiece and allowed to leave?"

"No. I require an assistant." The spellcaster rose from the throne and stepped down to the floor, his eyes on the dark shape faintly visible through the diamond. "You others, go and sit on the steps. I want no distractions."

"Raimeau, here," said Krunzle, indicating the gray-haired man, "is knowledgeable in many disciplines. He would make you a better assistant. I feel myself to be in the way, and would be pleased to withdraw."

Thang-Sha sent the thief an eloquent look and raised one finger—a symbol incised into its lacquered fingernail glowed a deep red. Krunzle hurried to the wizard's side and said, "I am at your service."

From the folds of his robe, Thang-Sha drew out a black bag, which the thief thought resembled closely the one from which he had originally produced

Krunzle's boots and sword and Chirk. The wizard undid the cord that closed the sack's neck and reached in, bringing out a rod of what appeared to be gold, as thick as two fingers. The rod's length, as he drew it out, was far greater than the depth of the bag; by the time it was all out, it was a golden pole. He handed it to Krunzle and said, "Hold that," then reached in and brought out another, then still one more, passing each to the thief. Finally, he drew out a large, conical piece of gold whose base was pierced by three holes.

Working quickly, with the thief's assistance, the wizard fitted one end of each of the poles into one of the holes, creating a tripod. This he erected over the smudge beneath the floor, adjusting it until it was positioned to his satisfaction. Then he brought a golden cord from the bag and attached it to a hook in the base of the cone.

"The finder," he said to Krunzle.

"The what?"

"The thing,"—his fingers brusquely indicated the talisman—"that I hung from the glass rod. And you'd be wise not to let your flesh come into contact with it now."

The thief retrieved the object, being careful not to touch it, and when instructed, held it so that Thang-Sha could contrive to tie it to the golden cord without letting his flesh encounter the dark metal.

"Good," said the wizard. He stepped back and regarded the object, which had begun to spin of its own accord. As they watched, it rotated faster and faster. Now the wizard took a tube of what appeared to be carved ivory from his bag. He studied the thing he had called "the finder" through the tube from several angles. "Very good," he said.

Krunzle was aware of a sense of expectation, not just from the wizard, but from the entity that he had carried about with him since the night in the Kalistocrat's mansion. "What is about to happen?" he said.

Thang-Sha put down the ivory spyglass and turned on him an expression that mingled unrestrained glee with boundless cruelty. "For me," said the spellcaster, "something wonderful and long sought after. For you . . ."—his gaze slid over all of them—"some necessary sacrifice."

The bald dwarf was first to his feet, reaching for the black-headed mace at his belt. But Thang-Sha gestured with a flick of his bony fingers and spat two syllables. Brond stopped and stood where he was.

Thang-Sha said, "Release the weapon and sit down. You two, also." The mace fell with a clang from the dwarf's nerveless grip, and the dwarf staggered back to sprawl across the steps. Krunzle could see him struggle to move, but the wizard's incantation had robbed the Noble Head of all his strength.

Raimeau and Gyllana had also made to rise, but never even got their feet properly under them before their limbs lost all vigor. They sat on the steps like puppets whose strings have been cut.

"Izmar's Directed Thralldom," said the wizard. "A most useful spell, though of only intermediate duration. Still, it will last long enough for today's purposes."

Krunzle had made no move. The wizard looked him over and said, "Wise. You will, at least, outlive them."

"You need no spell to constrain me," said the thief. "I am fond of existence and would like to continue it."

The wizard smiled. "Besides," he said, "there is still Chirk." He spoke to the snake. "Keep the man obedient to my every command," he said.

At the back of Krunzle's mind, the thief sensed something like a confirmatory grunt. The snake also constricted the man's neck for a worrying moment, a small flexing that Thang-Sha apparently perceived, for he nodded in satisfaction and returned to his work.

Krunzle felt a brief sense of warm contentment at the place where his thoughts and the snake's interwove. *You truly are your master's creature,* the thief said, inwardly, *aren't you?*

Thang-Sha looked up. "Do not be harsh to Chirk," he said. "I told you, his loyalty is unshakeable. He has been mine since I found him in the sorcerers' bazaar at Sothis, many years ago." He resumed inspecting the talisman and its supports through the ivory tube, then after a while said, "All seems as it should."

He returned to the black bag he had left by the steps and drew from it a small, thick book bound in age-cracked leather. He sat on the topmost step and opened the tome, flicked through a few pages, then became immersed in what he was reading.

Chirk, Krunzle said, *you said that disturbing the contents of the tomb would bring widespread destruction. Yet it seems that is what your master intends.*

The snake made no reply, but Thang-Sha looked up from his reading, placing a finger to mark where he had left off. "It said that? I applaud its perspicacity. But I suppose even a simple being like Chirk can sense the power inherent in the being beneath our feet." He went back to his reading, then broke off after a few more lines. "By the way, do not think to suborn Chirk against me. It is mine."

"I was only seeking to understand," said Krunzle.

"No, you were seeking advantage," said the wizard. "But since you will be the only audience for the most consequential act of the age, I will tell you what is to happen."

He set down the book and rose, coming to stand near the tripod and the rapidly spinning object suspended from it. "Beneath us is an entity of vast though as yet ill-defined power. It is left over from a bygone age, from long before the gods created humankind, from before dwarves and orcs and all the modern world's panoply.

"No one, not even I, knows the entity's true nature. It may have been a great wonder-worker of its kind. It may even have been a kind of god. What is known is that it commanded immense powers—old magic, deep-earth magic, the dark primeval stuff whose spells and incantations no human voice could ever speak."

"Then what use are such powers to you?" Krunzle said. He idled closer to the tripod and its small, spinning burden, peering at the latter through his slit-goggles.

"The spells themselves?" said Thang-Sha. "Useless. But the power behind the spells, the entity's great will, remains, still attached to its earthly remains."

Thang-Sha pointed at the spinning talisman. "And this object is connected to its will, so that power passes between them. Exactly how, I need to study further. But I do know that it casts the talisman out into the world, like a fisherman tossing a baited hook, then reels in whatever takes the bait. It brings the catch as close as possible, then drains them of their life force. Thus it lives, after a fashion."

"We found Berbackian, drained of all his substance."

"Again," said Thang-Sha, "I find you more knowledgeable than I expect. I may keep you and see what use I can make of you." He gave the thief a considering look. "Of course, I would have to modify you, to keep you tractable."

"I prefer my present personality," said Krunzle. "It is my life's work."

The wizard's expression promised little. "We shall see. Remove your sword and scabbard and put them behind the throne." When the thief had done so, Thang-Sha said, "Now, back to my preparations."

"One other question," said the thief. "The entity, whatever it was, called Berbackian to it. But what about the rest of us? And the orcs?"

Thang-Sha's face showed modesty clashing with pride; the latter won. "The orcs were my doing," he said. He offered Krunzle the ivory spyglass and said, "Look through that."

The man took the tube and put it to one eye, closing the other. Immediately the blue glare in the chamber faded to a mild background glow. His three traveling companions, seated to one side against the wall, were revealed to be tightly wound about with what appeared to be smoke-gray ropes. Thang-Sha himself was much changed in appearance—taller, smoother of complexion, and far more imposing—so that Krunzle realized that his wizened, diminutive aspect was merely a facade.

But the thing that drew the thief's attention was the tripod and the object hanging from it—or, rather, what passed between the suspended, spinning talisman and the floor beneath it: a column of multicolored light, as thick as a strong man's wrist, up and down whose length flashed a constant sparking, surging flow of bright energy.

Krunzle took his eye from the ivory tube and looked through the glare-suppressor: nothing. He looked again through the spyglass and saw saffron and alizarin crimson alternating with azure, silver transmuting to gold then evolving into purest white. "What is it?" he said.

"Power," said Thang-Sha, "purest power. The undiluted, sheer force of will of an entity to which space, time, energy, matter, and existence itself were once as mutable as clay in a potter's hands.

"The connection between the talisman and the entity in the tomb is constant. It grows in strength as the talisman brings its catch closer to this chamber. Once I knew where the talisman was, by scrying the whereabouts of Wolsh Berbackian, I was able to isolate the frequency of that connection—think of it as the note produced when a taut string vibrates—and once I had identified it, I could adapt some of its power to my own purposes."

The wizard spread his arms. "With such power, I summoned a legion of orcs to the environs of Mount Sinatuk, crushed their primitive minds and made them my slaves." He turned and smiled bleakly at the Noble Head. "I could not let your dwarves prevent the carrier of the talisman from reaching the heart of the mountain."

"But what of them?" said Krunzle. "And, for that matter, me? Three of us were drawn here by dreams: me of wealth abounding, Brond of reviving his nation, Raimeau of performing some great deed."

Thang-Sha shrugged and recovered the spyglass. "Not my doing," he said putting the tube to his eye and studying again the conduit of power. "Our friend down there"—he indicated the shadow beneath the floor—"reaches out to dreamers. Some of them respond. It is like a fisherman seeding the waters with blood and ordure to draw fish to where his lure awaits them. One will strike at the bait and be pulled in; the rest will thrash and trouble the sea, darting about aimlessly under the spur of unrequited appetite."

Krunzle felt a coldness descend upon him. "All my dreams, the desires that have drawn me through this life, they are nothing more than chum broadcast by some ancient creature that seeks souls to devour? To keep itself in half-life?" He looked over at the three prisoners. A terrible pain showed in the thin face of Raimeau; an even worse suffering had dulled the eyes of the dwarf. Only Gyllana seemed unaffected—but then the thief remembered that the dream that had drawn her here was not hers, but Berbackian's.

"It is a harsh world," said Thang-Sha. He tucked the ivory tube away in his robe. "Now, I believe the interflux between the talisman and its owner is nearing its maximum potency. Having fed, it will seek to cast its lure back into the world and begin once more the recling in."

The spellcaster went back to where he had left his black bag and began to rummage around in it. "I,"—he looked at the captives—"that is, we, will interrupt the flow, capture some of the energy, and store it in"—from out of the dark fabric he drew a globe of purest black—"this."

He flourished the stygian orb. It resembled, Krunzle thought, a great black pearl, except that it had no sheen, but was dull all over, like Brond's eyes, as he gazed inward at his life's dream debased. Thang-Sha carried it toward the tripod. At a small distance from the spinning talisman, he stooped and busied himself for a moment, and the thief saw that the black object had its own, smaller tripod of gold rods to support it. Thang-Sha set the globe on the floor, measured by eye the distance to the larger tripod, and made a slight adjustment.

Krunzle would have liked to examine the black orb through the spyglass. It seemed to him that the moment it had come out of the wizard's bag, the brilliance in the diamond chamber had dimmed—and that it still continued to dim further. He took the slit-goggles from his eyes and, though the space around him remained preternaturally bright, he was not blinded as before. The black globe must be absorbing some of the light.

Thang-Sha, finished with setting the object in place, had gone over to consider the three captives, stroking his sparse whiskers. "You'll do to start," he said to Brond, tapping the dwarf on the shoulder. "Arise and follow."

The hairless face showed no resistance, only brute despair, as the wizard guided Brond to the black orb. He ordered the dwarf to lie with his feet toward, and almost touching, the globe; his head was a short distance from the many-colored column of light that stretched from the diamond floor to the spinning talisman.

"Scooch a little this way," said Thang-Sha. The dwarf wriggled his shoulders and pushed with his heels to bring himself fractionally closer to the vertical stream of colors. "Excellent. We are ready." He backed away from the apparatus and pushed Krunzle farther toward the dais with a back-extended hand.

"Now," Thang-Sha said to the enthralled Noble Head, "reach out with one hand above your head."

A tear rolled from the corner of one eye as the dwarf did as he was ordered. His hand neared the colored stream and Krunzle saw a subtle change in the flow of energy: the column showed more red and yellow, while the blues and greens diminished. The thief had an impression that he was seeing a representation of mounting anger.

Then Brond's fingertips touched the stream. Two things happened: First the flow of colors was partly diverted, the blue and green continuing from the floor to the spinning talisman. Then a portion branched off to envelop the bald dwarf's body in a cocoon of crimson and saffron, from his fingertip to the soles of his boots. After a moment came a third effect: from Brond's feet to the orb leapt what Krunzle could only think of as a spark of pure black energy that crackled and flashed for several heartbeats. Simultaneously, the dwarf's whole body juddered and shook within its sheath of angry colors, his spine bent like a bow so that he touched the diamond floor only at the crown of his head and where his heels beat a vibrating tattoo on the unyielding surface.

Abruptly, it was over. The crackle became a hiss, then ceased altogether. The red and yellow cocoon of light winked out of existence. The flow of colors from the tomb to the talisman resumed its previous appearance. And in the place of the Noble Head of the Regulate of Grimsburrow the thief saw a smoking mass of black stuff, pocked and fissured, roughly the shape of a dwarven corpse with an arm stretched above its head. From it rose a stench the like of which Krunzle had never known; it seemed to invade the innermost recesses of his skull, searing and grating his membranes. Pinching his nostrils shut and breathing through his mouth brought only partial relief.

Thang-Sha showed no discomfort. Instead he was standing over the stinking object, the ivory spyglass to his eye, examining the black orb. Krunzle thought the globe had grown larger.

"Good," said the wizard, after an inspection from several angles. "Very good." He turned to Krunzle and indicated the smoldering husk that had been Brond. "Sweep this out of the way. We will perform another drain."

Gagging, Krunzle approached the mess. He reached for what was left of the corpse's outthrust arm, but it fell to ashes in his hand, leaving a foul-smelling, tarry residue. Another gust of stench rose from the charred remains, and he used his unpolluted hand to close his nostrils again. He kicked the mess aside, regretting the smears of filth deposited on his buskins, until the space between the colored stream and the black orb was clear except for some irreducible stains.

Thang-Sha, meanwhile, had been withdrawing the globe to a greater distance. Krunzle thought that the spellslinger probably meant for Raimeau to be the next sacrificial conduit. His surmise was confirmed when the wizard straightened and pointed at the gray-haired man. "You," he said, "come."

Raimeau stood, his face a mask of helpless rage. At that moment, an idea came to Krunzle, softly, like a whisper stealing beneath the curtain that separated his consciousness from the rear reaches of his mind. "I think," he said, "the woman would be better. She is more . . ."—after a moment the word came—"corporeal."

It seemed impossible to the thief, but the outrage on Raimeau's face actually deepened, even as he walked toward where Thang-Sha waited. The thin man's show of anger was matched, however, by the expression Gyllana now wore, though hers was mixed with disgust.

The wizard, however, looked from Raimeau to Gyllana and said, "Hmm, I think you are right. It would make a difference." To the gray-haired man, he said, "Go back to where you were," and with a beckoning finger, turned to the woman and said, "you, come."

Raimeau did as he was bid, still possessed by impotent fury. Gyllana rose, and Krunzle saw fear fill her face even as her limbs carried her toward where Thang-Sha waited. The wizard stooped and nudged the black orb a little closer to the stream.

No words formed in Krunzle's mind. The connection between him and Chirk was now much subtler than that. He simply knew what to do and how to do it, and he knew that he must not think about it. He took a step toward Thang-Sha, at the same time stretching his hand out to his side. The short sword left its scabbard behind the throne and flew into his grasp and, again without pause to think, he swept the blade around in a sidewise swipe.

Thang-Sha, seeing the motion from the corner of his eye, turned toward the thief, his fingers forming the opening arrangement for some spell, his mouth actually uttering the opening syllable. But then the ensorcelled point—ensorcelled by his own powers—met the bulge at the front of the wizard's throat and passed right through it.

The second syllable was never uttered. Thang-Sha choked, one hand going to the gash where the sword had severed his vocal cords. But in his eyes the thief saw not shock, but cold determination. The spiderlike fingers of his free hand formed themselves a fist then opened flat. A finger began to curl into a particular position, but Krunzle did not need Chirk's prompting to bring the sword up and down again. In a moment, the wizard's hand fell limp to the diamond floor.

The thief raised the weapon to sever the spellcaster's bald head from his neck, but he heard Chirk's voice say, *No! Bind him.*

The thief used the wizard's own belt to confine his arms to his sides, then lowered him to the floor. The stump of Thang-Sha's wrist had stopped bleeding, as had the slit in the front of his throat, which argued for the spellcaster still possessing usable powers.

We should make sure of him, Krunzle thought.

Soon enough.

The internal exchange brought Thang-Sha's head around, and the thief was glad to discover that the wizard could not kill with a mere look, else his life would certainly be fleeing his body.

He feels betrayed, Krunzle said.

His feelings do not concern me.

Meanwhile, Gyllana and Raimeau remained under the wizard's control. The thin man sat where he had been and the woman, having crossed the floor as bidden, stood beside her recumbent master. Both wore expressions of shock, but Gyllana's, as she looked down at the wounded wizard, was giving way to an obvious desire to do Thang-Sha harm.

What now? Krunzle asked the snake.

His bag.

The thief went to where the sack lay on the seat of the throne, opened it. A deep chill emanated from within it.

Say these words, Chirk said, and planted a string of sounds in the man's mind. Krunzle dutifully repeated them, feeling as he did so a strange rushing sensation from his feet to his throat, as if a great wind had passed through him. He shivered.

Your first spell? Chirk said.

Indeed.

You did well, then. The bag's defenses are annulled. Reach in and think about this: an image formed in Krunzle's mind, of a green jewel.

He remembered it from the night in Eponion's house. As the image became clear in his mind, he felt a cool presence in his hand. He withdrew it from the bag and saw that he held the emerald that had sealed Chirk's grip upon its own tail.

Touch it to me, said the snake. *Anywhere will do.*

From the floor, Thang-Sha attempted a sound, but could produce only a hiss of air through the slit in his throat. The noise did not distract Krunzle, who touched the jewel to the snake's metal skin. A sensation like pins and needles went through the thief's fingertips as the two substances met, and the jewel seemed to change shape and substance for a moment, as if he held not a gem but some great animal's eye—then he realized that, for the first time in days, his throat was unencumbered by a torc of bronze.

Chapter Fifteen
Chirk Unchained

He expected to hear a clang as the snake fell to the floor, but he did not. When he turned, he saw, standing behind him, a willowy, gray-skinned form that resembled nothing so much as a man interrupted in the process of transforming into a snake, or vice versa, clad in a loose garment of woven, shimmering gold. The snake-being's eyes, cool and dark as a subterranean pool, were level with his own. "Chirk?" Krunzle said.

The lipless mouth was ill suited to make a smile, but he heard a trace of amusement in the voice—deeper than the one he'd heard in his head—as it said, "You may call me that, if you wish, but it was never my name. You do not tell creatures like that,"—he indicated the bound spellcaster—"your name. It gives them power over you."

"He had power over you," said the thief. "You did his bidding."

"The jewel held the power," said the snake-being, "and only as much as I had given it."

"I don't understand."

"You have no need to." The being Krunzle had called Chirk bent itself in a curve and lowered its face to study

Thang-Sha. The wizard was struggling against the belt that confined him, while one hand attempted some magical mischief. Chirk reached into the man's open robe and retrieved the ivory spyglass, transferring it to his own garment. Then he gestured with his own sinuous limbs and hissed something complicated. The cincture around the bound man grew to become a cummerbund, then a sheath, then a long, tight tube of leather that confined Thang-Sha from throat to ankle.

"Still," said Krunzle, "I would like to know what I have been conscripted into." He paused to regard the still-struggling wizard, whose face was contorted with frustrated intent, and the still-paralyzed Raimeau and Gyllana. "And whether it is yet over."

Chirk glanced over at the man and the woman. "I could break the spell," it said, "but it would pose some risk to your companions. In any case, it will lapse in a short while,"—the black eyes glanced at Thang-Sha— "through its own internal dynamics."

It brought out the spyglass and examined the black orb, the stream of many-colored energies, the floor, and lastly, Thang-Sha himself. The wizard mouthed silent curses, to which the snake-being apparently saw no need to respond. Finished with his inspection, Chirk hissed in what Krunzle took for irritation, though for all he knew, it could have been gay laughter.

A moment later he decided the sound had expressed worse than irritation, for the snake-being swung its scaly tail to thump Thang-Sha in his side. The thief saw it as the equivalent of a well-earned kick, Chirk's delicate lower limbs not being designed to deliver much punishment.

"Trouble?" he said.

"It could be worse," said Chirk. It looked again through the ivory tube. "At least it's not irreparable." It gave Thang-Sha another smack with the tail. "But it will cost me a deal of effort."

As the snake-being spoke, a tremor went through the chamber, accompanied by a sound like ice crystals cracking on a winter-frozen lake when the spring sun begins to spread its warmth. Krunzle saw that a change had occurred in the floor of the chamber—or, more properly, the roof of the sarcophagus. What had been clear blue gem was now clouded. And the stream of light between floor and talisman had stopped.

"I will have to work fast," said Chirk. "Thang-Sha's stupidity has given the entity its best chance in more than a millennium to break free of the stasis that constrains it." The snake-being looked at Krunzle. "You will help me."

"I thought a better use of my time would be to take the wizard's bag and go fill it with blue gems at the last lava tube," said the thief. "On my way out."

"The bag is not a bag," Chirk said. "It is a being from another dimension, enslaved by Thang-Sha and forced to keep his arcane impedimenta out of reach of the covetous. The moment it is released from servitude, which it soon will be, it will return to its own plane. If you have been outraging its dignity by stuffing diamonds into its maw, when it departs, it will probably do so with you in its gullet. Besides, unless I undo the harm Thang-Sha has done, you will be worse than devoured—by that." The snake-being pointed at the floor, where a network of cracks was now visible—and expanding—while the dark shape beneath seemed to be moving.

"I am eager to help," Krunzle said.

It turned out that all that was required was muscle—Chirk being somewhat gracile in construction, and Thang-Sha an uncooperative dead weight. Krunzle dragged the writhing leather tube and its contents over to where the cabinet of gold vessels stood. While he was doing so, the snake-being levered up and out two concealed leaves that fitted flush against the furnishing's upper surface, expanding it considerably. When the extensions were braced and firm, Krunzle was instructed to hoist the silently raging wizard onto what now more resembled an altar than a cupboard.

"Face-up," said Chirk, and when the man had rotated the bound wizard accordingly, the snake-being said, "and now bring the orb. But be careful to touch only its gold supports. If your flesh—even so much as a hair—comes into contact with the surface, the thing will take what you would call your soul."

Krunzle gingerly retrieved the object. The gold tripod that held it was icy cold, surprising him so much he almost dropped it. But he recovered and brought it to where the snake-being indicated.

"Now the talisman," Chirk said, "but touch only the filament from which it hangs." The thief remembered what had become of Wolsh Berbackian and was careful to keep the talisman at a distance until Chirk took it by the golden thread and held it above the bound spellcaster. Thang-Sha's face went several different colors before settling on rage-red. His breath hissed from the slit in his throat even as his lips formed powerless words. So much magic was based on the wielder's will, born of spirit which was expressed in breath.

Chirk paid him no heed. "Be ready to hold up the orb," it told Krunzle.

The thief knelt and prepared to grip the ice-cold, golden rods beneath the black globe. Above his head, Chirk elevated the talisman and whispered a long susurration of sibilant sounds, a language that Krunzle had never heard, though he would wager its written form was the sinuous script that graced the talisman and the gold vessels beneath the altar.

"Pick up the orb and position it between the altar and the place where the colored stream came from," Chirk ordered, "but do not let your body block the path." When the man had done as bidden, Chirk voiced another string of hisses and placed the talisman on the bare forehead of Thang-Sha. The wizard's eyes spoke volumes—each a fat-spined book filled with the direst maledictions—until the metal form of a flower-headed snake sank sizzling into his flesh—then went even deeper, into bone, and his mouth opened in a scream that would never be heard.

"Hold it still!" said Chirk, as a crackling burst of black energy leapt from the altar to the orb. The thrust of its power was so great that Krunzle was pushed sideways, his feet sliding against the diamond floor, toward where the roof of the sarcophagus was visibly cracking and something dark—something big and powerful— surged against the failing barrier.

The thief struggled and shoved, his hands turning to ice as he gripped the chill gold supports, to press the globe back toward where Chirk waited at the altar. He had a glimpse of Thang-Sha's body, vibrating in the leather sheath that held it, a hole shaped like a flower with a coiled stem in his brow, dark smoke boiling out from the braincase.

"Here!" called Chirk, one boneless-seeming finger pointing to the altar while his other arm thrust the remains of the wizard to the floor. Thang-Sha fell soundlessly to the polished surface and broke into fragments of fuming black ash that spilled from both ends of the leather cylinder that had confined him. The talisman bounced free of the charred dust that had been his skull, its gold thread incongruously still gleaming.

"Here!" Chirk said again, and added a string of sibilants while performing a complexity of motion involving head, upper limbs, and tail.

Suddenly, Krunzle found the struggle against the orb's tombward pressure easing. He lifted the globe high and placed it, still on its gold tripod, in the center of the altar.

Raimeau and Gyllana had risen to their feet. Chirk, hands busy with golden vessels taken from shelves beneath the altar, said to Krunzle, "Get them over here, away from the tomb."

The thief beckoned the two toward where he stood, waving them away from the line between the orb and the sarcophagus. The snake-being, meanwhile, reached down and retrieved the talisman from the wizard's ashes, placed it into a shallow bowl of gold atop the altar, and applied a golden pestle to it. Though Chirk's supple limbs clearly had little strength in them, the talisman fell apart as if it were of no more solidity than the stuff that used to be Thang-Sha, rapidly becoming a gray powder.

Now the snake-being lifted a stoppered gold beaker from the shelves beneath the altar, removed its plug, and poured its contents into the talisman's dust. Krunzle saw nothing come from the container, but when Chirk stirred the gray stuff, it now behaved as a slurry. Throughout the work, Chirk kept up a monotonous chanting, sounds almost too soft for the thief to hear, and in a hiss-and-shush language he could not decipher.

Krunzle could tell, by the motion of the stirring pestle, that the mixture in the bowl had thickened. Chirk set down the pestle and sought among the altar's contents for another implement, coming up with a long-handled, shallow ladle. It elevated this in both hands and began another chant.

A sharp *crack!* spun the thief around. He had been aware of a continuous crackling from the direction of the tomb. Now he saw that where the diamond had been clouded, a long, deep, and jagged crack had appeared in the floor. It widened even as he looked, and something dark stirred in its depths.

Chirk hissed a string of syllables. The snake-being dipped the ladle into the shallow bowl and scooped up some of the gray goo. Carefully, chanting again, it dripped the stuff onto the top of the orb. As it touched the matte black surface the slurry seemed to congeal, dripping more and more slowly down and around the sides of the globe. Chirk ladled out more, then shaped the stuff into an even coating, until finally all that was left uncovered was the portion of the globe that nestled in the supporting tripod.

Now came another sound like breaking bones. Krunzle saw that the first crack in the sarcophagus's roof had been joined and intersected by another. They both widened. A segment of the broken diamond flooring heaved up. Something black, something that resembled an unholy hybrid of a flower's petal and a snake's head, was moving in the expanding gap.

"Quick!" said Chirk, indicating the now gray-coated orb. "It is breaking free! Turn the orb so I can do the remainder!"

Krunzle recoiled. "You said only by the supports!"

"It is safe now. But the rite must be completed before—"

The floor heaved now, and the thing that had been visible in the crack reared itself knee-high into the chamber. More of it was visible just below.

"Hurry!" said Chirk, indicating the gray orb on the altar.

But the thief hesitated, and the moment was long enough for the floor to split beneath him with a groan and a crack like a glacier calving. The diamond slid out from under him and he fell to one knee, with one foot dangling into the crevice. An acid stench rose about him, scouring out the inner passages of his skull. He fought to breathe.

Raimeau moved. The gray-haired man was suddenly at Krunzle's side. He stooped and seized the thief's collar, and with one great heave of his slim body, hoisted him out of the crack and flung him bodily toward the chamber wall. His motion brought him around to face the altar, and without hesitation, as if he had rehearsed it all in his mind, he reached and scooped up the covered globe in both hands and held it so that its uncoated base was toward the snake-being.

With deliberate speed, Chirk upended the ladle and poured the last of the gray slurry over the exposed black. Krunzle, watching from where he had landed, heard a hiss and saw the thin man abruptly stiffen. The thing from the tomb had risen higher, and its lily-like head had reared back, then snapped forward. Now a white smoke erupted from Raimeau's back, which was out of the thief's line of sight. He saw the former mine slave grimace and grit his teeth as he must have when the lash came down in the iron mines.

But, resolute, Raimeau held the globe as best he could in shaking arms, until whatever Chirk had set out to do was accomplished. Then the snake-being reached and took the coated object, and the thin man fell forward and crawled away from the cracked tomb, his jaw clenched against pain. Lines of smoking heat crisscrossed the cloth across Raimeau's back, and Krunzle leapt forward to strip the tunic from him. It stank of burning cloth and flesh, overlaid by an acrid reek of acid that brought a surge of bile back into the thief's throat. Quickly, he used the bunched cloth to wipe away the stuff that was still eating into Raimeau's scarred back.

The lily-head was now forcing its bulk out of the broken tomb. It reared almost to chest height now, but Krunzle suspected that he was seeing only the neck and head of the creature. A thicker, heavier mass was visible through the cracked floor. Its strange split head went back then darted forward, shooting a jet of colorless acid at Chirk. But the snake-being held the coated globe so as to intercept its spew, which dripped harmlessly to the broken floor.

The lily-head reared back again, but Chirk had already lifted the dripping globe high. With an unintelligible shout, the snake-being flung the coated orb into the center of the spread petals, into the maw of the creature from the tomb. The fleshy, petal-like palps closed reflexively around the missile, and as they did so, Chirk turned to the three humans and said, "Get down!"

Krunzle dropped to the floor, pulling Raimeau down beside him—or, if the truth must be told, between him and the thing risen from the tomb. He saw Chirk take a cylinder of gold from beneath the altar and rub it swiftly, softly muttering all the while. A line of sinuous characters entwined about the rod glowed the same color as the blue of the chamber, and a sound like a swarm of bees came suddenly from everywhere.

The petals were peeling back from the gray-coated orb, and the lily-head's sinewy body was rearing up as if to spit the globe back at the snake-being. But Chirk held aloft the golden rod then brought it down like a whip to point directly at the lily-head. A stream of coruscating white light, thick as a man's forearm, sprang from the end of the rod and struck against the orb in the lily-head's maw. For a second, then another, the light spattered, sparking, against the gray coating. Then the hardened shell split apart, spraying gray shards in all directions, and the matte black surface of the object beneath was exposed once more to view.

And to the touch of the creature rising from the tomb. The same lightless energy that had passed as a spark from Brond's body to the orb now blossomed around the flower-shaped head, forming a thick, roiling cloud of non-light. The snakelike body shuddered and convulsed, then the cloud rolled down the creature's body—and where it had been, nothing remained. The dense vapor followed the line of the creature's flesh down through the cracks in the roof of the sarcophagus, leaving behind only a stench.

Krunzle rose to his feet. Beside him, Raimeau and Gyllana did likewise. Chirk was standing over the broken floor looking down into the tomb beneath. The thief came to stand beside him, saw only a swirling mess of gray ash through the crack. "Is it finished?" he said.

The snake-being turned its head to look down on him. "Until the next time some addle-pated nibblewit thinks he can use the power that is confined here."

Chirk shook its head in a gesture whose fluid grace did not disguise its weariness. "I grow tired of doing this."

Raimeau, despite his obvious pain, sought answers. "What are you?" he said to Chirk. "What has happened here?"

The snake-being shrugged its almost nonexistent shoulders. "Nothing I can explain to you in this clumsy speech. Yet if I spoke to you in my people's way, you would hear my voice thundering in your head, and it would almost certainly drive you mad. So the short answer to your question is: nothing you need to know. Say that you fell into another's drama. And be thankful you are not exiting it as Brond did."

"But it will happen again?" said Raimeau.

"It will take a thousand years or more for—" Chirk interrupted itself, then went on. "I won't speak its name." It gestured toward the cracked floor, which was now reconstituting itself. "Its force of will will eventually reconstitute itself. Then it will reach out once more for those whose venality makes them vulnerable. One of them will find a way to the tomb and, as has happened before, some hubristic fool like Thang-Sha may try to make use of him." It hissed a sigh. "And then I will have to come back from wherever I lie dreaming and stop it again."

"Why you?" said Krunzle.

"It is a long story, full of things you would not understand. Call it my fate, laid upon me by one more powerful even than I. And be glad that yours is no longer tied to it." Chirk's lipless mouth formed something like a smile. "You are free now."

The snake-being turned from them and began gathering up the vessels and implements it had used in the process of reconfining the lily-head. It paused to recover a gold salver that had somehow found its way into Krunzle's shirt, giving the thief a pointed look. Then it closed up the altar and sealed the doors.

"You had best be on your way," it said to the three humans. "The tomb knows it must heal itself, and has already begun. The whole mountain will be affected. The dwarves' tunnel will not likely endure. I will leave by other means."

Apparently, Chirk's kind were not given to long, sentimental goodbyes, Krunzle thought. But, then, neither was he. He took note of Chirk's warning and rapidly recovered his sword and oil lamp, buckled on the former and relit the latter, and hurried out through the crevice to the tunnel, then followed it back the way he had come. He was aware of tremors in the rock behind and around him as he ran through the darkness, leaping over orc carcasses as he came to them.

He paused only in the lava tube whose semi-excavated walls were studded with uncut blue diamonds. He crossed it quickly via the trestle, whose shaking worried him. On the other side, a few stones the size of crab-apples stuck out from the wall. He was using the sword to pry them loose and had four good ones in his wallet when Raimeau and Gyllana caught up with him. The gray-haired man was weakened by his ordeal and the woman was helping him.

"Leave it," said Raimeau. "It's not worth dying for." The sounds of cracking and falling rock were growing louder, and the trestle shook alarmingly.

"No," said Gyllana to the thin man, "leave *him*. His greed will kill him, just like Berbackian's."

The comparison offended Krunzle. He left off trying to pry loose the last gem and offered Raimeau a shoulder to lean on, showing the woman a face that invited her to revise her opinion. She did not accept the offer, but thanked him for helping the burned man who had saved his life.

With the mountain groaning and shivering around them, and with rocks falling almost at their heels, they struggled up the long, dark tunnel until they reached the place where the dwarves' lighting resumed. Despite his protestations, they put Raimeau into the ore cart and pushed him up the gentle incline.

It was evening when they finally emerged from the tunnel onto the apron where the dwarven guards had died, dust billowing from the refilling space behind them. They found the dead neatly lined up on one side of the open space, and Skanderbrog seated on the log the orcs had used to shatter the great doors. The troll was disappointed to learn that the Noble Head of the Regulate would not be joining him.

"I thought it might be better if he went with me to get my sword," he said. "Do you think they will still honor his piece of paper?"

Raimeau said, "I'm sorry to say that, without Brond, the Regulate will soon fall apart. They're probably already squabbling right now." He shrugged. "Dwarves. What can you do?"

"If they don't make you a sword," said Gyllana, "I will have it done, in return for your escorting me home. The Kalistocrats of Kerse believe in rewarding good service."

"Excellent," said Krunzle, "so if I complete my mission and return you to your father, he will be generous?"

"He will pay you exactly the amount agreed," said the woman. "What was the negotiated fee?"

The thief bit his inner lip. "Never mind," he said.

Skanderbrog was sniffing at Raimeau's back. "Snake stuff," he said. "Wait here." He went down into the forest and they heard him rummaging in the undergrowth. Eventually, he returned, chewing something. He spat the contents of his mouth into his hands and said, "Bitterthorn leaves," then wadded the mush into a poultice that he applied to Raimeau's back. "Good for burns. My mother taught me."

The pulpy mass seemed to soothe the thin man's pain. "I bless your mother," he said.

"I was thinking . . ." Skanderbrog began.

"Unusual for a troll," Krunzle said.

The troll flicked one finger at the thief's chest. The impact knocked the man back two paces.

"I was saying," Skanderbrog went on, "that I've been thinking that living in the mountains, eating deer, and wrestling the occasional bear is a boring life, even for a troll king."

"And?" said Krunzle.

"And I thought I might team up with you two,"—he indicated the thief and the gray-haired man—"and see what lies down the road."

Raimeau's expression said he found the idea worth considering, but Krunzle said, "My plans are to give up the wandering life and open a rogues' academy, perhaps in Augustana or Ostenso. A troll, even an unusual one, would be of no more use than a bib on a boar. I am sorry."

Gyllana said, "How will you fund your academy?"

"With these," said the thief, holding up his wallet. He noticed that it felt curiously light. When he opened it, he found that the four excellent blue diamonds he had prised from the lava tube were gone. He looked about his feet in the gathering darkness.

"Our serpentine friend said the mountain would reconstitute itself," said Raimeau. "I suppose it has taken back what it considered its own."

"No diamonds," said Gyllana, as if to herself.

Krunzle had several things to say, none of them genteel. When he began to wind down, Raimeau said, "So, if you're finished, perhaps we should discuss Skanderbrog's kind offer. There must be all sorts of opportunities for two enterprising fellows and an exceptional troll."

Krunzle saw that his plans must change. But he had always prided himself on his adaptability, and now rose to the occasion. "We could start," he said, hoisting a thumb in the Kersite woman's direction, "by holding her for ransom."

About the Author

Hugh Matthews is a pen name of the science-fantasy author Matthew Hughes. His web page is at **archonate.com.**

Glossary

All Pathfinder Tales novels are set in the rich and vibrant world of the Pathfinder campaign setting. Below are explanations of a number of key terms used in this book. For more information on the world of Golarion and the strange monsters, people, and deities that make it their home, see the *Pathfinder Roleplaying Game Core Rulebook*, *The Inner Sea World Guide*, or any of the books in the Pathfinder Campaign Setting series, or visit **paizo.com**.

Absalom: Largest city in the Inner-Sea region.
Andoran: Democratic nation south of Druma.
Almas: Capital city of Andoran.
Aspodell Mountains: Mountain range to the southwest of Druma.
Augustana: Port city in Andoran known for its shipyards.
Avistan: Northern continent of the Inner Sea region, and the one on which Druma is situated.
Blackjacket: Slang term for a member of the Mercenary League.
Darklands: Extensive series of subterranean caverns crisscrossing much of the Inner Sea region, known to be inhabited by monsters.

Druma: Shortened name for the Kalistocracy of Druma, a nation built on the tenets of the Prophecies of Kalistrade, a pseudo-religion in which individuals view the accumulation of wealth as the highest possible goal.

Dwarves: Short, stocky humanoids who excel at physical labor, mining, and craftsmanship. Stalwart enemies of the orcs and other evil subterranean monsters.

Elves: Long-lived, beautiful humanoids who abandoned Golarion millennia ago and have only recently returned. Identifiable by their pointed ears, lithe bodies, and pupils so large their eyes appear to be one color.

Falcon's Hollow: Logging town in northern Andoran.

Five Kingdoms: The fabled original civilization of dwarves in the Five Kings Mountains, which have long since fallen apart as any cohesive political entity.

Five Kings Mountains: Major mountain range in Avistan, populated primarily by dwarves.

Fog Peaks: Uncivilized mountain range east of Druma.

Garund: Southern continent of the Inner Sea region.

Golarion: The planet on which the Inner Sea region is located.

Great Goldpan River: One of two great rivers in Druma, which flows down from the Five Kings Mountains near Highhelm to join the Profit's Flow.

Grimsburrow: Shortened name for the Regulate of Grimsburrow.

Half-Orcs: Bred from humans and orcs, members of this race are known for their green-to-gray skin tone, brutish appearance, and short tempers. Highly marginalized by most civilized societies.

Highhelm: Major dwarven city and capital of dwarven holdings in the Five Kings Mountains.

Inner Sea Region: The continents of Avistan and Garund, positioned on either side of the eponymous Inner Sea, which are the primary focus of the Pathfinder campaign setting.

Kalistocracy: The ruling caste of Druma, who control the official Resplendent Bureaucracy that governs the nation.

Kalistocrat: A follower of the Prophecies of Kalistrade in good standing.

Kalistrade: An eccentric mystic who lived thousands of years ago and preached the acquisition of wealth (along with strict lifestyle prohibitions and routines), creating the Prophecies of Kalistrade.

Kelldor: The current High Prophet of the Kalistocracy and leader of Druma.

Kerse: Capital city of Druma.

Kersite: Someone from Kerse.

Koldukar: One of the great dwarven cities called Sky Citadels, which long ago fell to invading orcs.

Macridi: Town in Druma, situated where the Great Goldpan River meets the Profit's Flow.

Mercenary League: Druma's well-paid and highly trained military force.

Mount Sinatuk: Volcano at the westernmost tip of the Five Kings Mountains.

Okeno: Island port city far south of Druma, known for its slave trade.

Orcs: A bestial, warlike race of humanoids originally hailing from deep underground, who now roam the surface in barbaric bands. Universally hated by more civilized races.

Ostenso: Port city in the devil-worshiping nation of Cheliax, southwest of Druma.

Profit's Flow: Major river in Druma, flowing from the Five Kings Mountains down to the enormous Lake Encarthan, emptying into the lake near Kerse.

Prophecies of Kalistrade: Pseudo-religion that holds the acquisition of wealth as the greatest goal of all thinking creatures, and guides this pursuit with several lifestyle prohibitions, routines, and other strictures.

Prophet: Somewhat slang term for a well-to-do follower of the Prophecies of Kalistrade.

Regulate of Grimsburrow: Relatively new dwarven commune in the western Five Kings Mountains which seeks to reclaim the ancient skills and glory of older dwarven empires.

Runt: Pejorative term for dwarves, used exclusively by taller humanoids. Considered extremely offensive.

Scrying: Using magic to view something from a distance.

Sky Citadels: Ten great fortress cities built when the dwarves first emerged onto the surface following their origins in the Darklands.

Sorcerer: Someone who casts spells through natural ability rather than faith or study.

Sothis: Capital city of the desert nation of Osirion, on the northeastern shores of Garund.

Taldan: Someone from Taldor.

Taldor: Nation southeast of Druma that was once an immensely powerful empire, but has lost many of its holdings in recent years due to decadence and neglect.

Tian: Someone or something from the Dragon Empires of the distant east.

Tien: The common trade language of the Tian peoples of the Dragon Empires.

Torag: Stoic and serious dwarven god of the forge, protection, and strategy. Viewed by dwarves as the Father of Creation.

Trolls: Large, stooped humanoids with sharp claws and amazing regenerative powers that are overcome only by fire.

Ulm's Delve: Small boom town in western Druma, founded to take advantage of recent gold strikes in the area.

Wizard: Someone who casts spells through careful study and rigorous scientific methods rather than faith or innate talent.

For half-elven Pathfinder Varian Jeggare and his devil-blooded bodyguard Radovan, things are rarely as they seem. Yet not even the notorious crime-solving duo are prepared for what they find when a search for a missing Pathfinder takes them into the gothic and mist-shrouded mountains of Ustalav.

Beset on all sides by noble intrigue, curse-afflicted villagers, suspicious monks, and the deadly creatures of the night, Varian and Radovan must use sword and spell to track the strange rumors to their source and uncover a secret of unimaginable proportions, aided in their quest by a pack of sinister werewolves and a mysterious, mute priestess. But it'll take more than merely solving the mystery to finish this job. For shadowy figures have taken note of the pair's investigations, and the forces of darkness are set on making sure neither man gets out of Ustalav alive . . .

From fan-favorite author Dave Gross, author of *Black Wolf* and *Lord of Stormweather*, comes a new fantastical mystery set in the award-winning world of the Pathfinder Roleplaying Game.

Prince of Wolves print edition: $9.99
ISBN: 978-1-60125-287-6

Prince of Wolves ebook edition:
ISBN: 978-1-60125-331-6

PRINCE OF WOLVES

Dave Gross

In a village of the frozen north, a child is born possessed by
a strange and alien spirit, only to be cast out by her tribe
and taken in by the mysterious winter witches of Irrisen, a
land locked in permanent magical winter. Farther south, a
young mapmaker with a penchant for forgery discovers that
his sham treasure maps have begun striking gold.

This is the story of Ellasif, a barbarian shield maiden who
will stop at nothing to recover her missing sister, and Declan,
the ne'er-do-well young spellcaster-turned-forger who wants
only to prove himself to the woman he loves. Together they'll
face monsters, magic, and the fury of Ellasif's own cold-hearted
warriors in their quest to rescue the lost child. Yet when they
finally reach the ice-walled city of Whitethrone, where trolls
hold court and wolves roam the streets in human guise, will
it be too late to save the girl from the forces of darkness?

From *New York Times* best-selling author Elaine
Cunningham comes a fantastic new adventure of swords and
sorcery, set in the award-winning world of the Pathfinder
Roleplaying Game.

***Winter Witch* print edition: $9.99**
ISBN: 978-1-60125-286-9

***Winter Witch* ebook edition:**
ISBN: 978-1-60125-332-3

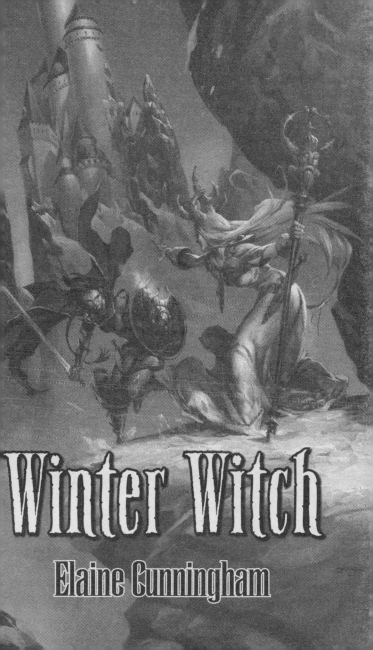

Winter Witch

Elaine Cunningham

The race is on to free Lord Stelan from the grip of a wasting curse, and only his old mercenary companion, the Forsaken elf Elyana, has the wisdom—and the swordcraft—to uncover the identity of his tormenter and free her old friend before the illness takes its course.

When the villain turns out to be another of their former companions, Elyana sets out with a team of adventurers including Stelan's own son on a dangerous expedition across the revolution-wracked nation of Galt and the treacherous Five Kings Mountains. There, pursued by a bloodthirsty militia and beset by terrible nightmare beasts, they discover the key to Stelan's salvation in a lost valley warped by weird magical energies. Will they be able to retrieve the artifact the dying lord so desperately needs? Or will the shadowy face of betrayal rise up from within their own ranks?

From Howard Andrew Jones, managing editor of the acclaimed sword and sorcery magazine *Black Gate*, comes a classic quest of loyalty and magic set in the award-winning world of the Pathfinder Roleplaying Game.

Plague of Shadows print edition: $9.99
ISBN: 978-1-60125-291-3

Plague of Shadows ebook edition:
ISBN: 978-1-60125-333-0

Plague
of
Shadows

Howard Andrew Jones

In the foreboding north, the demonic hordes of the
magic-twisted hellscape known as the Worldwound
encroach upon the southern kingdoms of Golarion. Their
latest escalation embroils a preternaturally handsome
and coolly charismatic swindler named Gad, who decides
to assemble a team of thieves, cutthroats, and con men to
take the fight into the demon lands and strike directly at
the fiendish leader responsible for the latest raids—the
demon Yath, the Shimmering Putrescence. Can Gad hold
his team together long enough to pull off the ultimate con,
or will trouble from within his own organization lead to an
untimely end for them all?

From gaming legend and popular fantasy author Robin
D. Laws comes a fantastic new adventure of swords and
sorcery, set in the award-winning world of the Pathfinder
Roleplaying Game.

The Worldwound Gambit print edition: $9.99
ISBN: 978-1-60125-327-9

The Worldwound Gambit ebook edition:
ISBN: 978-1-60125-334-7

the WORLDWOUND Gambit

ROBIN D. LAWS

On a mysterious errand for the Pathfinder Society, Count Varian Jeggare and his hellspawn bodyguard Radovan journey to the distant land of Tian Xia. When disaster forces him to take shelter in a warrior monastery, "Brother" Jeggare finds himself competing with the disciples of the Dragon Temple as he unravels a royal mystery. Meanwhile, Radovan—trapped in the body of a devil and held hostage by the legendary Quivering Palm attack— must serve a twisted master by defeating the land's deadliest champions and learning the secret of slaying an immortal foe. Together with an unlikely army of beasts and spirits, the two companions must take the lead in an ancient conflict that will carry them through an exotic land all the way to the Gates of Heaven and Hell and a final confrontation with the nefarious Master of Devils.

From fan-favorite author Dave Gross comes a new fantastical adventure set in the award-winning world of the Pathfinder Roleplaying Game.

Master of Devils print edition: $9.99
ISBN: 978-1-60125-357-6

Master of Devils ebook edition:
ISBN: 978-1-60125-358-3

Master

of

Devils

Dave Gross

A warrior haunted by his past, Salim Ghadafar serves as
a problem solver for a church he hates, bound by the
goddess of death to hunt down those who would rob her
of her due. Such is the case in the desert nation of Thuvia,
where a powerful merchant about to achieve eternal youth
via a magical elixir is mysteriously murdered and his soul
kidnapped. The only clue is a ransom note, offering to trade
the merchant's soul for his dose of the fabled potion.

Enter Salim, whose keen mind and contacts throughout
the multiverse would make solving this mystery a cinch, if
it weren't for the merchant's stubborn daughter who insists
on going with him. Together, the two must unravel a web of
intrigue that will lead them far from the blistering sands of
Thuvia on a grand tour of the Outer Planes, where devils and
angels rub shoulders with fey lords and mechanical men,
and nothing is as it seems . . .

From noted game designer and author James L. Sutter
comes an epic mystery of murder and immortality, set in the
award-winning world of the Pathfinder Roleplaying Game.

Death's Heretic print edition: $9.99
ISBN: 978-1-60125-369-9

Death's Heretic ebook edition:
ISBN: 978-1-60125-370-5

Death's Heretic

James L. Sutter

Once a student of alchemy with the dark scholars of the Technic League, Alaeron fled their arcane order when his conscience got the better of him, taking with him a few strange devices of unknown function. Now in hiding in a distant city, he's happy to use his skills creating minor potions and wonders—at least until the back-alley rescue of an adventurer named Jaya lands him in trouble with a powerful crime lord. In order to keep their heads, Alaeron and Jaya must travel across wide seas and steaming jungles in search of a wrecked flying city and the magical artifacts that can buy their freedom. Yet the Technic League hasn't forgotten Alaeron's betrayal, and an assassin armed with alien weaponry is hot on their trail . . .

From Hugo Award-winning author Tim Pratt comes a new adventure of exploration, revenge, strange technology, and ancient magic, set in the fantastical world of the Pathfinder Roleplaying Game.

City of the Fallen Sky print edition: $9.99
ISBN: 978-1-60125-418-4

City of the Fallen Sky ebook edition:
ISBN: 978-1-60125-419-1

CITY OF THE FALLEN SKY

TIM PRATT

PATHFINDER
CAMPAIGN SETTING

THE INNER SEA WORLD GUIDE

You've delved into the Pathfinder campaign setting with Pathfinder Tales novels—now take your adventures even further! *The Inner Sea World Guide* is a full-color, 320-page hardback guide featuring everything you need to know about the exciting world of Pathfinder: overviews of every major nation, religion, race, and adventure location around the Inner Sea, plus a giant poster map! Read it as a travelogue, or use it to flesh out your roleplaying game—it's your world now!

EXPLORE YOUR WORLD!

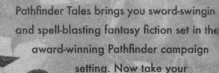

CHART YOUR OWN ADVENTURE!

The PATHFINDER ROLEPLAYING GAME puts you in the role of a brave adventurer fighting to survive in a fantastic world beset by magic and evil!

Take on the role of a canny fighter hacking through enemies with an enchanted sword, a powerful sorceress with demon blood in her veins, a wise cleric of mysterious gods, a wily rogue ready to defuse even the deadliest of traps, or any of countless other heroes. The only limit is your imagination!

The massive 576-page *Pathfinder RPG Core Rulebook* provides all the tools you need to get your hero into the action! One player assumes the role of the Game Master, challenging players with dastardly dungeons or monstrous selections from the more than 350 beasts included in the *Pathfinder RPG Bestiary*!

The PATHFINDER ROLEPLAYING GAME is a fully supported tabletop roleplaying game, with regularly released adventure modules, sourcebooks on the fantastic world of Golarion, and complete campaigns in the form of Pathfinder Adventure Paths like Kingmaker and Serpent's Skull!

Begin your adventure today in the game section of quality bookstores or hobby game shops, or online at **paizo.com**!

Pathfinder RPG Core Rulebook • $49.99
ISBN 978-1-60125-150-3